MW00464617

RIVER ROAD

RIVER'S END SERIES, BOOK FOUR

LEANNE DAVIS

LEANNE DAVIS

Raw. Real. Emotional
Romance

This is a work of fiction. Names, characters, places, and incidents are either the product of the author's imagination or are used fictitiously, and any resemblance to actual events, locales, or persons, living or dead, is entirely coincidental.

River Road

COPYRIGHT © 2016 by Leanne Davis

All rights reserved. No part of this book may be used or reproduced in any manner whatsoever without written permission of the author except in the case of brief quotations embodied in critical articles or reviews.

Contact Information: dvsleanne@aol.com

Publishing History First Edition, 2016

Print ISBN: 9781941522387

River's End Series, Book Four

Edited by Teri at The Editing Fairy (editingfairy@yahoo.com)

Copy Editing: Sophie@sharperediting.com

For Keith Stuhr
Every time I'm at The Property I keep expecting you to walk across the lawn swinging a golf club.
Or at the very least to be bugging me to get my butt out of bed to go golfing with you at Alta Lake.
Thank you for all of the memories and summers I will cherish for the rest of my life.

CHAPTER 1

~YEAR 4 FROM START OF SERIES~

*K*ATE MORGAN FOLLOWED THE curves of the road while a large knot formed inside her stomach. She imagined birthing labor must feel something like this. Not that *she'd* ever know. But still, she was convinced her nerves were mimicking the pain. She ignored the bile that nearly climbed up her throat as her pretty, little sports car came to a stop in front of a log home. It was perched on a mound like a king upon his throne, lording over the land that rolled and swayed all around it. The river glinted so brightly, it almost blinded her with white-gold. She could not believe she was doing this. Nor could she believe how she found herself in this situation.

How could her mom keep that kind of secret? She really didn't know the answer, much less, understand; and that pain, perhaps more than her nerves, made her stomach knot and cramp to the point she couldn't remember the last time she'd eaten a real meal.

Inhaling a deep breath, she kept trying to pep talk herself into opening the car door and stepping out. She was strong

1

enough to handle this. She had to do it. She was not responsible for the situation. Her mother was.

Damn her mother.

Why then, did the very thought of her mother, now dead, nearly cut her in half? It made the knot in her stomach sharpen like a knife before twisting inside her gut and taking her breath away. *Oh, Mom, how could you do this to me? But I miss you. So much...*

Don't cry. Not now. Now wasn't the time for grief, knowing she'd never see her mom again. She'd never learn the answers for why her mom would keep such a secret. Or what she was supposed to do about it.

She had no idea if coming there was right or wrong. Nothing felt right or wrong anymore. She didn't know if her grief-stricken brain was still even capable of making the proper decision. But here she was...in the middle of freaking nowhere, at a dusty ranch with not a soul around. At least, none that she could see. Lousy, piece of crap location.

So, grabbing the handle on her convertible two-seater, she climbed out. She had long legs. Ridiculously long. Standing damn near six feet tall, she never once slumped her shoulders to lessen her stature. She was proud and sure of every damn inch of herself.

At least, she was until today. Now, the thought of going to a strange house and introducing herself as the long-lost sister to its owner managed to make her usual confidence waver just a smidgeon.

Shit. What could anyone say to that? As far as she could read the situation, Mr. Jack Rydell, her *half-brother*, wouldn't know she even existed or consider the possibility. Same way she felt about him. Until two weeks ago.

She shook her head. Not now. She could not enter the psyche of her dead mother in order to figure out why she would have kept such a secret. Even worse, how could her mother abandon her own son? Turning her back on him as if he were an annoying cat or dog or guinea pig she no longer wanted?

Maybe he was a horrible kid and man? Maybe he was a serial killer in the making and she kept him a secret just to protect Kate. Could that be? Glancing around, Kate gave the ranch a passing grade. They weren't destitute. She sniffed; that didn't mean anything. There had to be some kind of compelling reason why this Jack Rydell was always kept from her. And why her mother ran from this place, literally never once looking back or returning or even mentioning it.

Perhaps it was the smell? A gust of wind tinged with the earthy scent of horses and manure wafted up her nose. She nearly gagged. She hated farm animals. Along with farms. Ranches. Chickens. Goats. Cows. Horses. Anything country. She grew up in a condo overlooking Elliott Bay in Seattle, and lived in a different condo in Fremont now, but a condo, never the less. Hell, the world needed farms and farmers and all that stuff; and she proudly bought only locally grown, sustainable, organic products from Pike Place Market. But she turned her nose up at living on a farm. No way. Uh-uh. Definitely not for her.

She slipped her sunglasses off and stared up at the ranch house. Nothing. No movement. Damn it. She—

"Excuse me, ma'am, I think you turned off at the wrong road. The resort is the next driveway."

Ma'am? Kate froze in horror over hearing the expression directed at her, rather than being startled by the unexpected deep voice that interrupted her surveillance. She spun around and cast her gaze right smack on the chest of a man. It was impossible not to stare at the broad chest, as it was bare and gleaming in a sheen of sweat. Her gaze descended instead of rising, and she couldn't help noticing how low the light blue jeans rode over his lean hips. A large, silver belt

3

buckle was the only distraction from his perfect abdominal wall. The voice, however, didn't totally match the chest. His voice was quiet, almost soft and so respectful with the *ma'am* attached to it. *Ma'am?* She lifted her glaring eyes to inspect the man's face. He probably had a good half inch on her. Maybe. She could totally eclipse him in heels, or even just a good pair of boots. It was impossible to get much of an impression. The white cowboy hat he wore was pulled down low over his forehead and deliberately shielding his eyes. His jaw was under its shadow, but she didn't fail to notice the square cut of it. Almost to the point of being boxy. His mouth was flat and his nose hooked slightly to the left as if it had had a bad break at some point. Interesting face, but not perfect. Not even all that handsome.

She mentally bitch-slapped herself for gawking at the man. He was her brother! Gross. *God, Mom! How could you not tell me?* she kept wondering.

"Are you Jack Rydell?"

An infinitesimal smile tugged at the man's mouth and he grunted his reply, which she took to mean "as if." The man lifted a hand to the brim of his hat where the white was grayed, no doubt, by the man's dirty hands often doing that very move. He tilted the hat back far enough so his eyes could totally meet hers. They were a bright hazel that glowed against the dark tan of his skin. She caught a glimpse of sandy-colored hair. "Sorry, ma'am. I'm not Jack. Mr. Rydell isn't here right now. You're not looking for the resort then?"

There it was again. *Ma'am.* How the hell old did she look to this cow hick? Forty? He had to be riding close to thirty and she was just barely past it. Resort? What resort? What the hell was he talking about?

"Uh... yeah. Sure. Of course. Jack Rydell runs it, right?"

"He and his wife, and all his brothers."

Brothers? She didn't know he had other siblings. "Are you one of them?"

His eyes never left hers, and she felt something shift in her stomach. It changed from a dull ache to butterflies. There was no mistaking the connection and electricity between them. Her breathing instantly sounded thicker and raced faster while her hands grew moist in a new kind of anxiety. He was hot. Harsh face or not, the man's body created an irresistible urge inside her to lick and caress it.

"No. I'm AJ Reed, their ranch foreman. I have nothin' to do with the resort. You'll want to go back out to the River Road and take a left. The resort's driveway is just a half mile down it. You won't miss the sign for Rydell River *Resort*."

Instead of the Rydell River Ranch. Yeah, confusing much? At least, it made her look legitimate. Resort, huh? Could she stay there? Instead of just popping into the Rydell home with, *Gee, I think I'm your sister, Jack?* Maybe a stay at the resort was a better plan after all. She could scope things out. See what Jack Rydell was like and if it was worth even informing him about their shared mother. She suspected there was something gross, or off about him, which was why her mother kept so silent. Perhaps she could stake him out, and see what was up.

And not only that, but maybe she'd like a quick joy ride on the fine-looking specimen of a cowboy standing before her. Her insides started to hum at that salacious thought. Yeah, maybe… a little game of giddy-up with Mr. AJ Reed.

"What does a ranch foreman do?" she asked, her gaze sliding with captivated interest from his eyes to the angular lines of his body. He wore brown cowboy boots under the scruffy jeans. Nothing finer in her opinion than a working man in a tight pair of ripped jeans. Sigh. Women had to go designer and risk breaking their ankles in heels, and men?

All they needed was a nasty pair of jeans and look at him! Undiluted sexual perfection.

At least, that's how he appeared to her. No man she ever knew walked around at two o'clock in the afternoon looking like *that*. The thought made her almost snicker out loud. Imagine Greg Danners, her co-worker and current fling, walking around her office with his shirt off, letting the sweat and dust glisten off him instead of wearing his usual black suit and neatly coiffed hair.

Resort, huh? Yes, she could use a vacation. She could work from there. Internet made life workable almost anywhere.

"Does this resort have internet and all that?" She glanced at the surrounding mountains with a glare of disgust. Stupid, confining mountains! They were tall enough to possibly block off any signals for the internet, although she didn't know exactly how things in damn, rural hick-hell ran.

He nodded. "All the amenities."

"A pool?"

"Well, no, there's no pool. But the river's right there," he nodded off towards it.

"Ick. Who knows what kind of bugs and yucky stuff are in it?"

"Probably a whole lot less harmful than chlorine," he replied dryly.

"But I can get online. Right? It's not dial-up or something backwards like that, is it? I need a high speed modem."

"Uh... sure?" His eyes started to dim as his gaze skittered away from hers. Despite her ceaseless drilling, she suspected he didn't actually know the answer, but he didn't want to push a potential customer away.

"Well, back to River Road then, huh? Pretty easy address for you all, isn't it? 1227 River Road, River's End, Washington?"

His eyes returned to hers. "Yeah," he mumbled, adding, "longest one I've ever had." His gaze again left hers. Was he shy? She studied his face, and he never once looked back at her. He seemed unsure of what to do under her intense scrutiny. He shuffled the weight of his hips over his feet, and kept shifting from one foot to the other. Was it merely embarrassment? Or was he painfully shy? Such bashfulness seemed a stretch for a specimen of man like him. He could give her a hot flash and make her think she was in early menopause just by looking at him. Imagine a guy like him being shy! He could blind a woman with the sheer bulk of his shoulders and the perfect U-shape of his pecs. Hot. Hot. Hot. Lick him up and down, that kind of hot. Yet he was so soft-spoken as he nervously shifted his feet? Something didn't fit.

"Well, I'd best get back to it before Mr. Rydell returns."

"Back to what? Again, what *does* a ranch foreman do?"

"Uh, anything and everything. Right now, we're thinning the orchard. I'm overseeing that."

"So you're a farmer too, huh?"

His smile was small as he glanced at her and then away. "Sure. Whatever needs doing."

Sounded like a good guy to have around. He obviously had no airs about what he should or should not be doing. He turned and said, "Ma'am, have a nice stay."

"Oh, I will," she said, smiling at his back, already deciding he would play a definite part in her *nice stay.*

She turned back to the house and saw no more movement. Okay, on to the resort. She was anxious to see who Jack Rydell really was and what the hell he was all about. Then she'd decide whether or not to divulge the fact that she was his half sister.

CHAPTER 2

*A*J REED WATCHED THE silver sports car crunch over the drive until it disappeared. Wow. Nothing like the women around here. That woman was exquisite. A tall, long, crystal vase among a sea of broken pottery. She was as tall as him. Right in the eye she looked at him. Her blonde hair was cut in some crazy, short but sophisticated style. Kind of long bangs with a short back and a silver, honey color. It made her blue eyes seem huge and cool in her face. She wore a lot of makeup, which he wasn't too keen on. But she made it look good. No doubt. Her long legs were barely confined to a pair of jeans that molded over their long leanness. Her tank top left her equally slender, smooth arms exposed. The muscles were nicely defined on her arms. She was intimidating. The kind of woman he really didn't associate with much. Obviously, she came from the city.

Of course, it wasn't like he ran into women very often. Not around there. It was all men he oversaw and worked with. A few of the Rydells had wives and one had a girlfriend, but he didn't associate with them much. He'd never been very good with women. He didn't have a way with words, obviously. He always struggled to think quickly or appear charming under pressure. He was lucky not to become tongue-tied when speaking to any woman like the one who just stopped by.

Once, he had no problems with the opposite sex, but that was back when he was on the rodeo circuit as a bull rider; drinking, gambling and raising hell in whatever little town he happened to find himself. In that loose atmosphere of anonymity and gallons of alcohol, he'd always been full of himself. That false confidence unfortunately didn't carry over when he finally sobered up and turned to clean living. Back then, his biggest problem was merely a matter of choosing a different woman almost every night. Lots of cowgirls or wanna-be cowgirls played groupie to him as well as the other cowpokes after they performed. Being in towns for only a day or two or three, back then, it was easy to love 'em and leave 'em.

Then… Well, then he did that stint in prison. That ended his rodeo career, his drinking, his partying, his womanizing, and sadly enough, his confidence.

As far as he was concerned, however, that was a positive. There was nothing redeeming about his youth, or the man he'd been before. Not like the man he was now, head foreman and dedicated employee of the Rydell family. A title he proudly clutched. He was finally someone. He had a job, a safe place to live, and more importantly, an *address*. A real, permanent address. Even if someone else held the deed.

AJ never had a permanent address before, not one that he could remember. His earliest recollections were of trailers, bedrooms, motel rooms, everywhere and nowhere. His dad dragged him from one gambling game to the next, then one rodeo to the next. AJ dutifully followed the Reed family morals and legacy to a tee. His dad sometimes relinquished him to the state, abandoning him in foster care for extended stays. But he eventually always came back and took AJ with him again. AJ's schooling was sporadic at best, continually interrupted and left unfinished. The only person on the Rydell River Ranch who knew that, however, was Jack. AJ told Jack everything before Jack even hired him, including his interrupted education as well as his stint in prison. Being upfront and honest, AJ emphasized how the prison sentence was deserved. He was guilty. Strangely enough, Jack appeared to show a surprising compassion for AJ. Jack didn't seem too concerned about his lack of education or his ex-convict status. He allowed AJ to stay on a probationary status at first with explicit instructions that AJ avoid the family house and not be allowed near any finances or money.

But later, Jack gave him access to his personal office, the petty cash funds, and even started letting him make repairs at the main farmhouse. It bolstered a deep loyalty in AJ. He felt obliged that a man as upstanding and honorable as Jack Rydell would give him another chance, and then go beyond that to actually trust him. Jack truly, and with an open heart, allowed AJ to prove himself. AJ responded by striving to prove his loyalty, work ethic, and physical strength each and every day for the Rydells. They had become his family, from a distance of course, since he wasn't really related to them. He might have been uneducated, but he was no imbecile. He was confident he possessed average intelligence, and clearly understood what his place and status with the family were. But they were all unfailingly polite to him. They were as respectful to him as they were to the reverend and even toward each other. AJ responded to their upstanding behavior by trying to emulate them as much as possible.

He flung his hat back on his head and adjusted it lower to cover his eyes. He preferred it that way. It dulled the effect of another pair of eyes staring at him. Well, hell! Why was he standing around now thinking about a model-worthy woman before retreating into the vast, bottomless, and hollow memories of his misbegotten youth? There was work to do; livestock to manage, hay bales to move, and he had a meeting with Jack later on.

There was always something to do and AJ loved that fact. In the off hours and on weekends, Jack asked him to do some side work by helping to build Joey Rydell's house, currently under construction.

AJ glanced up towards the blue sky, bright with the morning May sun. Simmering heat was starting to evaporate off the dirt and fields. It would surely be a warm one today. May could be the best month, with its pleasant sun and cooling breezes; if they were lucky, even a light rain that lasted only an hour or two. And other times, the day would foreshadow the stifling heat that became as oppressive as a tight lid sealed over the land.

He grabbed the bandanna in his back pocket and wiped it over his face. Didn't matter. Rain or heat, he could work in any kind of weather. He'd done so his whole life. His best qualities were having the arms of a gorilla, the back of a mule, and the determination of a thoroughbred. Unlike his gambling, feckless father, AJ worked. It was the only honorable thing he did, and all he had to offer others, and society at large. He felt he owed a bigger debt to the community than the eighteen months he served in prison, so he worked.

Jack had started him off at minimum wage, as most ranch hands weren't very skilled. However, he quickly singled AJ out and began to raise his wages by degrees. Every six months, like clockwork, AJ received what he considered a generous, almost undeserved pay hike. He was earning nearly the same as a guy in a worker's union. Considering he had no more than an eighth-grade education, that seemed pretty generous to AJ. Jack explained that good, loyal, trusting foremen were hard to find and golden to keep. AJ never knew how to respond to such a compliment. He didn't get it; so he merely did the work Jack asked him to do.

When Ian, Jack's brother and right-hand man, decided to leave, Jack tapped into AJ like never before. Side by side, they managed everything: the horses, the alfalfa, the orchards, and all the building maintenance. Ian's departure turned out to be the best thing, career-wise, to ever happen to AJ. Then, to his surprise, the brother who was third in line, Shane Rydell, started to stay around the ranch more than he ever had before. Shane never so much as shoveled a scoop of horse shit or fed a grain of barley to a horse for years.

However, he began to settle down after meeting the local school teacher. He married her and started to work alongside Jack. Shane was inadvertently pushing AJ backward. He returned to being more of a ranch hand than Jack's right hand man. It was a bit of a disappointment to AJ, but he fully understood. Family first, family always, and blood was thicker than water. He would have expected nothing less of the Rydells.

In that time, they expanded the ranch, erecting a series of cabins that eventually became the Rydell River Resort. It was all at Ian's instigation. AJ was fascinated by the venture and eager to help even though he had no idea of the big picture. Ian just came out one day and said they were going to start clearing the land by the river, which was not too far from the cemetery. After that, they were digging and clearing the site according to Ian's specifications. They built footings, and concrete trucks filled them, forming the foundation. All of it was new to AJ, who'd never done any real construction work from the ground up before. Both Ian and Jack were patient, showing him how to do different things, the purposes of all the tools, how to use the laser-level to square things up, the safest way to do the prep work, and how to minimize the costs.

They didn't have to take time from their busy schedules to actually teach AJ or give him the required skills. But they often did. Low and behold, all the little squares of concrete were soon framed and the cabin roofs were put on. Finally, AJ learned they were building cabins and planning to open the ranch up to people as a vacation destination. AJ never pried before then. He always knew it was *their* place, *their* family, *their* stuff, *their* horses, and *their* buildings. He didn't want to overstep any boundaries, despite how he was salivating with curiosity. *What was going on? Why were they doing this?* When Jack finally explained the plan to him, AJ's surprise must have shown on his face. Jack even apologized for not realizing AJ didn't know what they were up to. He always insisted that AJ just ask, and speak up; it was fine, and he was glad for AJ to know what the plan was.

Still, AJ didn't broach the subject. He held his tongue, because he knew his place.

He wasn't about to jeopardize that.

As for learning the cabins were part of a new concept, the Rydell River Resort, to say that AJ was shocked was putting it mildly. That Jack would let any fool, stranger, thief or con-artist—like AJ's dad, for example—have access to his land, his horses, and his river was beyond reckless. Jack explained that the family was expanding and the decision was not just Jack's. He described how they intended to respond to the entire family's needs, not just Jack's. AJ reacted by finding even more reasons to respect the man he worked for.

After the cabins were all finished up, they opened up their private land to strangers. Vacationers from around the state and beyond came there. Most were coasties from the west side of the state, looking for sun, heat, and horses, i.e., the country experience. As if it were a freak phenomenon or tourist attraction. The Rydell River Ranch was a working horse farm, which made it monumental for some people to experience. AJ didn't fully understand the urge; it was merely work to him. And home. And his life. It was never a photo op for AJ.

Jack specifically asked AJ, along with Pedro, Caleb, and Jordan, the other ranch/resort staff, to please leave the guests alone. No sleeping with the women; no making friends or enemies with the men. It wasn't out of snobbery because they were considered the ranch hands or hired help. It was because Jack did not want the possibility of any lawsuits arising, and aimed to keep things running as smoothly as possible. He hoped to limit the ranch and resort's contacts and crossover as much as possible.

Since AJ had no desire to hobnob with *vacationers,* never having done such a thing in his damn life, he was more than comfortable with that. The resort was on the high side of the main house, with its own access, cabins, check-in office, and grounds. A white fence separated it from the fields, pastures, his own living quarters and river access, barns and working roads. All AJ's domain, essentially. He saw it as his boundary line of freedom. The resort was his idea of hell.

So seeing that woman today wasn't something he often encountered. No one ever missed the turnoff before. It was the first driveway the vacationers saw from the main road. And the resort had a huge sign that was pretty hard to miss. AJ shook his head. He knew little of the amenities. He thought it best to mention the encounter to Jack, and hope she didn't leave. He feared he might have scared her away with his bumbling knowledge.

AJ quickly loped towards the orchard. He went to the barn seeking a new sprinkler head to fix the one that was busted by Pedro when he accidentally hit it with the mower. With the sprinkler head in hand, he found the crew moving down the orchard rows with pleasing efficiency. He turned off the water line and started fixing the sprinkler head for the next few minutes. When it was repaired, he turned the water back on. It pumped up from the river into the orchard before spraying out of the heads in lazy circles, catching the sunlight in colorful prisms of refreshing, little rainbows. Nodding with satisfaction, he caught up to the crew and started helping them thin the orchard. They already did the pruning early this spring, before anything bloomed, but Shane decided this particular section needed more thinning.

They ended their chores for the day, and stored the tractor, the mower, and the old farm truck in the barns before placing all the other implements into the proper tool sheds. Always a neat and tidy ship, that was what the Rydells ran. AJ was sure to keep everything in tip-top shape and exactly where it belonged so the Rydells could use it at any time.

Jack was in his office in the main horse barn. AJ knocked on the half-open door. "Hey, Jack, do you have a moment?"

Jack pushed away from the small desk he was sitting at. "What's up?"

"Just letting you know the orchard's done. There are only a few more limbs to prune on a small number of trees, but Pedro said he could handle those the rest of the week."

"That was quick. You must have pushed them hard."

"Just a few days' work. Nothing special about doing a job."

Jack smiled. "I wish everyone agreed with what a full day's work is as you and I do."

AJ stood there, his hat in his hands, which he always removed before Jack. Sign of respect. Jack was maybe in his late thirties, and not that much older than AJ's own thirty-two years, but the position and stature Jack demanded and deserved was light years ahead of AJ.

"What's up next?"

Jack leaned back, lacing his hands together behind his head, and his chair squeaked. "Get Caleb and Jordan on the sprinklers tomorrow; got some hot weather moving in, so

15

let's make sure the alfalfa gets plenty of water. Found some goat's tail growing along the east pasture. Damn stuff will take over before you can blink. Can you get them out there scouring for it around the area?" AJ wasn't sure of the actual name for the prickly weed that wasn't native to the valley, but consistently popped up in their fields. Its prickles were long enough to cause serious problems. Any time they found one, they combed the area to pull out as many as they could find. They didn't dare risk the chance of it spreading. "They'll get it done."

Jack's lips pursed. "Only because you'll be on their ass. Never understood how they could be Kailynn's blood. But you keep them tolerable, at least. And Ian stays off my ass for that." Kailynn was Ian's girlfriend. The two brothers, Caleb and Jordan, were a bit lazy and unenterprising. However, they were good enough farm hands as long as AJ stayed glued to their asses.

"They're good guys."

"Yeah? Matter of opinion. But Erin said there's a big group coming into the resort tomorrow. They reserved most of the stable horses for a long ride. Could you help her out with that tomorrow?"

AJ nodded. "'Course. If Erin needs it." His heart dipped. He had no love for the paid horseback riding. The inexperienced riders didn't handle the horses right or appreciate them if they did manage to ride them even marginally correct. But Erin, Jack's wife, who ran the horseback riding for guests, was every bit as upstanding to AJ as Jack was.

"Thanks." Jack cleared his throat. "Well, hell, all these damn changes..." he grumbled. AJ crossed his arms over his chest. What was his next task? "Don't get me wrong, I'm grateful for Erin and Allison, but damn! You won't believe the latest thing they got together and decided."

He bit his lip, trying to imagine little, five-foot-nothing

Erin ordering Jack about. She might have been the only one who could get away with it. "What?"

"They wanted to hire a landscape artist. Here. For this place. Can you even imagine? What the hell? I know what they are. But designing how and where we grow stuff? Here? I'm confused; it's as if they didn't realize we're a goddamned working ranch. And we *grow* stuff. Important stuff. *Food.*" The reproach was thick in his tone. "I couldn't even argue. Then Shane, the wimpy little jerk, agreed it wouldn't be a bad idea."

"Uh, what is it? The artist, I mean? Do they plant stuff?"

"Oh, first, they design it, which costs a fortune too. Anyway, I told them no. We can buy our plants at the local nursery and I can dig a hole as well as the next guy. So..."

AJ sighed. "So that means I'm now a landscaper?"

"Well, no. *We* are. You and I. I wouldn't just punish you without taking some of it myself. But yeah. They want to landscape all around the main house, our houses, and all the cabin areas as well as where the guests might walk." Jack sneered when he muttered *guests* in lip-curling disgust. AJ dropped his head, pressing his lips together to keep his own smirk from showing. Jack was as much a fan as AJ in his "affection" toward the resort people.

"You know, if not for my brothers, and their right to have wives and kids so our kids will have something to do with this place, I'd never have built a goddamned hotel here. It's like they come here to pat us on the head, and say how cute we are with our little horse farm out here in middle of nowhere. If it were just my decision, it would have forever remained the Rydell River *Ranch.*"

AJ nodded, a little squeeze tugging near his heart. But Jack wasn't alone. Jack had three brothers, two sons, a wife, and now a sister-in-law and another one probably someday. He had plenty of responsibilities, as well as people whom he owed to take into consideration. AJ couldn't fathom it. There was no one in his life. His dad, sure, until he was sixteen, but that barely came to a combined total of three or four months out of the entire year when AJ was actually with him. "But it's not just you, and therefore we need to start landscaping the place."

"Indeed we do." Jack stood up. "Walk with me, I'll show you what they have in mind. All the ranch or orchard work comes first, of course. Start this whenever you have some free time. If you choose to work at it on your own time, you can, just be sure to keep your hours and charge me."

He followed Jack, and they started out of the barn. They always saw eye to eye. Both slipped their hats on as the sun grew brighter to the left of them. "You know, I'm not an artist when it comes to plants. You'll have to tell me what you want and where."

"Like I know one bush from another," Jack mumbled.

"Well, I sure don't."

They started towards the main ranch house. It was nothing less than magnificent to AJ. Rising from a small mound, lush grass fell down all around it. A porch surrounded the two-story log home that had a central river-rock chimney and other accents of river rock all around the base of it. It once housed all the Rydells, but recently, Jack and Erin built their own house further down the river. Ian's house was nearby also. Shane moved with his wife, Allison, into a house near the orchards, overlooking the rest of the ranch. The youngest son, Joey, only lived in the main house whenever he came home on leave from the Army. Right now, and for the first time ever, the house was unoccupied. AJ heard Jack mumbling in the last month or so, about his brothers turning it into some kind of restaurant or gift shop for the guests. They had yet to convince Jack to do that, however.

Jack stopped and stared at it, squinting against the light. AJ wondered if Jack missed living in the house he was raised in, as well as his own two sons. "It's apparently not fancy enough with just the grass. They concurred it needed more flowerbeds running the length of the porch and an island right here in middle of the lawn. Then they want me to pave the driveway and parking area, just to keep the dust down. Like a little dust ever hurt anyone. All these fancy-ass sedans and SUVs don't appreciate their gleaming exteriors having a little real earth on them. Anyway, from here, we'll put the same flowerbeds... which are actually bushes with bark or gravel around them... the *landscaping,* I'm told, over here." He kept walking around the ranch and pointing out where the next beautifications were to occupy. Eventually, they were standing before the ten mini-log cabins that hugged the river's edge. Like tiny clones of the main ranch house, they had small, covered porches on the front, and viewing decks off the back. The views were of the river that ran down the ravine from the cabins.

"And right off, Erin wants flowers outside along all the cabins. So the grass will need to be removed in front, the soil tilled and... the flowers freaking planted." Jack nearly shivered at the word "flowers," as if Erin were asking him to pole dance in front of a crowd. "All the flats of flowers are under the lean-to near Shane's shop. You can't miss them."

"I'll get started tomorrow." *Flower gardening.* AJ cringed at the idea. He agreed with Jack. Having all grass made it easy. They had an industrial-sized mower deck that regularly tagged along behind any number of their tractors, and a smaller, riding mower to use around the buildings. It still cost plenty in gas, maintenance, time, and manpower just to keep the grass mown. Now all these new landscaping needs? They turned to leave. "Hey, there was a guest, a tall lady who pulled into the ranch house today. She had all these questions about the resort, which I'm not real familiar with, so I might have steered her wrong. I'm sorry if I mighta scared her off."

Jack shrugged. "No. Erin mentioned a single lady checked in. No worries." They walked off towards the barns and turned to separate. Jack added, "Thanks, AJ. You're a life-saver, both for what you do around here, and because I can trust you. You always mention every little thing you think could be of significance. That means a lot to me."

He nodded. "Just doing my job."

Jack nodded. "And doing it well."

AJ went towards his trailer, which Jack had recently upgraded. He lived for a few years in a small trailer from the nineteen-sixties. With a brown and orange interior, it was terribly gaudy to the eyes, and only a shelter. Jack—well, actually, Erin—gave him permission to stay in her trailer as of a few months ago. It was far nicer, with its own bedroom and the color scheme was from the early nineteen-nineties, a pleasing mauve. Erin kept it spick and span for she still loved the place where she first lived on the ranch. Allowing AJ to live in it was as big a compliment from Erin as AJ could imagine any of the Rydells bestowing on him.

It had a private deck, and the whole trailer was covered so he could live there in the winter without the snow pack collapsing its roof. Whereas the other trailers for the ranch hands were regularly stowed in one of the giant outbuildings when the employees were laid off for the winter, AJ stayed on and helped Jack year round. Year round, stable work. Literally. It made his heart swell as he tried to believe it.

For the first time, he had a stable job and the same address *all year*. It was profound. Something he had dreamed of, but never pictured actually accomplishing. *River Road*. His address. He even received mail here. That was another first for him. Before, he'd always kept a post office box, since he moved around so much with his work. Most winters, he found temporary employment doing any odd jobs he could scrounge. To have stable, steady work now was a relief and unlike anything he'd ever known before.

AJ entered the trailer as the sun began to set over the mountains across the river. It blackened the valley and trailed orange in the water. Tossing his hat to the side, he stripped his shirt off to head to the shower and wash off the day's dust, sweat, grime and dirt. Later, as he sat on the small deck, *his deck* for now, he ate a sandwich and drank a glass of milk as he marveled at the perfect day. He just didn't see how life could get any better than a day like today. A full day of work, a place to stay, and all alone. No bunkhouse or roommate. His own space, entirely. And a view like that which now encircled him. The chirping of crickets and nightly silence. A few lights shone across the river as the residents of River's End, the small town across the river, one-by-one began to light up their houses. Families living in unending peace and quiet.

Although he had no family, he finally had the respect of one. AJ also got to have acres and acres of land around him, along with the sporadic smell of horses in his nostrils and the happy prospect of doing all of it again tomorrow. He was respected and relied upon. That trust, which he received from all the Rydells, was something he cherished. His name and his reputation were all he had in the world. He wasn't a smart man, or a worldly man, or a man with any type of family or connections. All he had was his integrity.

After growing up with a man who had none, and living for years without any, himself, it became his sole goal in life now. Prison showed him how not to live and he didn't want to spend another day confined. That was another AJ Reed who landed himself there. He bummed around for a few years after his release. Most people didn't want to give him a chance once they realized he was an ex-convict.

A big guy, with huge muscles, he involuntarily intimidated more than a few. Along with his criminal history, AJ understood why most were wary of him, and nervous to give him any chance or a break.

But Jack Rydell did. For no real reason. He didn't have to. AJ certainly didn't deserve it. But Jack took a chance on him, and AJ would never forget that. As far as AJ was concerned, the Rydell family had his permanent loyalty and he had their backs until the day he died, or they didn't want him there anymore. Whichever came first.

Yes, integrity was all AJ had. The words Jack said left a smile on AJ's mouth as he tilted his head back to gander at the emerging stars above. Yup, he just couldn't foresee his life ever being this good, nor could he see it ever getting any better than this.

It scared him to think that way. He shied away from those thoughts. The hope. The belief. He never had stability or respect before. So to have both, now, at the same time? It was like winning the lottery to AJ. And he'd never do anything to tarnish either or change it one iota.

CHAPTER 3

*K*ATE STRETCHED OUT AND yawned. Finally, she managed to find one decent thing about the place: it had nice beds but the dinky cabins were entirely too small. She walked through the front door directly into the living room consisting of only a couch, a flat screen TV on the wall, and a small chair with an ottoman. The four-seat table was almost directly behind the couch, with just enough space to walk into the kitchen area. Small too. A sink, prep area, fridge, stove, and microwave. The bathroom was beyond that. Up the stairs was a loft with a large bedroom. Kids were supposed to sleep on the fold-out couch below. Lacking any walls, it was all open, so in Kate's estimation, any family would have to adore each other to tolerate such accommodations.

She checked in for two weeks. Throwing caution to the wind, she used her credit card, called work, and ordered them to send someone with the files she specified. Then she immediately set up the kitchen table as her temporary office.

Rising from the bed, she hastily flipped the covers back and put her slippers on when she saw how late it was, judging by the sun's position. The worse part was, she'd yet to meet any Rydells. A young girl named Jocelyn greeted her at the check-in desk and gave her the key to her room. She was proficient and emotionless. With spiked blonde hair, tinged in white ends, she had tattoos trailing her wrists that partially covered her arms. The girl also had an uncomfortable-looking piercing through her tongue and two more on her lower lip.

But she was in killer shape. Defined arms, hard with muscles, rippled through her white muscle tee, which she wore over a dark tank top. With a tight, athletic body, and a funky outfit, she topped it off with red cowboy boots. Kate almost asked how she managed to get such a rockin' body, but the girl was all business. Polite. A cool customer.

"Any of these mythical Rydells actually around here? Or is that just some kind of figure-head name for the resort? Maybe none of them really live here."

The girl's tongue played with her lip rings and she shrugged. "Nah, they're the real deal. Erin runs the horseback rides and Jack and his brother work the ranch. Horses don't feed themselves, you know. It's not just a fun tourist distraction. It's the real deal."

Kate felt insulted, as if tourists, like her, or any other guest of the Rydells, were somehow careless or oblivious that people were actually working there while the rest of them vacationed. The annoying clicking of the girl's tongue ring against her teeth as she raised her eyebrows almost in challenge soon had Kate gnashing her teeth. She could not abide rude, snotty youth who thought they were somehow superior to her. As if they had done anything in this world except mooch off their parents. But Erin? She must have been a Rydell.

"Can I go on one of the horseback rides?"

"Sure." Click. "Just gotta book it and pay up front."

Kate eagerly paid for the ten o'clock ride that morning. Then, she scoured through her suitcase and sighed. She had nothing to wear that was suitable for the back of a horse. Her jeans cost more than the rental fee of her room, and her spiky ankle boots had three-inch, sharp heels. She pulled the jeans on, eventually settling on a tank top she brought to sleep in. She packed her clothes with the intention of meeting her brother, not to take a vacation on a freaking dude ranch like a city slicker.

She had eaten no food and saw no café or restaurant. Stupid. For goodness sake, what was she supposed to eat? But first, there was the ride. Squaring her shoulders; she decided she could handle it. They at least provided the complimentary coffee grounds and coffee maker.

While making the coffee and dreading facing a horse ride, she tried to gear up to face it. She thought about the predatory assholes at work who assumed because she had big tits, albeit fake, but still *her* tits, she had no brains. And because she chose to dress in a revealing fashion, she wanted to be harassed.

They soon learned she was just the opposite of that. She gave out enough attitude and tongue lashings to stop any nonsense. So she figured she could probably handle a domesticated horse. Convoluted argument to convince her to not be afraid to ride a horse, but it worked.

Reconnaissance. She was just scoping out the lay of the land, getting a feel for the enemy. She had to remind herself she was strategizing. It was worth the risk of potentially ruining her boots and pricey jeans. However, the boots would be a damn shame. She glanced down; they were cute as hell even on her size ten feet.

She slammed her cup down and started out the door, walking up the graveled pathway that conveniently led towards a large, covered horse arena.

Wobbling, she cursed the damn prickly bits of gravel on which her narrow, spiked heels couldn't get any traction. She was liable to twist her ankle. Had these people never heard of such earthy inventions as concrete? Pavement? Asphalt? You know, civilization?

Inside the arena, she saw a dozen horses, all saddled, standing hitched to the long wall, their tails intermittently swiping their butts and hindquarters. Some stomped and blew out air noisily. She started over towards them when something caught her eye. Stopping, she carefully walked closer to the wall that separated her from the arena. It was a boarded wall that looked scarred and scraped on the inside. From what? Years of horse hooves kicking it? She shivered, picturing the damage the massive animals might inflict. *Not like dogs, and that was for sure,* she thought with a tingle of apprehension. Throwing her shoulders back, she straightened her neck. Since when did she get scared? Jangled nerves were for sissies. It was simply a useless emotion.

She kept thinking about the man from yesterday. DJ? JR? No, that wasn't it. Some initials. Anyway, the Rydells' ranch foreman. He carried a saddle in his hands, lugging the equipment as if it weighed as much as her purse. Approaching a horse, he deftly planted the saddle on the horse's back with a speed that was impressive. Making quick work of cinching it around the horse's belly, Kate had no idea what particular skill he was demonstrating, but he did it with the speed of a pro.

He paused and grabbed the lead rope and halter on the horse's head before leaning closer, and swiping his mouth along the horse's neck. Kate's eyebrows rose and she drew closer to the arena. Did that big, burly, muscled man just kiss the horse? And was he now talking to it? Yes! Of that she was certain. His lips moved. Lifting his big, flat, wide hand, he patted the horse's neck, sliding his fingers along its mane.

Was he comforting it? She quickly ducked below the level of the wall where he could see her and crept in closer.

"...clueless city jerks. They can't help it if they pull the reins too hard, or confuse you with their lack of instructions. We have to forgive their ignorance. I'll get you a special treat later for your ordeal, 'kay?"

Kate was close enough to catch the end of the conversation. She forgot to be stealthy in her shock at seeing a grown man kissing and soothing a horse. Right out in the open. And not some well-groomed professional, but a rough-and-tumble, sweaty, dirty (but in a good way) cowboy. He wore a shirt today, and it clung to the wet parts of his back from sweat. Dust covered his bare arms and his jeans hugged his ass.

"Do you think all city people are jerks? Or just the ones paying to stay here?"

The cowboy's back jerked upright, and he spun around. His reflexes were quick and impressive. His hat was again pulled down low as he scanned the line of the wall until his eyes landed on her, mid chest. She leaned forward, resting her elbows and forearms on the fence. "Sorry?" he asked when his gaze met hers.

"The conversation you were having with the horse? I was wondering if you considered all of us ignorant jerks, or are there some tolerable ones?"

He flushed and his cheeks went ruddy with color. Dropping his head, he pointed the toe of one of his boots and drew a little circle in the sand of the arena. "No, ma'am. Sorry. I was just... this one here, well, she gets a little nervous with all the new people and crowds. I was just... trying to soothe her, and calm her down a bit."

Comforting her? The horse? Kate bit her bottom lip to repress the grin. The man... AJ! Yes, it was *AJ*. He was a bit unusual and not what she expected from a brute of a man

27

like him. He was blushing because she caught him sweetly comforting the horse. She might have even kind of liked that in him; but again with the *ma'am* shit? She didn't like that one bit.

She waved at the horse. "Then why put us ignorant jerks on her back?"

He glanced up. "Um. It's Mrs. Rydell's call as to which guests we take. There are thirteen today... um guests, today, so we used some horses we don't take out as often, a few like this."

"We?"

"Yeah." His gaze skittered all around again. She riveted hers on his face, his chest, and finally, his crotch. That was because his worn jeans cupped him so enticingly, it was impossible not to give him at least a warm, loving glance of appreciation. Not that the shy cowboy noticed it. All of her flirting was wasted thus far. She sighed and walked around the corner of the arena. One side was lowered, where the horses were tethered to a long bar that ran the length of the wall.

She leaned against the wood column supporting the roof. "So let's not put me on the back of the one who gets nervous and doesn't like crowds. Turns out I'm one of the clueless, ignorant city gals."

Pursing his lips, he glanced at her and then away, as if he couldn't stand to allow his eyes to remain on her. As if he were incapable of it. "I, uh, didn't mean that. I was just... I mean, I don't pay much mind to what I'm saying when—"

"Talking to a horse?" She bit the inside of her cheek to keep from smiling.

"I don't really think that about the guests or anything. You guys are important to us. The Rydells, I mean. I'm not one of them, but I just try to—"

AJ's eyebrows wiggled downward. Lord! It struck her

then. He was worried she might tell on him. Only it wasn't any small concern to him. His facial expression looked stricken, and his face seemed a degree paler. After a giant breath, he visibly sought a new train of thought.

"Hey, cowboy, I was just kidding around with you. I don't care what you talk to the horses about. No harm, no foul." She smiled softly. "Your opinion of city people is safe with me."

His head nodded. "Thanks, ma'am. I appreciate that. But it's really not my opinion..."

"It's the horse's?"

His face jerked up. Finally, after a long, drawn-out moment, a slow, small smile appeared on the man's lips. "Yes, ma'am, how the horse feels."

She uncrossed her foot from the other and stood straight up. In the distance, she could see a crowd coming towards her. "Can't blame her. When I have a job to do, I like to surround myself with only the best available. Experts. Not novices."

"That's about it."

"Looks like the rest of them are coming."

"You're with them?"

"No. Not me. I'm all alone."

He cleared his throat, moving his hand to his neck and rubbing it. "Well, it seems that you're the one I was waiting on. Erin's taking the larger crowd and I'm taking... you. You're the one who paid for an introductory horse ride and lesson, right?"

With Erin Rydell. Kate ground her back teeth and pursed her lips as she dropped her face to hide her disdain. God damn it. She wanted to just meet a freaking *Rydell.* But what could she say? Sorry, cowboy, but only the girl will do? "Yup, that's me. I thought you said you were the foreman."

"I'm whatever they need me to be."

She almost bit her tongue to keep the flirty retort inside her mouth. He said it with a completely serious and blank face. "Meaning?"

"I help out wherever I'm needed. Mrs. Rydell had a big party coming today, so I helped her saddle up the horses. This is a lot for one time, you know, all at once. Then, you signed up for a ride, so first thing, they hit me up to take you."

"So I'm taking you from your real work? Is that what I'm kind of picking up on here?"

"Nope. I'm here to do whatever needs doing. Today, that happens to be you."

Dear God? How could she not smirk? Laugh? Say it back? Say what was on the tip of her tongue? He was flirting and his sexual overtones were about as subtle as bullhorns, yet she was pretty sure he didn't even realize it.

"AJ? Ready?" A woman's voice called from across the open arena. AJ turned towards the door leading into another closed building. *Probably a barn or store room*, Kate supposed.

"Yup. You're good," he called across the way. "Let 'em in whenever you're ready."

Kate straightened and stared at a small girl with long, dark hair; a blur of flannel shirt, jeans, and a black cowboy hat. That's all she managed to glimpse of her *sister-in-law*.

He glanced back at her. "We'll get the crowd all mounted before I can properly get you started. Do you mind waiting? I don't think Jocelyn realized she booked the group and you at the same time."

"No. It's not a problem. I'll watch. This city girl could use a bit of an education. Never been to a place like this."

He nodded and didn't say anything for long moment. Then he sneaked a glimpse at her and looked quickly away. "For real?"

"Totally. I doubt I've ever been this close to a horse before."

He leaned over and grabbed the leather strap of the horse he'd been talking to, easily petting her nose as he briefly glanced at Kate and then away again. "Where you from then?"

"Seattle. Born and raised."

"Yeah? Never been there. Never been over the Cascades, actually. But Mrs. Rydell, she's from there, born and raised too, I believe."

Erin was a city girl too? The one she saw yelling? The one who was all controlled around horses? Go cowgirl. How did she end up here? More importantly, why? Kate could not fathom what would make any girl stay on at a place like this.

And AJ here, never venturing to the west side of the state? Where more than three fourths the population lived? That was odd, unimaginable. Crazy. The thought made Kate shiver as she imagined being trapped here.

Hearing the raised voices of the crowd entering the arena, she saw Erin following right behind them. Kate's gaze fastened on her. She was a small woman. Both in size and presence. Tiny boned, even her face seemed pixie-ish. Her hair fell to her waist in a rope-like braid. Beautiful. She smiled easily as she started with the first horse and rider. AJ left the corner where they were talking and went over to help. Erin began by taking an inventory of who'd ridden horses before and their history. Kate wondered how many of them lied. It was an elaborate process, but the two worked in tandem to make it appear seamless and streamlined.

Kate would have been a mess of straps and animal gear. The two easily lined the horses up once the rider was mounted. Most of the horses danced around a little bit, taking a step forward or back, but nothing erratic or unnerving. Kate's palms sweated as she began thinking about herself doing that. Erin got on a horse, which she rode in front of the group, and gave a ten-minute demonstration of the riding basics and how their horses were trained.

She was, in a word, masterful. And in complete command. She made it seem effortless, in fact. Then, taking the lead, she started out of the open gate of the arena while AJ worked to get the rest of the horses in a single file, relatively nose to butt, following each other.

Amazingly to Kate was how the horses did just that, obediently following Erin out of the arena, towards the driveway and up across a pasture. Kate approached the gate where AJ stood, watching them go.

"She's good."

"She took to it like a natural."

"You mean, she didn't grow up with them?"

"No. She was terrified of them at first."

"Why did she come here then?"

"Just… life." He fidgeted, moving around anxiously before he started to back up. He couldn't easily talk. Apparently, no gossiping for him either. She sighed. So far, her reconnaissance mission had yielded zero, nada; nothing of real value, that is.

"Look, if you have other work to do, I can wait until they come back and go with… Erin, isn't it? Anyway, I'm on vay-cay, so I can do whatever, whenever. No hurry or schedule to meet."

"Jack asked me to do this now, and I'd rather not change the plans."

"Right."

AJ disappeared and came back, leading a horse. He swiftly tied a magical knot, and off he went again, returning with another. Kate stood back, waiting. He didn't fill the silent gaps with any conversation.

Yeah, not the best horseback riding coach. No wonder

that was Erin's domain. She easily talked and smiled and jabbered to all thirteen guests the entire time. AJ could saddle the horses in minutes flat. He'd saddled eight horses already that morning. She was exhausted just watching him, but he didn't act as if it were any different than her wandering to the coffee bar for a snack.

AJ's gaze rarely acknowledged her. Yet, it wasn't in a cold or disinterested way. It wasn't rude either. It was more like he suffered from unsureness. He didn't seem at all comfortable around her. He was quiet. There was no doubt about that. But watching his shoulders flex and move, and his giant, broad back lifting and bending soon had her insides contracting with lust and want. She could use his tongue for lots more than talking.

Finally, he patted the gray horse. *It was a girl*, Kate thought, as he finally acknowledged Kate still standing there. "So, they're all ready to go."

She walked forward, and his gaze dropped to her feet, then shot back up, frowning. "Uh, ma'am?"

"What?"

"You sure? About those shoes?"

She kicked a heel up. "About these? Hell, yeah. They are cute as hell, am I right?" His eyebrow arched. He was one serious guy, she'd give him that. She sighed. "I was kidding. I know what you meant. I don't have anything close to cowboy boots."

"Most people don't. Just sneakers will do."

Sneakers? She had a pair of special order Nikes that she used entirely for running. As if she'd wear those works of art out here where manure bits were mixed into the sand. "It's these or flip-flops."

"Okay. Just be careful. Don't need a twisted ankle. The roads ain't too good for walking in those things."

Those things? She cringed. They were three-hundred-and-fifty-dollar boots. And those things weren't at all appreciated here. In fact, he seemed to visibly disdain them. As if. She stood nearer the horse now, staring up at it. Even though she was tall, she still had a good distance to look up.

He was close, holding the horse's head. He had flat, wide, kind of fat hands, actually, for how muscular and broad the rest of his body was. She liked his hands. They seemed... She didn't know, but they seemed capable of gentleness and caring. Something about the way he stroked the horse's neck appealed to her. Kate was thinking of him stroking her in some way. But it wasn't all a sexual response. It was more like intrigue. "What is that thing?"

"What?"

"The thing on the horse's head?"

"Bridle."

"Bridle, right. So you got a good hold?"

"Yup. Grab the saddlehorn, put your foot inside the stirrup, and pull up."

She did so, hauling herself up before settling on the saddle. He nodded as he walked closer and took her ankle in his hand. He gently pulled it from the stirrup and began working on the leather and metal fastener. "What are those?"

He was just below her. When he looked up, she could see his eyes under the hat. "Adjusting the stirrups. You're a lot taller than the last lady that rode this one."

"Probably more than most riders."

"Probably."

He finally tucked her foot back inside the stirrup and didn't notice her scowling. Charm wasn't his forte, and she could vouch for that. He adjusted the other stirrup and told her to stand up on them before he asked her how it felt.

As far as she knew, it was fine. Never mind that she feared she was flying up in the air. He came closer and gave her a quick tutorial. He showed her how to pull ever so gently on the reins, where to place her heels and the commands she needed to use. "Don't worry; you'll be following my horse. We only bring out the most laidback, older, well-trained, and trail-ready horses for the guests. So don't expect too much excitement."

"What does that make your horse?" Her eyes tracked him as he swung up with such ease and agility, it surprised her, given his linebacker bulk and muscles. His stirrups were already adjusted. "Mine? It's not like any of those." He eyed hers. "Mine's a lead horse."

"Is it your personal horse?"

He shook his head. "No. They all belong to the Rydells. Ready?"

She nodded.

AJ made soft, clicking sound and swung his horse around. It was a magnificent mahogany color with a black mane and tail. It pricked up its ears at the sound and began a little shuffling dance. AJ pulled back on the reins. "Whoa, easy, girl. Easy." He had a light touch with the reins. The rest of his body didn't even move.

Her horse simply started walking. Kate didn't have to click her tongue, or push into the horse's flanks or move her hands. She grabbed the knob that AJ referred to as a saddle-horn and let out a small exclamation, scrambling to accustom herself to the back and forth rocking of the horse's gait.

He glanced back. "All good back there?"

"Fine." Maybe that was an exaggeration, but at least she was staying on. The horses leisurely walked across the road, starting up a gentle incline that criss-crossed back and forth. The horses' hooves clattered over the rocks and bits of wood and branches. The trail was very narrow, weaving through the sagebrush until they reached the top of the hill where it flattened out to meander through the pine trees.

They were red-barked, and the morning sun gleamed over their straight, dark green needles. It was so peaceful, and lovely, really. She relaxed her grip on the horn, holding only on to the reins. Her whole body started to undulate with the slight swaying and repetition of the horse's calm, sure steps. She let out a long breath. Wow. It was strangely peaceful, almost nice.

AJ wasn't much for words out there either. She watched his straight back swaying easily with the horse's movement. He mostly rode one-handed. This was a *job* to him, she got that. The trees opened up and they started down again, now that the mountains were visible once more. The white peaks of the Cascades were miles off, capping the uneven stacks of ragged mountains.

After a good fifteen minutes, AJ merely glanced back to check on her, and she asked, "So, are you from around here?"

"No."

She rolled her eyes at his back, sticking her tongue out at him. "Then… where are you from?" She was trying to guide him into normal, conversational rapport.

"Uh, nowhere, really. Dad toured in the rodeo, so we traveled a lot."

"How'd you end up here?"

"Followed the work."

"How long have you been working for the Rydells?"

"Just about four years."

She sighed, sucking on her lower lip. The guy wouldn't give a fricking inch. What good was he if she couldn't get anything out of him? He had no curiosity about her whatsoever, which was a little offensive. She usually let a guy know if she were interested in him with her strong signals, which most men usually picked up on. They flirted and conversed with her in exchange.

Had she ever been so overtly denied such a response? She

wasn't exactly sure that AJ was denying her. Perhaps he had nothing to say, and no real interest in conversing. Maybe he was that dull. Maybe he was uninterested in anything but his own life and ranching?

She let her attempt at conversation die a natural death. Zoning out, her eyes ate up the scenery. Crossing a ridge with a sloping hill below them, she admired the gentle roll and sway of the land where the river bisected the valley. She took in a deep breath of the warm air. Okay, for country, rural-hick-hell, it had some pretty spots in it. Watching the horizon, she jerked when her horse suddenly jumped, shook, and took off with a little leap. Without thought, or any understanding of what was going on, she was on the horse one moment, and the next, she was eating the ground.

The world spun and swirled in colors all around her. Landing flat on her face, the air was rudely expelled from her chest and she lay there, stunned.

What happened?

Her brain started to make sense of it. She'd fallen. She was off her horse. And flat on her stomach. Hands touched her back. "Ma'am? Are you all right? Can you move?"

She lifted her head off the ground. Dust coated her lips and filled her mouth. She spat several times and motioned toward her chest. She was suffocating, and hurting. Shit! Was she choking? What was that horrible sensation?

His gaze followed her hands. "The wind was just knocked out of your lungs. Give it a second. You'll be okay."

She gasped in a hitched breath and finally got up on all fours so she could try and breathe. Then she sat back on her heels. AJ squatted next to her. His hand remained on the center of her back. The warmth of his handprint radiated all over her skin. There was a tenderness in his soft rubs. Just liked he cared for the horse. She kept her face pointed down, trying to regulate her breathing, so she could continue more easily. Finally, the urge to gasp and the feeling of being strangled started to dissipate. Her breathing returned, and she tilted her head to the side. AJ Reed, in all his muscular bulk, was kneeling next to her with his hand still resting on her back. "Do you even know my name?"

His gaze shifted from the top of her back, where he'd been watching her, to her face. "What?"

"It just occurred to me, you keep calling me *ma'am* because you have no idea what my name is."

His lips twitched. "That's what most concerns you right now? Are you okay?"

"I'm going to live. Now, do you?"

"Um," he muttered and his gaze skittered away from her. "I'm sorry, Jocelyn didn't write it down and I couldn't remember. I didn't want to be rude. They usually take down the names for the ride."

Her eyebrows arched up. "Kate. My name is Kate Morgan. You could have asked me. And no more with the horrible *ma'ams*. It makes me feel like I need a shawl so I can sit on a rocking chair on the front porch of my cabin."

"Okay, Ms. Morgan."

She rolled her eyes. "Kate. Just call me Kate."

He didn't. He suddenly seemed to notice his hand was still resting, warm and comforting, on her back. The heat of it permeated the material of her tank top. She sighed, glancing down. It was ruined. Dirt blackened it. "What happened to me? I was sitting up and staring out at the gorgeous view—" *You, actually,* but she didn't say that out loud to the shy cowboy. "And then, I did a face plant on the ground."

"Horse shook and jumped. It got startled and you slipped off like an icicle melting off a steam room."

"It was so fast. I couldn't react in time."

She finally examined her face and came away with dirt

and grit on her fingers. She lifted her ruined top and wiped it, leaving a black mask imprint of her face. "There goes a small country's budget."

"What?"

Kate showed him the white material. "This brand of shirt. It's ruined. Forever a rag now. Shame, too. This was a killer find, and I got it at a clearance sale, plus half off that. You'd celebrate with me if you'd only seen the original price." *Plus, it makes my tits look killer.* But she withheld that comment out of respect for her shy cowboy's sensibilities.

"Maybe it's a good idea not to wear clothes that cost so much out here."

"Really? Can I borrow some? Because I don't have any, which is why I'm wearing these."

"You didn't consider that while you were packing to come to a horse ranch for vacation?" His tone implied she was incomprehensibly stupid to him. He was so close, his jaw was easy for her to inspect. Little whiskers covered it, so he must not have shaved this morning.

She imagined his scruffy cheeks running over her thighs, rough and scratchy to the sensitive, delicate skin, going higher, and higher… She mentally banished her thoughts when she began fantasizing. Could any man cause quite the visceral and physical reaction inside her as this one did?

Then again, maybe if she met a few more who looked like him, and worked with their hands and had muscles and were dirty and sweaty… Well, hell, she would have to fan herself soon if she didn't stop.

"I wasn't sure what I was packing for," she grumbled. He rose and put his hand out, palm up. Again, she was struck at how appealing his hands were. She put her hand in his, the red manicured nails and slim, long fingers looking so elegant against his stubby, wide ones. Like a small, delicate flower growing through the rocks on a mountain. He gently tugged and pulled her up to her feet. She wobbled on her boots. "Or that I'd stay."

"And yet, you're staying?" he asked softly. He had a low, deep voice, but the tone he spoke in now was reservedly low, and she had to intensely focus on his lips to make sure she clearly heard him.

She stared eyeball-to-eyeball at him as a small, smirk lifted one side of her mouth. "Oh, I'm staying."

He let go of her hand and cleared his throat. And like that, the moment was broken.

Behind AJ, the horses stood with their heads down, their jaws working the long strands of grass clumps, grinding the mouthfuls they swallowed, only to do it over again. Their reins hung loose and relaxed over their long, bent necks. They looked as peaceful and calm as the surrounding pine trees and natural scenery. "Well, I see the experience traumatized them as much as it did me," she scoffed.

AJ sauntered over to them. He grabbed both of the horses' reins and walked them towards her. They easily followed him without any resistance. "Are you afraid to get back on?"

"Oh, hell no. No four-legged animal decides if I ride it or not." Her voice was filled with gusto, even though her stomach was filled with nervous butterflies now.

He nodded and held her horse still as she scrambled back onto the saddle. She gripped the saddlehorn this time, completely determined not to let it go. Her body was jarred and her head was still ringing. She would surely hurt tonight. And need a hot bath and big glass of wine.

He let her reins go before remounting his own horse. "Good. Now just be sure to pay attention at all times. It can seem very peaceful up here, and they are great horses, but they can easily startle at any time. They don't mean you any harm, it's just a reflex for them. So just…"

"Hold on for the ride?"

"Something like that," he said with the smallest, flirty smile. It was there, but gone just as quickly as she blinked. Then he whipped his horse around and moved in front of hers. Okay, the cowboy thing was hot. Never before had she considered it, but yeah, it was *Master and Commander* kind of stuff. Man against nature. Primal. Sexual. She sighed. All this man did was keep making her go there.

She finished her ride with relative pride, clutching the saddlehorn and squeezing the reins until her fingers ached, but she stayed on. When they re-entered the ranch, she could see the last of the large group that Erin took riding. Most were already gone and dispersing towards the cabins. That left... only Erin.

As they entered the ranch from the driveway and stopped just outside the arena, Erin came sauntering out of a little room off the arena. The horse tack must have been stowed there, Kate suspected. Erin leaned her slim shoulder against the side of the building, using her hand to shade her eyes as she watched them ride up. Kate envied the narrow width of her shoulders. Kate's were wide and just as stout as the rest of her. She was tall and thin, but not thin-boned by any means. Her shoulders might have even been a bit too boxy.

"Hey, AJ," Erin called. "How was the ride?"

He stopped his horse and stood, swinging his leg around. Erin's gaze landed on Kate. She jerked off the wall. "What happened?"

Kate touched her cheek. "Good lord. How bad do I look?"

Erin walked forward and grabbed the horse's nose, the bridle, as AJ called it. "I'm sorry. My name is Erin Rydell. I'm—"

"The owner? Therefore the one who is liable and worried I might be an unreasonable, selfish asshole who decides to sue you for a random, stupid accident? Don't worry, I own a business too, I get it. I fell off the horse due to my own carelessness. Not AJ's, not the horse's fault, certainly not the ranch's and therefore, not your fault either. Believe me, I plan to drink a bottle of wine and forget this even happened. I'm not planning to hash it out anywhere, especially in public."

Erin's facial expression showed her shock, surprise, and finally, a genuine smile. "Ah, well, I wasn't going to say that. But yes. I'm responsible for the horseback rides here."

"And the owner?"

"No. Jack is the owner."

"Isn't he your husband? I'm sure I heard Jocelyn say that." No, Kate knew that before she came, but why wouldn't this woman claim this place as hers? Her job and her right? Why give her husband all the credit? Like she's just a lucky little lady because she is supported there?

"Yes. This ranch belongs to his family."

"And therefore, it's legally half yours," Kate said as she swung her leg down and got to her now shaky feet. Her butt and the backs of her thighs shook and cramped. Damn horse. She hung on to the saddle. "You all seem concerned. I'm guessing that since AJ here didn't know my name, nor did Jocelyn, apparently, take it down, I'm guessing there must be some kind of liability form you usually have guests sign before riding your horses. Get it for me and I'll sign it now. No harm, no foul. I'm just embarrassed, but not looking to cause any trouble."

Erin visibly released her breath and held up a paper. "Yes. Thank you, Mrs. Morgan. Jocelyn did forget. I assumed... I think AJ assumed..."

"Read me the highlights until the feeling returns to my ass."

Kate was too busy staring at her feet while wiggling her toes to make her blood circulate. So when Erin didn't reply, Kate glanced up and Erin's face was almost white. She stared down at the paper, as a weird, almost horrified expression appeared on her face. AJ suddenly, quickly, and faster than she ever saw him move, grabbed the paper from her. It made a *whoosh!* sound as it flapped and he held it in one hand.

Wow. These men around here... Kate would have kicked them in the shins the way they seemed to strong-arm Erin. The ultimate condescending treatment for *the little woman*.

AJ started to read. Liability issues, not Rydell River LLC responsibility if she got hurt, blah blah, blah; the legalese continued.

Kate held the horse while she nodded. "Sounds all legit. Hand me a pen and I'll—"

"What's going on? Why do you look like you're holding a meeting?"

The male voice came from outside the arena's walls. It was blocked by the ass end of the horse Kate had ridden. She was still holding on to its saddle as her aching, jarred body staggered with weariness.

It was his voice.

For some reason, Kate was sure of it that time. This wasn't any ranch hand or foreman or stranger. No, the authority and confidence in his tone, expecting an answer, had to belong to Jack Rydell, the owner of the ranch, the resort; Erin's husband and her own half-brother.

His head appeared first, rising above the top of the wall, turning into the arena and past the horses. He wore a tan cowboy hat and a chambray shirt. He came fully into view then, his long legs and extended torso, and he appeared to be in good shape. He was surprisingly neat for a guy who shoveled horse shit all day. His jeans were unripped and clean. He was tall, like AJ and her. His body was lean and sinewy. Handsome, but a different kind of handsome from the brute strength of AJ and his boxy, rough-hewn face. Jack stopped right beside Erin, leaning down to swipe a kiss on her forehead.

"She fell off the horse," Erin blurted out. Kate glanced at Erin as she gazed up at him, her eyes foggy with concern. "I forgot to check. I was taking the larger group out, and at the last minute, we had AJ step in—"

"And I forgot to check too."

Kate stood there, her head turning from Erin to AJ and back, before rising to look up at Jack. Good God. It seemed like they were both little mice and the big, bad cat had just entered the room, deciding which one he should attack first.

Kate rolled her eyes. Jack's first impression didn't bode well for Kate. He seemed to strong-arm the help, as well as his wife, judging by the way they both seemed so anxious to justify a stupid, clerical error.

"It's not your job, AJ. It's mine."

"Actually, it's Jocelyn's," Jack countered in a quiet tone, his mouth turning into a frown.

Kate rolled her eyes, but faced the horse, so no one saw. "So he was reading it to me while I was dismounting. What's the big deal? I told you all I'd sign it. No harm, no foul."

Jack's gaze finally shifted to her and he stared into her eyes, without flinching or shyness. His gaze swept over her, taking in all the details of her appearance. But he wasn't checking her out. She'd have to give him credit for that. He didn't stand there ogling her in front of his wife.

Jack stepped forward, stretching his arm out. "I'm Jack Rydell. I—"

"Own the place? I've heard your name from many different sources. Kate Morgan." She stepped forward too, right into his personal space, and pumped his hand up and down with a vigorous, healthy shake. She nodded her head as she said her name, giving him direct eye contact. No mousey little woman here. She intended to make sure this macho, old-fashioned asshole understood that right off.

"No, no. My family owns it. I'm more the... the acting operations manager. Anyway, sorry you took a spill. Are you sure you don't need to get checked out at the hospital, Mrs. Morgan?"

"No. I'm a little bruised and got the wind knocked out of me. Used to happen when I fell off the swing on the playground. I certainly don't need any medical attention. Just give me your form and it's signed. No one needs to take blame or responsibility for anything."

AJ handed it to her and Erin scrambled off before returning with a pen. Kate took both and scrawled her signature. "There. Your ranch and resort are safe from any lawsuit from me."

Jack smiled. "Thank you for understanding."

"And not being an unreasonable asshole. You're welcome. Sad you all have to be so diligent, isn't it? Providing a rare treat here, and some people go off and be stupid and all. I run a business too, I get covering one's ass, Jack." She held his gaze as she said his name. None of this *Mr.* and *Mrs.* shit.

Jack's smile widened. "No comment on the stupid people. We have *guests*. But yes, some can be... interesting. What business are you in?" Somehow, his emphasis and tone when he said *guests* suggested how little he thought of them, and therefore, Kate too, for being one.

"I run a consulting company that streamlines businesses from their operations to the way in which they market their products."

"Based in Seattle?"

"Yes." Wow, one minute of conversation and Jack knew more about her, including her name, than AJ had gleaned after over an hour spent all alone with her.

"Well, I appreciate your willingness to sign our paper-work, even after the fact."

Why? Because he would have beaten up Erin or AJ for not obtaining it beforehand? He seemed too heavy-handed. Jeez. Erin was his wife, not his employee.

"Sure. Now I'm going to take some pain meds along with some alcohol."

He stepped aside. Erin smiled as she moved to take Kate's horse. She heard Jack say, "AJ, can you mow the lawn over by the cabins before lunch?"

"Yes, I'll get right on it." Kate kept facing forward, but she imagined, silently, that AJ saluted and snapped his heels together in response to an order from the great Jack Rydell.

So far, she wasn't impressed. She liked his ranch hand a whole lot more than she did her own brother.

CHAPTER 4

$\mathcal{K}$ ATE SHOPPED FOR FOOD, along with some more casual clothes and shoes to survive her stay at hillbilly hell. She brought it all home and popped two ibuprofen tablets to help alleviate the pain of her jarred muscles from the morning fall. She also slipped on the pair of jean shorts and a tank top she had purchased. They were both made of cheap material and she planned to throw them away when this experience ended.

She checked her emails and answered all the essentials. Leaning back, she sighed as the afternoon sunlight streamed into the small cabin. She wandered out to the small deck and stared down at the river. Swollen and discolored with snow melt, there were sticks and even large trees bobbing down the rapidly flowing water. She walked back in, grabbing the cowboy boots she bought. They were a bright pink that she thought were cute as hell, compared to all the brown, dirty ones she'd seen thus far.

Walking down the road, she ducked under a white fence that ran the length of the land as far as she could see. The sign read "No guests beyond this point. Rydell River Ranch employees only." She headed towards the river to avoid anyone. There were all kinds of buildings up ahead. Some were enclosed, and several must have been barns, judging by their shape. There were also lots of carports with everything from tractors to old trucks parked under them. She meandered past the fields of green and observed the horses grazing.

Some lifted their heads towards her disturbance, but most ignored her and kept grazing. Eventually, she came to a large building with a giant sign on it that said "Rydell Rides." Huh. Looked like a bike shop.

She peeked in as she got closer. A giant of a man with a long, black ponytail, tattooed arms, and a leather vest caught a glimpse of her. He rose up from where he knelt, working on a bike.

Smiling, he stepped from the building and leaned against the door. "You don't look like you got a bike for me to fix."

She smiled. He beamed at her with an easy tone and a flirtatious smile. "Nope."

"You saw the sign, I assume."

"You mean the one that forbids the guests from going beyond it? Yup."

He nodded, winking at her as he turned back towards the motorcycle behind him. "Okay, then watch out who catches you."

She laughed. "You're not going to kick me out?"

"Free country. Just don't steal nothin'."

"Are you another Rydell brother of Jack's?"

"Shane." He smiled. "Third in line. Ian comes between Jack and me. Joey's the baby."

"Hmm. Your poor mother. But nice to meet you, Shane, I'm Kate."

"Well, howdy, Kate. Touring the place?"

"Yes. It's quite big actually. And lovely."

"Yup. Well, I'd love to chat with you all day, but I got a deadline. Have a nice stroll, Kate."

Why couldn't he be her brother? So nice and amiable? He was less about rules and more about being friendly. *Sigh.*

She walked towards the muddy river and found another cluster of houses. It was a little cul-de-sac almost, but country-style. There were two finished houses, set back with lush green lawns, freshly planted trees and newly scattered bark.

There was another house half-finished across the way from it. Each had at least a half acre or more surrounding it. There were other spots that had been recently cleared. Would these become vacation rentals? Now, they were talking along her taste. She would have loved to stay in any of these houses, versus the little rustic cabin she now occupied. Strange.

She kept walking along a widely used trail. Weird, since the guests weren't allowed there. She heard noises and voices yelling, along with the splashing of body limbs in water. The trail swerved around a curve before opening before her. She saw a wide, sandy access to the raging river, and the brown, smooth mountains dipping down and up. Capping the entire scene were two boys frolicking. One was younger, and the other was a teenager. Both had red hair. Her heart twisted as she watched them.

There was no mistaking the older kid had to be Jack Rydell's son. He looked just like him, only twenty years younger and leaner. She blew out a breath of air. She never considered that Jack and Erin might have children. Or that she had nephews, at least one anyway.

She stepped forward, the sun glaring into her eyes. The boys noticed her and stopped horsing around. They were knee height in the water where they wrestled, although the older boy had the obvious advantage. They stopped dead, their arms still interlocked in a complicated move. Water dripped off their hair and down their sleek, slim, bare chests.

"Uh, hey." Kate tried for nonchalance. Sure, she wasn't supposed to be there, but how was she supposed to figure out what and who her brother was if she didn't snoop? She definitely wasn't on vacation here, so the sooner her reconnaissance was finished, the sooner she could go back to civilization.

The older one spoke. "Guests aren't supposed to come down here."

She waved her hand around. "Shane gave me permission."

The older one's shoulders dropped and he removed his hands from his little brother as he stepped out of the water. He seemed to take Shane's permission as some kind of signal that it was fine for her to be there. Thank you, friendly Shane.

He grabbed a towel and started drying off. His pale coloring revealed the blush that easily started at his chest before rising up into his face. She almost told him not to bother with any adolescent embarrassment around her. After all, she wasn't a pretty, older woman, she was his freaking aunt.

"I'm Kate."

"I'm Ben, and that's my little brother, Charlie." Ben waved at his brother with careless interest. Kate's heart flipped as she studied the youngster. They were her nephews. Wow. Ben was old. Late teens, at least. How? She was thirty-five and not even remotely considering children.

"So… you're Jack and Erin's sons?" Damn, she'd give Erin credit; she aged well. She'd have guessed Erin's age at no more than late twenties.

"Jack is our dad. Erin is our stepmom."

Hmm. What was the story there? Did Jack drive away the boy's mother? Or kill her, and bury her body somewhere around there? Lots of places to do that. She still wasn't convinced he wasn't some kind of nefarious wife-killer. There had to be some credible reason why her mother would not tell her anything about him. Why would she abandon her firstborn child, and her only son? It didn't fit with the mother that Kate knew. The one who raised and loved and spoiled and comforted her. Her best friend and champion.

And now she was dead and the pain persisted as if a chunk of the river rock sat weighing down her heart. But no. Not now. She could not feel this pain right now. She needed to be here. She had to focus on the task at hand. Figuring out why her mother hid it.

She had to stay busy and in the now. She had to ignore the pain that losing her mom threatened to draw her into. She had a feeling it would be a deep, dark, black pit. But no. Not yet. She would not feel the pain. She refused to feel it. Instead, she held on to the anger that burned hot and thick inside her body, like jet fuel on fire.

Her anger was so fantastically bright and deep that it smothered all her other emotions; including the sad and painful ones. Her anger was like a flash explosion inside of her. How dare her mother hide a goddamned sibling from her for thirty-five damn years?

"I didn't realize he had sons. It's nice to meet you." She put her hand out and Ben leaned over to shake it with a small smile.

Charlie came out with a shy twitch of his lips and said, "Hey," then dropped to his knees in the sand before sifting streams of fine white sand through his fingers over and over.

Ben was talkative. She learned that Jack had three brothers, Ian, Shane, and Joey. Two were gone. Ian lived with his girlfriend in Seattle while she attended the University of Washington and the other was just finishing his stint in the Army.

She discovered Ben had just graduated and shockingly, was engaged to be married. She twisted her head around at that announcement. Who in the hell got married on purpose after graduating high school?

She asked if he knocked the girl up, and was tersely informed with a stiffening of his back and neck, along with a glance of disdain, that no, he and Marcy, as it turned out, were very much in love and wanted to get married. No baby in their plans... yet.

She bit down hard on her lip to shut herself up. She had no right to comment on the teen, but she wanted to know exactly what was wrong with him? What teenage boy, and the kid *was* an overgrown boy, *wanted* to get married? It made Kate shudder.

Imagine getting married before you could even grow facial hair. It was unheard of to Kate. What kind of backwards household did Jack Rydell run? How could he allow his son to be married before he could even formulate real thoughts? It was asinine in Kate's opinion. Someday, she hoped to find a way to tell Ben to grow up and get a freaking clue. He was setting himself up for failure.

Go to college or travel or just get a job, and do something that didn't include mooning over some piece of ass. Have more ass to even begin to understand if it were truly love. She could not imagine what would possess any family to support such a notion.

Kids got on her nerves with their endless energy, dirty hands and faces, and demanding needs. But Ben was tolerable, and Charlie was quiet enough not to drive her right out of her mind.

Finally, she sensed she'd worn out her welcome, although running into the boys had provided a wealth of information she hadn't counted on. Wiping her butt off after sitting on the sandy, bleached driftwood for a good half hour, she found her way back to her cabin. Getting there made her smile with pride when she actually did it. Greg Danners. Wonderful. She needed the work he brought with him to keep her sanity, and she could also use the goddamned distraction his body provided.

He smiled, still sitting in his car, and getting out only when he spotted her scooching under the fence and strolling towards her cabin.

His smile was bright and his suit was stupid, considering the setting. He was still handsome, however, and would have to do for tonight. "What the hell are you doing here, Kate? This isn't you."

No, it wasn't. But no one had any clue about Jack Rydell and her discovery of her half-brother. Not one soul knew. And she wasn't ready to change that yet. So she smiled and shrugged. "Just needed a change of scenery."

He nearly frowned in displeasure when she stopped and her boots kicked some dust on his black, polished dress shoes. "You couldn't find a place with running water and electricity? You and I have completely different ideas of a vacation. I about fell off my chair when you called to announce you were taking a two-week vacation. Unheard of, but here? Why?" His tone was dry and he raised his eyebrows with unbridled curiosity.

She stuck her tongue out and took the bag he offered her that held her precious work. Finally! Something to do. "Because I needed a change."

"Oh." He let a lingering pause settle between them. "Because of your mom?"

"Yup. All because of my mom." She passed by Greg and walked into her cabin with him close behind. He knew she had recently lost her mom, but didn't know about the hole it had ripped in her chest. She kept it light and easy, as if she were only mildly sad. He didn't know two figs about her or

53

her real life. Only because of her mom was she there. That was no lie.

~

AJ STARTED EARLY when he tore out the grass that went all the way up to each cabin, front and back. He was working quietly, so as not to disturb anyone. It was tedious work. Using a straight edge and shovel, he cut squares in the grass, and using a pitchfork, simply lifted the squares up and stacked them off to the side. Later, he planned to bring the loud tractor up to load all the sod squares.

Meanwhile, he had to get the small flowerbeds ready for planting and bark or decorative stone to fill in around them. Now Erin was talking about using little, fancy river rocks. AJ bit his lip while Jack described it to him earlier that morning. He grumbled about all the rock they had right at their beach, so why buy the damn stuff? But Erin thought that river rock was *too big*.

Jack wasn't happy about it. Working away, by nine o'clock the sun finally slipped over the mountain above River's End. The warm rays hit AJ's back and he could feel the inevitable heat of the day through his t-shirt. It was going to be another hot one today.

He brushed the sweat gathering on his forehead and tucked a bandanna around his head before throwing his hat off to the side.

He glanced up when the door to the cabin suddenly burst open as if the intruder wanted to shove it off its hinges or shatter the glass inside. Then... well, he should have realized who it was by the vigorous energy used to merely open the door. It had to be Kate Morgan.

She was a bundle of energy. Quick, energetic, and confident, she seemed as though she were entitled to explore the ranch, and AJ would have bet that was how she lived her life. Loud and sure and *there*. There was no mistaking Kate's presence.

He sensed it didn't just include her vacationing there. Yet, she wasn't obnoxious or rude or annoying. She was mostly just bold and brash, living her life, it seemed, with a vigor he couldn't imagine. He was slightly intimidated by her. Sure. He wondered what person in their right mind would not have been.

She stepped out onto the deck, unaware of him working right below it. He sighed. He supposed he'd better let her know he was there. She walked to the edge of the railing and leaned on it, a coffee cup gripped in her hand. She placed it on the railing as the steam spiraled from it.

AJ glanced up and quickly averted his gaze. She wore only a man's long, white button-up shirt that ended at her mid-thighs. What thighs. Her legs went up to her neck, it seemed. They were longer than his, he was pretty sure. Bare now, her thighs were slim and shapely. Her breasts pushed against the thin, way too thin material. She wore no bra. Just two bright, pointy nipples pushing like fire pokers through the flimsy material. Her blonde hair was tousled all about on top of her head. It made her eyes look as big as an owl's.

He wasn't usually attracted to women with short hair. But on Kate? Nothing else would work. It so matched her fast and furious personality and the presence she had in every place she went. Confident, bold, and brassy, yet it also high-lighted the delicate line of her jaw and small ears.

He scraped harder at the grass, his shovel hitting a large rock and making a loud ding. Predictably, she leaned over the railing to investigate. He didn't look up to observe her. He didn't need another look at her naked breasts sheathed in only white gauze, or so it seemed.

Sexier than being naked. His body wanted badly to react

to her, but he remained bent over, working hard at not reacting. He hefted up the boulder, a round river rock that was embedded in the sandy soil and tossed it off towards the bank, out of the way.

"Oh, good morning, AJ. I didn't realize you were there. Hard at work again, I see."

"Morning, ma'am," he muttered by rote.

"Kate." Her tone was insistent and quick to correct him.

He nodded, peeking at her face, then looking back down. "Right. Kate."

"What is it you're doing there?"

He'd worked around the cabins since they were built. Mowing, weeding, spreading gravel or fixing miscellaneous repairs or hardware. Never once did one guest say hello to him or ask him what he was doing. He'd give her that, she wasn't snobby.

"Removing grass from the front and back. They're landscaping this area."

"They?" she asked skeptically. "Or do you mean you?" She sipped her coffee and leaned against the railing, her elbows and forearms flat while the coffee cup sat between them. At least, the cup covered the gap in her shirt that exposed her flesh. Her cleavage. Her elegant neck and the smooth, rounded white—

He shook his head, riveting his eyes on the dirt he was removing. "I suppose I mean me."

She was just slightly above his head. Her gaze skimmed over the view. "I'll give this place kudos; mornings this nice don't often come to Seattle. Beautiful morning. Is it often this gorgeous?"

He paused to lean against his shovel. "Yeah. Most of the time. Fall is cooler, and in winter, there's two feet of snow right here, but even then, the sun often shines."

"You here all year then?"

"Winter? Yup." The thrill of that knowledge hadn't ceased to zing through him yet. A permanent address.

"Kate, where the hell is my shirt?"

AJ froze and his entire body paused. She wasn't alone? Shock must have registered on his face. A man stood in the open back door, wearing black trousers, but no belt and no shirt. For a city guy, he had a pretty good build.

AJ frowned, embarrassed that he hadn't grasped the situation. He thought she was single. Not that it mattered one way or the other to him. He wasn't even interested in her. No. No way. But he had assumed wrong.

"I'm wearing it, obviously. Don't get your tighty-whities in a bunch," Kate grumbled back, glancing toward AJ and rolling her eyes.

"Can I have it? I need to get back now. I have a meeting at three."

"Well, I *could* return it to you now and possibly give AJ here a thrill, but why don't you just cool your heels until I finish my coffee? I have to prepare the Langenton campaign anyway. And since it's my company, and the meeting is on my behalf, if I make you late... who's going to complain?"

"Kate..." The man's voice trailed off in frustration. "You don't always to have to remind me who's boss, do you?"

"Actually, I do. It's part of the pleasure I get from it." She finally moved off the railing, crossing her arms under her breasts. AJ chose to face towards the river because he was getting too much of a thrill from staring at a woman wearing another man's shirt.

The same man who also got a thrill from her. Or at least, AJ had to assume that was so. AJ grabbed the squares of grass and started to walk away to stack them, if only to put more distance from her. "Because let me tell you, the insurance premiums I pay are the totally *un-fun* part of being the boss. Now, Greg... please let me finish my coffee in peace."

AJ kept walking, but he heard their muttering before the back door slammed shut. He wondered why the man would so easily leave a half-naked woman on the porch because she ordered him to? AJ would…

Do nothing. He'd do nothing, because she was a guest, and she had a boyfriend, and Jack said not to mingle with the guests, and because AJ couldn't remember the last woman he'd been with. So he'd do nothing. Besides, he didn't really want to do anything anyway.

When he went back to the grass patch, Kate was again leaning over the railing. "So, AJ, what do you all do around here for some fun?"

He squinted up towards her. Why the hell would she ask him? Like anything about him seemed fun? Digging up grass wasn't exactly the ideal pursuit of any party animal.

"Uh, I ride horses. Quads. Target practice. The rodeo. I guess, that kind of stuff."

"I have to say I haven't done any of that except ride the horses and you know how well I'm *not* at that." She flashed a quick, easy grin at herself and he almost forgot about the see-through top when her dazzling white teeth shone in a full, huge, wonderful smile. "But target practice? Like what?"

"Shooting guns. Clay pigeons. Or a box sitting on a fence post, whatever."

"Do you have a gun?"

"Uh." He scratched his head. She sounded shocked. It raised the hair off her head, she was so shocked by his proclamation. "Yeah… not so unusual. I hunt quail, grouse, some duck and pheasant. So I have a couple of shotguns, sure."

"Hunting. Guns. Dear God, it's for real then? I see this stuff advertised by outfitters and the like. But here you are, living it."

He shifted his weight on his feet, feeling somehow more uneducated and stupid than he usually did.

"Do you think you could show me sometime?"

"Show you what?"

"Let me try shooting one of your guns at a target. I've never even been that close to one. My parents were both avid anti-gun activists. So I have this unreasonable fear of them… but also a morbid curiosity. So… would you?"

"Would I…" He nearly scratched his head some more from not believing she was serious.

"Show me how to shoot a gun."

"Um, I really can't. Jack doesn't like us, you know, fraternizing with the resort guests."

"Jack doesn't what?"

He could feel the heat of a blush climbing up his neck. Did he use the wrong word? Fraternizing was right, wasn't it? But it was not like he could be sure. It wouldn't be the first time his ignorance embarrassed him, but with someone like Kate? He kicked the dirt near his toe. "You know, hanging around them. Separation between staff and guests. It's one of his rules."

"What about the horse rides?"

"That's different, that's work."

She scowled at him. "That is freaking ridiculous. I've never heard of anything so insane. What a damn tyrant. Like adults can't decide who they want to be around? Yet you're fully allowed to dig around the cabins we're in, just not fucking allowed to fraternize with us?"

Okay, maybe fraternize was the correct word. But why the hell was she so inflamed? He backed up a step, having no idea what to do with her. She had a lot of personality, and got riled up like a freaking machine gun. "Again, yeah. That's my job. So, I'll ah, just get back to it here."

She took her coffee and threw out a third of the cup in a

splash over the railing. It landed in the freshly dug dirt. "That's really insulting, AJ. Aren't you insulted?"

Was she still going on about Jack's rule? He had no idea what the damn deal was.

"No. He's running a business. I respect that."

"Well, *I* don't have to." She suddenly spun around and away she stomped. He stared at the slammed shut door, wondering if she was mad at him.

KATE DRESSED QUICKLY in one of her new ranch outfits. Shorts again, her boots, and a t-shirt. She marveled that she had never dressed that way before. T-shirts did great things for her chest. She rushed into the little check-in office.

Jocelyn was manning the front desk again.

"Can I rent a quad?"

Jocelyn glanced up at her snarled question. Kate didn't like being told what to do, but especially at a place where she was staying. And by her own brother, no less. "We require a small deposit. You'll get half of it back as long as you return the vehicle undamaged. You have to sign some paperwork for insurance reasons and take a quick tutorial, which I can gladly give you."

"Oh, the paperwork. I sure as hell hope you learned your lesson. I can't imagine how Jack Rydell had your ass over that."

Jocelyn's head tilted. "Well, no. He just reminded me to double check next time."

"What's with all the work going on around my cabin?"

"Oh, that's because of Erin and Allison. They want to fancy up the place. Jack's complaining, but it will be nice. I hope you weren't disturbed."

"By AJ? The man's a damn shadow. Ghost. Snake. I don't

know. Whatever moves around without making a peep or complaining or even voicing basic human rights," she grumbled. Kate was offended on his behalf by her brother's tyrannical actions. First taking over for Erin as if she were a damn idiot, and then insisting AJ couldn't even talk to guests?

"Oh, AJ. He is quiet."

"Don't tell me half the old married women here aren't out on their porches drooling over him," she muttered, scowling at the image. She'd seen some women in their retirement years. She just bet they all enjoyed a nice fantasy of eye candy in the quiet, hardworking ranch hand.

"Well, don't we all?"

"Do you have something going on with him?" The thought made Kate resist glaring at Jocelyn as if she had any business to ask, let alone care if they did.

Jocelyn dropped her head, shrugging her shoulders as she let out a little, embarrassed laugh. "Well, not from lack of trying. But he nearly pats me on the head and tells me to run along. He says he's far too old for me, but I don't care..."

"How old are you?" Kate studied the girl. She was all tattooed and pierced, so it was hard to tell. She might have been older than Kate first thought.

"Twenty-one. AJ's thirty or something. So I guess he's old. But old like that..."

AJ's esteem just shot up. He turned this hot little girl down? Yes, Jocelyn was hot in a wild, rebellious, crazy way. A way AJ had turned down! Good man.

"Well, I hope you didn't get into any trouble because of me. And I'll plan on that quad around two, okay?"

"It'll be pretty hot then. You going alone?"

"No. I'm going to find someone here to go with me. But let me guess, it can't be AJ, right? Because Jack forbids it?"

Jocelyn's smile was quick before it disappeared. "True. But in all fairness, it's the same no fraternizing rule for all the employees, not just AJ, from me to all the ranch hands. Have you seen the other workers? AJ is just the tip of the iceberg. It would be one hook-up after another if too many women mingled with the guys who work here."

"Well, it still seems impossible that someone can insist on that." Kate turned and left the office, determined that stupid Jack's rules wouldn't hamper her sudden inclination to enjoy one AJ Reed.

No matter who told her not to. Because the first thing her brother would learn about Kate was, she did not tolerate anyone telling her what to do.

KATE WANDERED around the beach and the ranch until finally she found Erin working with a horse in the circular arena. She leaned on the gates and watched for a good hour or so after Erin walked over to chit-chat and gave her permission to stay. Snapping up the opportunity to try grilling Erin again, she didn't find out anything more of great interest.

Kate mentioned the rented four-wheeler and hinted that she needed someone to go with her. Erin claimed she only rode on the backs of them, but promised she'd find someone. Kate crossed her fingers, hoping she'd suggest AJ.

It was so foreign to Kate to pussyfoot around a guy like him. She didn't play games, or send others to do her work, or hope the guy would be here or there. She just usually went out with the guy. She asked him for a date or if he wanted to sleep with her. That was usually her way. Never just flirting and being subtle or hoping.

But scoping her brother's ranch and doing reconnaissance came before the hot ranch hand with whom she'd like to pass her time.

She caught glimpses of Shane walking into the main

house. He waved at her, and later, another man passed her who was heading towards one of the outbuildings. He was cute too, but didn't quite hold her attention the same way that AJ did.

Finally, Erin came over to the fence. They chatted about the ranch. Kate got an earful about the history. For over a hundred years, the Rydells had been there, and the damn river was even named after one of their ancestors, Clint Rydell. She learned how Erin came to the ranch and found the four brothers living together, alone, while raising Jack's two sons.

"Where was his wife?"

"Jack's first wife died when the boys were three and ten. She had a heart condition. She died almost unexpectedly."

"Oh. That's very sad. What happened to their parents?" She held in the sigh. It didn't change the fact that Jack was a controlling, misogynistic pig, or that he could still be a serial killer, which would justify why her mother hid his existence and ignored her son. Kate still clung to that reasoning, because if that weren't the case, she'd have to start dealing with what that made her mother.

It meant that her mother had abandoned her own child.

Kate wasn't sure how to accept that knowledge in contrast to the image and the experience of the mother *she* knew and loved and dearly adored.

"Their parents died together in a car wreck when the boys were young, and Jack was merely twenty. He pretty much raised his two younger brothers, but especially, the youngest one, Joey, who was only five. Jack was more of a father figure to him."

Kate's face scrunched up in displeasure. Oh, great! He was a sad, tragic hero with dead parents, no wife, and raising three young kids all alone? Crap. Still didn't mean his personality wasn't terrible. He could beat up Erin or the kids.

He could be mean and stingy and awful to them... Perhaps her mother was right.

"Where are you from?"

Erin leaned over the railing, rubbing her hands together, and lifting her face as she stared off towards the river, taking in a deep breath. "Seattle."

"How'd you end up here?"

Her smile was small and quick. "By accident, really. I came after my brother, who was working here. I stayed after he left."

"And snagged Jack."

She laughed. "Nobody snags Jack. But yes, we eventually fell in love."

"Idyllic story."

She snorted. "Oh, good God, no, it wasn't. I slept with his brother, and my brother stole a bunch of money from them, and disappeared with my car, stranding me here."

"You?" Kate burst out laughing. Now they were talking, and she felt a sudden kinship with Erin she wasn't sure she *could* feel. "Which one? The big one? Shane?"

"No. The young one. Joey. The one Jack thinks of as his son."

Kate shook her head. "How do you get past something like that?"

"Lots of patience, and lots of avoidance of the subject. It helped when Joey returned to the Army about then, and he hasn't been back for more than a few visits."

"What will you do if he comes back to stay? What will Jack do?"

Erin shrugged, easily. "Welcome him."

"You're telling me Jack doesn't care? He isn't crazy with jealousy? I'm not sure I could handle that. My sibling and spouse?"

"I'm telling you Jack knows what I feel and for whom."

Kate flushed. "Sorry, I'm prying. But this place is kind of fascinating."

Erin's smile was indulgent. "I must say you are by far the most curious guest we've ever had. Shane mentioned running into you and the boys both said you ended up down at our beach. All these questions about us..."

Her words trailed off. Kate kept her stance casual and easy. "I'm on vacation all alone and come from the city. I love the city. I have no idea what to do with myself here. I'm desperate for human interaction. Call it being bored and you all are the only distractions."

Erin laughed out loud, hitching her foot up on the bottom rung of the fencing. "Why are you vacationing all alone here then, if you don't like it?"

"Oh, I like it. Surprisingly, I do. But it's so foreign sometimes, it feels odd. Like I'm a duck waddling around a football field. I'm harmless, just a curious kind of person. Especially about that which is so strange to me. You know what I mean?"

Erin nodded. "Yes, I felt like that about this place from the start. Being from Seattle too, it was nothing I had any knowledge of."

"Yet you stayed?"

"I fell in love with this place, the lifestyle, and the family as much as I did Jack."

Maybe she just wanted to live there and Jack was a good man to be with in order to make that happen. Kate still wasn't convinced. Erin straightened off the rail. "Oh, there's Shane. He could take you up on the four-wheelers."

Kate sighed. She wanted AJ, but accepted the big, long-haired Shane. He was an amusing companion. She could hear more gossip. She soon learned all about his wife Allison, and baby, Rosie. In fact, that was all the man talked about each time they stopped zooming up and down the old logging

65

roads and canyons. By the time they got back, she had dust pouring from every pore, hair follicle, and crevice in her body.

She had loved it, however, and the faster, the better. Kate managed to master the machines far quicker than riding the horses, and soon they were racing hell-bent down the dusty, abandoned roads, and up into the hills until they roared down into the ranch, at full throttle in a race for their lives.

Shane won by just a tire length and had Kate ranting and raving as she got off and threw her helmet down. Shane laughed and grinned at their bickering before it drew the other ranch hand—Caleb, Kate believed his name was—and later, even Jack, who frowned at her. He probably didn't like all the fun happening.

AJ was stacking farm implements in one of the barns nearby and his neck twisted as far as it could when he caught her shriek of laughter after shutting the vehicle down. Passing by him, she blew a kiss and continued on towards her cabin.

He worked all day on the lawn in front of the cabins. She made it her business to spend the afternoon by wearing her skimpiest bikini. It had triangles on top that let her breasts peek out on both sides and a small bottom. It was simple, classic black, but she added some heeled sandals that only made her legs seem that much longer. She lounged on her deck for several hours, sunbathing and spraying baby oil on her skin until she was all slick and shiny.

Closing her eyes, she sighed as the sun warmed her skin and the heat seemed to sizzle off her. Finally, this was her idea of a vacation. Later, she sauntered up towards the ranch, strutting a bit, perhaps, and garnered a few whistles from ranch hands who smiled back with a wave. She also got a few stares from the male spouses of guests. She made it her business to make sure AJ, busily loading the grass squares onto a tractor bucket, noticed her by fluttering her fingers at him.

She was forced to talk to Jack when he stepped out of the barn as she passed it after a substantial chat with a dusty ranch hand named Jordan, whom, she learned, was Caleb's brother.

She had all eyes on her. She was almost sure that AJ had noticed her, but she couldn't figure him out. He didn't glance at her. Or let his eyes linger on her or even seem to pursue her. Didn't he feel the same connection that she did?

Finally, Kate gave up and went to bed, spending the next few days repeating all the learning and talking and traipsing around the ranch. No one stopped her, but she got lots of odd looks. She assumed no other guests made themselves quite as at home there as she did.

They weren't policing her, but they did give her a few concerned looks. She worked daily on her tan, making sure she was always in AJ's proximity when she did so.

But the oppressive heat often drove her inside, where she tackled her work. The place really did need a pool. The river was raging and dirty with snow melt, the big sticks and even trees drifting past the shore. It was useless now for cooling off in, especially where the guest's beach was located. It wasn't half as nice as the one she found her nephews on.

If this place belonged to one of her clients, she'd give their marketing efforts a complete make-over. The Rydells could be making a killing there. She grudgingly had to give them that. It was a unique spot that provided a totally unique experience for tourists. For city people like herself, they weren't just on vacation. With a pool, they could capitalize on a relaxation spot and more, the unparalleled experience of actually witnessing how the ranch ran right there. The horses literally grazed all around them in the vast tract of sweeping farm land that encircled them. The horses were the key, and she'd definitely maximize their novelty in all marketing suggestions.

Not that the Rydells were sophisticated enough to hire her. Still, her ideas were bursting in her mind to share.

Finally, however, AJ was digging holes in the cleared area and planting trees. He said hello to her, but kept his face down and his mind on his work, no matter how much she tried to distract him. Frustrated and growing bored, she considered leaving. Then she pondered the idea of revealing herself to Jack. Then... well, she didn't know what she really wanted to do.

Other than AJ. She really wanted him. Maybe it was time to make that happen.

CHAPTER 5

*T*HERE, AT A TABLE, sat AJ Reed. Kate's blood started to warm and simmer. He could have it nearly boiling in minutes. Had she ever been so physically attracted to a man before? No. Not even when she was younger. Not even in college. There was never a man so physically hot to her. Maybe it was all the difference she saw in him. He had a neck as thick as her thigh. His shoulders made him appear square and bulky as he sat in the chair. He made the normal, average-sized chair look like a toddler seat.

Sitting alone at a small table in the corner, he was quiet and unobtrusive. His hat was still on as he stared down into the glass of clear liquid before him. His hand came forward and his fingers encircled it, lifting the glass and making it look like a thimble to his lips. He took a small sip before he set it back down and did it all with an ease and almost mannerly way that didn't totally match his bulky, red-necked country persona. He wore the same ripped, snarled-up jeans, cowboy boots, and a t-shirt with a picture of man lassoing a horse on it.

Bored out of her ever-loving mind, Kate strolled towards

AJ, glad for the distraction, but was disappointed when he didn't even glance up or notice her seductive saunter. However, a few other patrons, similarly dressed as AJ but without the appealing looks, eyed her walking up. She intended for them to see her too and smiled her greetings at their appreciation of her effort.

She was wearing a cute-as-hell jean skirt she found at the same place where she got the pink boots. Together, they made her forever long legs look awesome as hell too. The tank top showed off her boobs, which were rounded and plump, surgically enhanced, and one of the first investments she made after securing her condo, car, and investment property.

They were a personal reward after she took care of all the boring stuff. And her breasts *were* exquisite, even if she did say so. From a small A cup, she now had two large, plump Ds. She filled out the top, and her bright red bra lace peeked over the edge of her ribbed tank top. She didn't want ridiculous boobs, just a good-sized handful. Sexy. And their perkiness helped a lot too.

Still, AJ missed it all. She sighed. He was a tough nut to crack. Harder than she first anticipated.

"Hey there, cowboy. This seat taken?"

He glanced up, almost jerking to attention, as if he'd been lost in contemplative thought. What did a ranch hand contemplate? What kind of deep thoughts crossed his mind? She couldn't fathom what they might be. When to feed the livestock? Where to store the poop? When to cut the hay or whatever green crop grew in the fields, which they constantly watered? She gathered it was important stuff, like her office equipment, laptop, printer, and iPad were for her.

He swallowed and stared at her, a surprisingly quiet man. She ignored the fact that he didn't answer, and scooted right in.

"Is this like a honky-tonk bar? Never been in one. There's one in Seattle called The Achy Heart, but I never hit it. My friends went though, did the step-dancing stuff, what do you call it?"

"Line dancing?"

"Yup, that two-step stuff. I can't do it. Can you?"

He shook his head. "No one dances here. It's just a tavern. Mostly just working hands. Don't get too many of the tourists in here."

She glanced around and nodded. "I'm seeing that." She let out a long, exaggerated sigh. "I see too, I wasted my cute-as-hell outfit. Showering was dressing up to be here, huh?"

His gaze barely glimpsed her before resting back on the glass. The position of his hat only allowed her to see the tip of his nose and lips and chin. He was good at hiding, she'd give him that.

The waitress came by and grumbled, "What do you want?"

"Whatever he's having," Kate said, pointing at AJ and trying to get him to raise his head and engage her.

He did. Then he frowned and shrugged when the waitress's eyes landed on him, waiting. "Water. No ice."

He didn't even crack a grin. The waitress sighed. "Great. Two waters, no ice; coming right up."

Kate bit her lip, she was not expecting that. She asked, "Are you a recovering alcoholic?"

He finally met her gaze with little surprise. "No. I just don't drink much."

Huh. He was such an enigma to her and what she expected. She motioned to his nonlethal drink. "Wasn't expecting to drink water. I need something stronger; be right back."

She jumped up and scooted after the waitress to order a drink with some alcohol. The waitress nodded, her expression much happier; no doubt at the possibility of earning a tip at some point. Kate leaned on the bar and the man next to her smiled, his gaze centering on the substantial cleavage that spilled out of her tight shirt.

She smiled back. "Dream on. You're older than my dad." Though her dad was dead too, the man got the point. Nevertheless, he smiled with appreciation at her, despite being caught, and she returned the smile. She got her drink and headed back to AJ, feeling frustrated when his gaze didn't follow her or linger on her walking. Nothing. It was like AJ was immune to all of her enticements.

Sure, it happened, but not when she felt that kind of chemistry with another person. Their eye contact left her skin feeling flushed and heated. That could not be imagined just on her end. She wasn't cocky enough to assume all men fell at her feet in adoration. No. Duh! She knew when she was attractive to men, as well as when she wasn't a man's type. The ones who liked sweet, girl-next-door types weren't usually interested in her.

She sipped the drink as she sat back down before lifting her leg and slamming her heel on the table. "What do you think of my new shit-kickers?"

His head jerked up when her foot thumped the table. Exactly as she intended. She wasn't being ignored. She would figure this man out. Most men weren't too hard. Sex and sex. Especially if they were attracted to her.

Never before had the physical appearance of a man turned her on so much, and without even touching her. She usually demanded a bit of damn finesse and attention in the form of dates and compliments, petting and some kind of adoration. Never had she felt so turned on by a man who rarely met her gaze or said her name or even acknowledged her presence. Yet it wasn't silent and rude, like some men could be. No. Apparently, AJ was just that quiet. And shy almost. That still stunned her.

"AJ? The boots?" she pressed.

"They're pink."

"Pink and fantastic."

"Better than those spiked things, I suppose," he finally relented, and added, "You'd have twisted an ankle at some point if you kept wearing those."

She slammed her glass down and removed her foot, leaning forward. "That's some good stuff. Sure you don't want any?"

"I'm sure."

She waved to the waitress for another round and turned back to her shy, quiet cowboy. "So AJ, what are you doing in here, looking all contemplative?"

He sipped his water. "Trying to relax."

Good lord, she could not get anything out of him. Usually people, men especially, warmed up to her, but not this one. Country music crooned in the background, one song after another. This one was moaning on about lovin', fishin', and huntin'. She laughed. "This music. Just fits the damn scenery here. It's all I've ever heard since I got here. One sad song about losing a wife or husband or dog after another."

"Yup, it's pretty popular 'round here."

She finished her drink and her blood started to heat up. Meanwhile, AJ shoved his water away. Water! Sitting in a tavern to sip water. How funny. He rose up to his full height and adjusted his hat. "Well, enjoy your evenin', Kate."

Her lungs deflated as she blew out a sigh. What a letdown. After days in this country, rural hell, she still had nothing to show for it. She was missing her mother and feeling so out of sorts, she couldn't even get this man to crack a smile or show a spark of interest in her. He passed around her and started towards the door; her back was toward him. The waitress served Kate her last shot just then, and Kate swiftly downed it. Then she slammed the empty glass on the table and fished around in her small purse for some cash, which she tossed down as she slid her chair back. With a renewed sense of purpose, she rose and started across the small room, her boots clicking on the plank floor. Damn, she would not be so ignored.

It was very dark in River's End. There was one central streetlight in front of the church. The rest of the lights that broke the darkness were only citizens' porch lights, and a few more distant farm and ranch lights. Her eyes adjusted to the gloom. The river splashed down the embankment where the tavern was perched.

"Hey, cowboy? Give a girl a ride?"

AJ glanced at her from where he was just sliding into the truck he drove there. She thought it belonged to the ranch. It was green and old, with a boxy back end and big, wide tires that lifted it higher off the ground than normal trucks. There were no running boards.

He stared at her through the windshield before giving her a slow nod. His reluctance was real. She'd driven her own car, but left it as she jumped inside the truck, glad for her long legs. Her skirt rode up when she slid onto the vinyl bench seat. Two tears in the seat made it uncomfortable and the synthetic fabric stuck to the backs of her thighs. She scooched up and down to get comfortable, yet each time, it felt like her skin was being pulled off. "God damn. You should have warned me not to wear a skirt on this seat. It's like a cheap laser-hair removal."

His gaze flickered to her legs then. Even AJ wasn't totally immune to her body parts and the way she wiggled all around. Her skirt was short and high. His view rose to her chest and higher. "What about your car?"

"You can bring me back tomorrow," she said, smiling with

confidence. "I downed another shot. Probably shouldn't drive, not even that short distance."

He nodded. "Okay."

Shifting the truck into gear, within minutes, they were back on the bumpy driveway of the ranch. The main house porch lights and yard lights were on, but no one was around. AJ drove past it all and down towards the work buildings until he finally stopped under a carport. The silence seemed louder than the rumbling of the old truck. He slipped the keys out and turned towards his door without even a slight glance her way. She sighed. Okay, this was going to take bold, decisive, obvious moves. But she could handle that.

He pocketed the keys and stood near the truck's rear end that stuck out of the carport.

"So where do you live?" Kate inquired.

He nodded and pointed toward the left. She glanced over and saw a long trailer not too far inside the yard. It seemed private enough that he had plenty of his own space. There was a deck leading up to it. Not ideal, but not terrible, either; it could do for tonight.

"Oh."

He had the nerve to step around her. She gnashed her teeth. He was either completely obtuse, or simply confused. How could he not sense what she was about? Enough with her feeble attempts. It was time to accomplish her goal.

She stepped right back in front of him so he had to stop dead. He frowned at her, and their eyes were level with each other. "AJ, do you find me at all attractive?"

"Uh, I don't know. It's irrelevant. Jack forbids his employees, such as me, from mingling with any of the ranch guests."

Irrelevant? Didn't AJ feel the heat sizzling between them? And how dare Jack decide with whom his grown, adult employees could or could not have sex. She'd never heard of such a rule. What a complete power-tripping asshole her brother seemed to be.

She sucked in a breath and prepared to go into battle against her tyrannical brother, if only for AJ. She stepped forward. So tall, she managed to make AJ take a step back into the wall behind him. His hands came out to cup her elbows, and no doubt, push her off him. *No can do, cowboy,* she almost announced with a smirk. But she didn't want to scare him off, lest he literally run from her.

She stared right into his eyes. Such pretty eyes for this rough, weathered man. Hazel in color, they appeared unsure as he stretched his neck back as if to give himself more space. She leaned forward so her fingernails touched his forearm and trailed her index and middle finger down his left arm. It excited her to be so close to his bulk, especially when he suddenly stiffened at her touch.

"Kate..." His voice sounded wary. He was warning her, but she ignored him. All he had to do was step to the side and deflect her passes. His throat twitched as he swallowed. Nerves? It fascinated Kate to know she could make this big beast of a man feel nervous. But she was beginning to really believe she could.

"AJ," she mimicked his tone. Then she smiled at him and rubbed her fingernails up his arm again, adding her other hand. His breathing visibly increased. She followed his arms up to his beefy, tight biceps towards his shoulder and then made a line down his chest. Slow and steady, her nails and then her fingertips pressed into his skin. His breathing hitched, and his stomach quivered when her skin touched his abs. Lower and lower she descended, fixing her gaze on her hand.

The heat of his skin scorched her through the thin layer of his cheap t-shirt. He nearly gasped when she didn't stop at the waistband of his jeans, but went right over them and touched him. He immediately pushed back against her searching fingers with hard heat. Impressively hard heat. She glanced up at him. His mouth dropped opened and his breathing became fast and short.

She stared him in the eyes as her other hand joined her exploring one and she undid the silver belt buckle.

"This okay if I do this, cowboy?" She asked her gaze lowering between them.

He gulped his gaze riveted on hers, and nodded yes.

She was efficient, especially considering she didn't normally encounter such an obstacle as the belt. Then her fingers touched the bare skin at the snap of his jeans. Taut and rigid, his muscles pressed into her fingertips and she sighed with pleasure as she unsnapped his jeans and slowly peeled them back to reveal more of him. He wore tight underwear that cupped his now straining manhood.

She nearly licked her lips. *Perfect.* Hot and proudly presented for her approval. Her stomach warmed as liquid heat filled her and made her nether region wet. She reached in and touched him, pulling him out of the underwear and exposing him to the air. He sucked in a breath.

Shocked?

She was pretty sure he was just by the look in his eyes. He was turned on, but confused and still didn't trust her. He thought... what? She was messing with him? Would she back out? Oh, no. She definitely wanted this man and she wanted him now.

She ran her hands over the steely, warm length of him, shutting her eyes. Oh, he felt so perfect. Warm and big. She tugged on him and his hips jutted up towards her. With quick hands, she grabbed the condom from the back pocket of her purse and used her teeth to open it before dropping the wrapper to the ground. His gaze jutted up to hers in surprise when he heard the sound. She grinned and waggled her eyebrows. Always the prepared girl scout when it came to sex was she. There were no accidents or thoughtless risks in her sex life. Just fun. Lots and lots of fun.

She dropped down and put her mouth on him. She was sure that astounded him. He grunted in appreciation, however, and his hands, those big hands that she loved, landed on top of her head and started messing up the short strands. She loved sex hair. Her hairstyle almost looked better after sex than before. She licked him, sucked him, kissed him gently and swallowed him deeply. Cupping him, she moved her head up and down in a frantic rhythm, trying to give him maximum pleasure. The kind of pleasure she felt just by looking at him.

He finally surrendered to his feelings. His hips zeroed in on her mouth and his head fell back against the side of the barn with a soft thump. Groaning, his hands kept brushing, twisting, and even tugging on her hair. Satisfied that she'd given him the best blow job of his life, Kate let him come inside her mouth, with the condom on of course, before she promptly removed the results.

She didn't need that. After she finished, she slowly started to rise up again. Her knees were indented with the pattern of gravel on the ground beneath her. That was a first. In the heat of the moment, she hadn't noticed. She'd probably have bruises tomorrow to show for it. But the thought merely cheered her up, and did not embarrass her. It meant she finally succeeded with AJ.

He straightened up and slid his hands off her to reach for his pants. She sighed. Oh, no way was AJ done. She wasn't finished yet.

She glanced to the left, where the hay bales were stacked, and spotted one on the end that would suffice. She started kissing him before he could react. Nearly hungover from the orgasm he just had inside her mouth, he let her tongue touch his and she groaned in pleasure at the wet, hot heat. He didn't respond at first, but his hands suddenly cupped the back of her head. She moaned into his mouth and stepped forward, making him back up until the hay bale hit his legs. She pushed him down to a sitting position. Startled, he turned around to see what he hit. Then his gaze came back to her. She smiled, taking the bottom of her shirt and shucking it off. His gaze was fully riveted on her chest. She tugged her bra down and let him ogle her perky, round breasts. She had huge, brown nipples. He swallowed slowly and his nostrils flared as he kept staring.

She scooched her skirt up and straddled him. Gasping, he realized she had no underwear on. She took one breast and pushed it toward his mouth. "Suck it," she demanded.

He did. His mouth latched onto her and she moaned, burying her fingers in the strands of his hair just as he did to her. She let her head fall back in ecstasy as his wet mouth found her nipple, and his teeth alternately nipped at the hard, jutting pebble of her breast. "Harder, AJ," she mumbled. He nearly inhaled her nipple on command. She bounced on his lap and he grew harder under her until she nearly cheered in appreciation. "Oh, I like that. The other now."

Replacing his mouth with one hand, he switched sides. She leaned her chest into him, her blood burning, no, *scalding* at his attention. She was almost dizzy from it. She couldn't wait, she was so turned on. Her entire lower half was filled with blood and swelling in urgent need, desperate for release. She grabbed his hand and pulled it down between her legs. "I can't wait. Touch me. Now. Hurry, AJ."

He kept his face pressed against her breast as his hand quickly found her center. Sliding his fingers inside her as she groaned, her mouth parted and stayed open as ecstasy filled her entire body. Her orgasm was that quick and hot and fulfilling. The heat was so intense, it felt like it could shoot right out of her fingertips. It traveled to every corner, crevice, and nerve ending of her body. Her lips detached from his as her head bobbed back in pleasure too intense to even care what he was doing or what she looked like.

On and on it flared. She finally started to come off the burning high, and AJ stilled. Her eyes were closed. She sighed in total contentment. With a groan, she opened her eyes, blinking. There was a yard light outside the corner where they were half hidden. The light sifted between the slats of the wood, just enough for some illumination. Tipping her head forward, she smiled and leaned her lips towards his mouth, only this time, in a slow, easy kiss without any tongue. No slobber, no neediness. All the while, she was digging in her bunched-up skirt pocket for the other condom. Relieved when she grasped it, she pulled away from him and held it up. "Found it!"

He stared at her hands and again swallowed, but didn't raise his eyes to hers. His hat had fallen between the wall and the hay bale. She deftly opened the condom wrapper and slipped it over him as he strained, hard and steel-like, toward her. Lifting up her hips, she slowly sank onto his shaft and closed her eyes, holding onto his broad shoulders for support as she took him in her wet, swollen body. She nearly hummed with pleasure. She grinned and leaned forward to kiss him in a languid effort.

Lifting up her hips, she dropped back down on him, only harder. His neck strained. He sucked in a sharp breath. She squeezed her walls around him and he suddenly reacted by flipping her over onto her back, and completely amazing her. The world spun and tumbled when she was lying on her back, hay straws poking into her bare skin as his mouth engulfed her breast. He was now between her legs, and fully in control. His hips pushed hard. She threw her leg up over his shoulder for better leverage and nearly screamed at the new position.

He closed his eyes, finally losing himself in the act with her. At last, he was completely participating as he pushed hard inside her, making her back slide up on the prickly hay and abrading her skin. Slamming into her over and over again, like a wild piston on overdrive, he kept drilling into her, scraping the insides of her. She was astonished by his sudden participation and the fierceness of it. She closed her eyes, preparing for the wild, crazy, hot, hard ride that hammered inside her, on the threshold of pain, but making her burn with pleasure.

She surrendered completely to the experience then, spreading her arms wide and gripping the edges of the hay bale while striving to capture and withstand the impact of the man pounding into her. She was breathless and groaning and moaning as the orgasms started to erupt like molten lava, simmering and spewing out of her core. Her blood was nearly boiling when it coated her body in hot sweat and fired up all her nerves, ending in pleasure. AJ, the big, hulking, strong, quiet, unreadable AJ, came into her body with a final, hard, back-breaking push. He had his eyes closed and his teeth clenched, and Kate would not have been surprised if he began to pound his chest like a caveman, since it was that kind of total orgasm.

She lay there, slowly releasing the hay bale from her tightly clenched fists. Blinking, she stared at the open rafters above her. There was an occasional hoot and the fluttering of birds or bats, from the higher beams. A contented silence filled her stunned, spent haze. She swallowed. Sex. Complete, uninhibited sex. No sweet tenderness, or worry of pleasuring each other or even knowing who the other was. It was all about nerve endings and touching. It was hot and furious and fabulous.

She dropped her leg from the heaving, sweating, man at her south end. He closed his eyes, his shoulders dropping in a kind of odd moment. What? Was he feeling defeat? She'd swear that's what his body language told her.

His shirt was still on, and his jeans were all bunched up at his knees. He leaned over a few inches to grab them, and tugged them on while turning from her as he buttoned them and buckled his belt. He stayed too long turned from her. She shifted her legs, wondering if her spread-eagled sprawl was unlady-like. But her body had practically melted after her climax, and now she felt languid. She could not imagine feeling better than she did right then. She slowly drew her thighs closer together and lifted her hips to pull her skirt lower. Slipping her bra back over her breasts, she sighed as she stretched her long arms over her head.

"AJ?" He still hadn't turned back towards her. She sat up, concerned. "Hey, AJ?"

He finally looked at her, but his expression was strange. Was it regret? She swore it must have been some kind of lament. She got to her knees and leaned towards him, touching his arm with just her fingertips. "Are you okay? Did you like it?"

His mouth puckered and he nodded his head in the positive, but then looked away.

She slid her legs to the ground and her pink boots made a soft *ping*! on contact. "I did. I don't know why you're acting so worried, but I liked that, every single minute of it." She rose up to her full height with a genuine grin and began looking for her shirt. There it was. Wadded and wrinkled after landing in the dirt from being hurled against the wall of the barn.

"I never knew a woman to…"

She glanced up at him as she shrugged into the tank top. "Enjoy sex? What? Who do you usually sleep with?"

"…come on so strong."

She wiped off the dirt. "Oh, AJ, honey, that wasn't strong." She laughed at his stricken expression. "Strong would have been if I tried it on the first day, like I fantasized doing."

He kept his gaze away from her. She sighed again. She wasn't sure how to deal with his shyness. Was he regretting that? Who could regret the physical release and pleasure they both just received… and not once, but twice?

She turned and quickly dispatched the used condoms and wrappers by crushing them in a tissue she pulled out from her purse, which had fallen to the ground just outside the truck. He cleared his throat and shifted his toe forward, tracing circles in the dirt with the tip of his boot. Why all the hesitancy? "Is there something wrong with you having sex with me?"

Her hands rested on her waist, elbows out, her mouth turned down in frustration. What was this reaction? Regret? Why? Because she didn't simper and preen like it was all shocking and boring? Didn't he like knowing how much she wanted it? She reveled in it and enjoyed coming just as much as he so vigorously did.

"Don't you have a boyfriend?"

"Boyfriend?"

"The guy that was here three mornings ago?"

Her mouth dropped open. He was worried she was cheating? And it obviously bothered him. She let out a snort. "Greg? He's not my boyfriend. I don't cheat. I am a single adult, and I can sleep with whomever I choose."

His mouth puckered again and he chewed on his lower hip, his expression still perplexed. She shrugged. "I don't know what your problem is here, AJ, but we are two consenting adults and that was a great lay. What's the problem?"

"I just don't do that."

"You don't do what? Usually have great, hot, incredible sex?"

"Sleep with someone I don't even know."

She tilted her head. That was not something she expected from the man's lips. She stepped back, realizing in an instant she made all kinds of unproven assumptions about him, since he was a rather hot and well-built ranch hand. She assumed he was callous, careless, and had sex pretty easily and whenever available, just as AJ seemed quite shocked that sex didn't mean more to her. Emotionally speaking, that is. She cocked her head. She was acting like the typical guy stereotype and he was playing the guilt-ridden, hurt, typical girl role. Interesting... They both had unspoken expectations and were almost offended that the other wasn't living up to them.

She shut her eyes, nearly in a panic then. "Did I press too hard?"

He shook his head. "No. I don't mean that. I did participate. I don't think I was thinking about wanting to do it. I never intended to do it with you, but once it started... I mean, you were a shock..."

She sighed and walked over to sit dejectedly on the hay bale they'd just made love on. "Oh, crap. Look, AJ, I'm thirty-five years old. I have a healthy, active sex life. It isn't something that embarrasses me. I feed my desires."

"And I don't. It's just... it goes against my beliefs."

"What do you mean, your beliefs?"

He sighed and came to the other side of her before sitting down on the hay bale. She suddenly felt weird and sorry for her actions. Almost to the point of feeling stupid. Chills broke out over her arms, and she longed for some damn clothes, now that the sexual haze was over. She rubbed her bare arms. Wishing for, at least, her underwear.

He noticed her discomfort and got up and opened the

truck door. He returned with a wadded-up, flannel, red-and-black-checkered shirt. He held it out to her with a solemn expression. Feeling suddenly almost awkward with him, she reached out to take it, and rose to her feet. She slid her arms into it and wrapped it around her front, huddling under it as she sat back down. "Thank you," she said quietly.

He nodded, sliding back to sit near her, still looking chagrinned. She appreciated the sweet gesture and almost shy way his mouth nearly smiled. He rubbed his hands up and down on his thighs. She shut her eyes. He was nervous with her. Unsure. Strange. Looking at him, you'd expect him to be a swaggering, cocky alpha, out to fuck her like she just insisted he do. But now? She worried it wasn't AJ Reed at all. He was almost embarrassed... or ashamed of what he'd done with her.

"AJ? What did you mean? Your beliefs?"

"I don't sleep around. I was waiting..."

"Waiting for what?" Puzzled couldn't begin to describe how she felt. No way was this man still a virgin. She could tell by the way he responded to her and to sex. He was a man who'd done it before. There was no hesitation, and no lack of knowledge or experience.

"A little over three years ago, not long after I started working here, I joined the church across the river. They're nondenominational, but the pastor there is pretty amazing. Anyway, I've been following their beliefs ever since. I never had any before that. They... the church, I mean, changed my life completely. I was headed down a bad road. Had been for years. Gambling, drinking, having indiscriminate sex..."

"Oh, my God," she muttered softly, shutting her eyes and feeling completely horrified. He was a born-again virgin? She leaned forward, nearly burying her face in her hands as heat literally scalded her chest, neck and face. She rarely got embarrassed. She derailed his plans? His religious beliefs?

She exhaled a sigh. She never even considered that possibility. It was those stereotypes at work again, granted, but still, she wasn't usually so wrong. "Were you like, waiting until you got married or something?"

He shrugged, his giant shoulders lifting up and back down. She dared to glance at his profile. "I was going to say something. But you were so quick to…"

Get on my knees and give him a blow job? Strangely enough, she didn't think AJ would actually say such a thing to her.

"So you haven't had sex in…?"

"A while," he finished.

"As in years?"

"Yes. As in years." She shut her eyes again, groaning in near pain, not ecstasy. She never considered anything like that. Was it any wonder that once she reactivated his sexual desires, he morphed from the nearly shy, sweet, quiet AJ to the man pounding her into the hay bale? She'd done the equivalent of waking a sleeping giant.

Shame coursed through her body. Not once could she remember, even going back to high school when she first had sex, did shame over the act ever enter her consciousness.

"So you're Christian? The real kind? Belief in the Bible and all?"

"Yes."

"And before that you weren't like this?"

"No. I was not a very good person."

"Like you perceive me to be perhaps? Not a very good person? After all, I was down on my knees with a man I've known less than a week, right?"

His gaze traveled from her knees up to her face and his expression shifted to surprise, by the way his eyebrows lifted, and his brow wrinkled. "No. I don't perceive that at all about you."

"Really? Because I'm not Christian. I would never forego

86

sex for any religion, Jesus's, Allah's or Buddha's. And as you witnessed, I've had it twice this week alone. So you must consider me a raging heathen." Her heart was now heavy in her chest and it weighed her down. She hunched her shoulders to conceal her boobs.

"No. I don't think anything like that. I couldn't quite figure out why you were even coming on to *me*."

"Because you're ho—you're very handsome, AJ. I think maybe I tried to turn you into the stud I was fantasizing about. But I really liked talking to you, too. You're a bit surprising. I mean, you're very quiet. Very withdrawn. Very religious, as it turns out. Nothing about you is what I expected. And that's fascinating in anyone. And you're different than any man I've ever met. In my world, *you* are pretty amazing."

"I haven't done a lot of good things in my life."

"So Jesus led you to do good deeds?"

"Yes."

"And in exchange for that, you became celibate?"

"I guess. I mean, I was. I didn't label it, however. I just didn't sleep with anyone."

"Celibate cowboy." She blew out a deep breath. "Not what I was planning on, AJ."

"You were planning on something?" He finally tipped his head enough to catch a glimpse of her face before staring down at his feet again. His boots were parted and dust covered the tips.

"A girl doesn't show up without underwear and a pocketful of condoms without a plan."

"I'm not sure what to say."

"Join the club," she muttered, exhaling her disappointment. Somehow, she felt almost like she'd done something wrong. But she shook off the guilt. She certainly hadn't forced AJ. At any moment, he should and could have considered his devotion to his beliefs. They weren't her beliefs, and she had no idea about his, so again, not her fault. Even if it did shame her.

"So you regret that?"

"Well, I'm not celebrating it." He leaned forward, resting his elbows on his knees, his head hanging down.

"Now, I feel like *I've* done something wrong." She crossed her arms over her chest, catching the ends of the long flannel and bunching them in her hand.

"No. You didn't. I mean, it's probably a stupid thing anyway. I just was trying to improve myself."

"What do you need to improve?"

He shrugged. "From what I was before."

"What were you?"

She tilted her head, studying the back of his shoulder and the arm that was nearer to her. "I got in a lot of trouble. I used to ride bulls. Performed in lots of rodeos. Lots of drinking, drugs, women, and gambling."

She wanted to lean forward and touch his arm. It was right there, so close, and he seemed so strangely sad and disappointed in himself. She expected some celebrating and swaggering, not quiet reflection as if he were trying to figure out his belief system for life. "I didn't know that."

"Well, I was promiscuous. I've been tested for HIV and all that, with no long term repercussions. But for many years, it was all a blur. It doesn't make me too proud. To remember. Or to be like that again."

She rolled her eyes although he couldn't see it, and leaned forward and touched his bicep, wrapping her fingers around his muscles gently. "AJ, this doesn't make you like that again. It isn't being promiscuous to sleep with one woman in... how many years?"

"Three."

"That's not promiscuous. And for the record, I don't

consider myself to be either. I admit, this was a little quicker than most of my... we'll politely call them liaisons. But really, you aren't going to morph into whatever monster has you fearing sex now."

He tilted his head to catch her eye. "Prison. Prison keeps me from doing the things I was doing that led me there. And this act was reminiscent of that."

Her breath caught and her neck jerked reflexively. Okay, she hadn't expected prison. It wasn't something she thought about or even considered in someone else. She swallowed. "Okay, but it wasn't a drunk or drug-involved encounter. It was merely two people enjoying each other." She licked her lips. "What, ah, what were you in for?"

He leaned back to stare at his boots. His tone was completely soft and controlled. If she closed her eyes, she could imagine his deep, smooth voice and cadence belonging to a professor of literature, preparing to lecture an intimate group of students in some elegant room, not the muscle-bound, dusty cowboy sitting on a hay bale in a dark, cold barn.

"I got into a bar fight. I was drunk. I barely remember it. Bottom line is, I hospitalized this guy with a concussion. He was five-foot-eight and barely one hundred and sixty pounds. I looked like this then. Probably was even in better shape. What business did I have physically fighting with some little guy like that? I fully regret what I did to him. He had a wife and a little kid. He missed work and I was respon-sible. I don't want to forget what I'm capable of. Never again. I pleaded guilty, did my time, cleaned up, and swore I'd never drink another drop of alcohol again. Nor—"

He dropped his hand on his thigh, palm down, and began rubbing absently at the denim. Kate let hers fall on top of his and he nearly jumped at her contact. His entire body seemed to be in some kind of fight or flight mode. She felt his thighs tensing, and his hand stopped moving, as if completely frozen under her mild, innocuous contact. Especially after her very recent, not-so-innocuous contact. Her nails were painted pink to match her boots. Her long, tanned fingers and nails looked ultra-feminine against his fat, wide hands. She gripped his fingers in hers. He had adorable hands, really. Considering how big and broad he and his muscles were, his hands were kind of meaty and fat compared to the rest of him.

"Nor have sex? I promise you, this doesn't make you suddenly capable of inflicting violence. It doesn't make you unrecognizable to the man you were two hours ago."

He didn't clasp her hand in return. Nor did he withdraw it either. "I was going to say, nor act out of control again. This was out of control. I didn't plan it, I just acted. No, I *reacted*. I did what felt good. I don't trust my instincts. I don't trust myself to do things without my control."

She kind of got where the celibacy came in now. He was scared of surrendering to his baser urges or needs. He thought it… what? Made him violent? Turned him into a vicious criminal? She didn't see it. Nothing like what she witnessed in this man.

"It wasn't out of control. You didn't throw me against the wall or try to choke me. You did exactly what I asked of you, urged you to do, no, in fact, begged you to do. It was totally consensual, wanted, and I initiated it. You couldn't have planned it. I appreciate your line of thinking here. But I hope you realize the difference between a drunken bar fight from long ago, and pleasurable sex with me. And I hope when you think about it, you'd agree that if you were planning to end your celibacy, it was a damn sensational way to do so."

His lips twitched. She smiled when he finally lost the forlorn scowl. She leaned against the side of him, bumping her shoulder against his, and gripping his hand tighter. "It was spectacular. I dare you to tell me you don't agree with me on that part."

He nudged her back. "I will agree on that part."

"I'm freezing. Can we worry about your soul a little more in depth tomorrow?"

He jolted up. "Tomorrow?"

She slid onto her feet, wrapping his shirt tighter around her. "Well, you can't compound the sin by just calling it a one-night stand, can you? Wouldn't ending your stint of celibacy and all be more justified if it happened in a more substantial relationship? Meaning, at least more than two days?" She grinned at him after her explanation. "And I was hoping you'd walk little ol' me across this big, dark ranch. I don't really want to go to the cabin all by myself, not now."

He stood up, his gaze flickering everywhere but on her. "Of course. I didn't know it would bother you."

"Not in the daylight or even when we first got back. But it is a lot of ground to cover and it's very late. There's something spookier about late at night. After most of the guests have gone to bed. It's like the time animals should start to roam about. Or bats. I don't like low-swooping bats."

He was quiet as they exited the carport. She glanced around, relieved to see no sign of anyone. A few hours ago, she hadn't cared. But listening to AJ's compelling, deep reasons for why it should not have gone down like that, she now, retroactively, felt pangs of shame.

He didn't speak as his boots crunched over the gravel next to hers. Once they arrived at her cabin, he held back, like he was the hired help and not allowed to use the front door. She stopped on the porch step. He shuffled his feet and cracked his knuckles, fidgeting all around. She wanted to kiss him. No, she wanted to pull off his shirt and bring him inside with her. But what he told her made her feel ashamed for even having the urge.

"Goodnight, AJ."

He tugged his hat lower on his head. "Good night, Kate." Simple. Easy. Done.

However, she wasn't so sure that was the case. He stepped back, spun on his booted heel, and left her at a fast clip. She had a lot more to consider than she had realized. It hadn't gone at all like she expected. But strangely for her, he might have garnered more of her interest than she typically felt about a man. He might, she admitted, have grudgingly earned her respect. He was a convict. The word didn't match the man, but it was something she'd have to think about, mull over and see how it fit. Or what she thought of how it fit. But the extreme life changes? Yeah, she kind of admired them, even if three years without sex seemed like torture to Kate. Still, she could almost understand the urge to do so with that control thing he talked about.

*a*J GOT UP AT seven and showered, dressing in the only outfit he had that wasn't ripped, stained, or work-worn. To church, he always wore the same dark slacks and blue button-up shirt. That outfit was reserved for church and only church, and he carefully washed it each week in preparation for the next Sunday. Services began at ten, and he was always on time. He sat in the same pew, four rows from the back, six from the front. He drew no attention to himself, but he wasn't hiding in the back, or trying to avoid participating. He listened to the preacher speak about Bible verses and he sang along with the hymnal.

Guilt sat heavily on his heart. He didn't actually believe he would be struck dead by lightning, but he couldn't deny a sense of general displeasure and disappointment with himself. For three years, he lived completely sober; no alcohol, drugs, prescription or otherwise, no swearing, no fighting, and no sex. It was all a healthy package to AJ's way of thinking. He had abandoned all the wild, reckless living that might have sounded fun and exciting and what someone like him would seek, but it really was lonely. Most days, he felt sick or hollow over whatever he'd done the night before.

However, in the last three years, he could remember every single day, and every thing he'd done. He had real conversations and real connections. And although he didn't have anyone special in his life, he lived in a place that people knew and respected him. He had an address that his hard work and integrity earned him. That was enough for AJ.

What he did last night with Kate wasn't something he wanted. He was out of control and satisfying a baser urge inside him. And while many people did so and enjoyed it, as Kate was saying, when he did, it seemed way too far. It led him to remember long benders of sex and alcohol, and gambling to get money to fund it. He often woke up puking or staring in wonder at a naked girl he had little memory of. It wasn't fun when he tapped back into it. He believed his genetics predisposed him to overindulge in the urge to have sex, or drink, or fight, or gamble.

Kate Morgan had been driving him nuts since her arrival. The body and face were enough to make a monk break his vows, but when she wore that micro-bikini that made her long body simply go on and on and on, it was almost impossible not to fall at her feet and worship her. But AJ resisted. No lurid stares. No ogling. He kept his eyes diverted, and his mind and hands occupied by the work he needed to do. The savior of his life was work, the ranch and the sense of community he found in the church. He never belonged to anything before. Joining something like the church was humbling.

No, he didn't partake in church socials or even really talk to anyone. The preacher didn't invite him over for dinner or anything else, but he went to church and enjoyed it all. Sometimes, while watching the young families and little kids running around the church lawn, or yawning in their pews, or throwing spitballs behind their parents' backs, he imagined what it was like to be part of a family. He understood he never would be. He just liked knowing that families like those around him in church existed.

But not in AJ's world.

Sleeping with Kate was a fluke. He sensed by her presence at the tavern and coming over to his table that she might have been interested. That's why he hightailed it out of there as soon as he could. He never expected her to follow him, much less, to so boldly and crazily put her hands on him.

It happened so fast. She was touching him intimately and all his rational thoughts fizzled and dissolved. The only thing left were his feelings. So many overwhelming feelings. He hadn't dealt with them in so long, he forgot he could have said no. He could have managed his desires. But like the old days, he did not. The old days that led him to HIV clinics to be tested after nights of unprotected sex. Or getting patched up by some bar girl after another drunken fight. Or being hauled off in handcuffs to prison after breaking a bottle on a man's head and giving him a serious concussion.

So it wasn't lightly that he'd broken his commitments. In church, while listening to the sermons he'd never heard before the last three years, he became accountable to someone, and something. As it turned out, he realized he was never accountable to anyone before. Since his father encouraged such behavior, and bought him a damn hooker for his thirteenth birthday present, how was he supposed to learn right from wrong? Without any kind of restraint? Or any kind of respect for others, especially women, and most of all, himself?

He had no sense of purpose when he got out of prison, and knew he needed to find something to live for. Being trapped behind bars was a strong motivator. He couldn't tolerate that possibility again. He needed lots of space, air, and sky. Though he deserved his sentence, his entire life became dedicated to finding a way to become a better person. Different.

He succeeded in all that here at River's End. That is, until Kate Morgan pulled in that afternoon. As a dirty ranch worker, sweaty and uneducated, there was no reason to believe someone like this exquisite woman would even notice him beyond the directions to her destination. He was admittedly beyond flattered when she seemed to flirt with him. He knew she was hitting on him. He also understood it was because of his body. No other reason. She liked his muscles. After seeing her city guy, he understood what appealed to Kate. Along with the extent of Kate's interest in someone like AJ.

And he fully intended to make sure nothing came of it. But then… it did. However, it didn't have to happen again.

KATE'S HEAD popped around the corner of his trailer before he saw her body. She smiled, nearly sheepishly. He jerked upright in the lawn chair he occupied.

First, because she was *there*, and second, because she looked almost uncertain. Something he never observed in her before. She stepped on the bottom step of the stairs that led to the deck where he was sitting. Her pink boots clunked down on the wooden surface. She wore jeans shorts tonight. They made her long legs seem all the slimmer and more shapely, not to mention, they were cute as hell. Even if he restrained himself and managed not to ogle her as if she were a piece of cheesecake, he didn't want to be like that anymore.

She walked towards the small table beside him. From her back, she withdrew two glass bottles and set them down with a *thunk!* Water dripped down the sides of them. He glanced up at her, then at the bottles, about to protest until he realized they held lemonade.

Without asking, she sat down in the other lawn chair. "Hello, AJ." Her gaze was strong and bright on him. She had incredible eyes. Blue and bold, capped by delicate, almost white eyebrows that she darkened some days, although not on others. He noticed too much.

"Hi, Kate," he answered, shifting his butt around. Her presence made him uncomfortable. He was much too aware of her body, and therefore, his own. Plus, she was intimidating as hell. Whatever her life consisted of, it wasn't like his. It wasn't living in a damn trailer, or carrying around manure and dirt for a living.

She leaned forward, popping off the bottle caps on the drinks and handing him one while taking her own. She swallowed a long gulp, lifting her eyebrows as if to say, "your turn." He took the cool drink and did the same. It was real lemonade, sour and sweet, and so refreshingly cold in the heat of the afternoon.

She set hers down with a soft clunk and wiped the moisture on the back of her arm. He didn't expect the almost childish gesture. "So, how was church this morning? I assume that's where you went."

He nodded. "It was fine." He had no idea where they stood now, or what to say or do. Kate stopping by on Sunday afternoon at five o'clock was like they were friendly neighbors about to engage in a regular chat. Never mind that they shared the craziest, wildest kind of dirty sex he'd had in years... in so many years.

The tip of her tongue came out and moistened her lower lip. "So did you confess?"

"Confess?"

"For being a fallen man?" Her smile was quick, lifting one side of her mouth up.

He cleared his throat, and leaned forward to wrap his hand around the cool drink and stare at the label, anything to divert his eyes from staring at her. Her hair was tousled; the blond strands that should have looked manly didn't. Instead, it seemed like his hands had been combing through it, just like last night, while her head…

That was why he hoped Kate Morgan would end her vacation today and go home. He had a few too many fantasies leaning her way. Now that he had images, pictures, and feelings to match the fantasies, he was overwhelmed by how easily his body responded to her. "It's not a Catholic church. There is no confessional," he mumbled. The humor she found in something that meant everything to him really set him off.

"Oh, so you intend to just carry on now as a sinner?"

His jaw clenched harder. "Well, I guess. I don't know. It isn't like anyone polices it. I was only trying to be a better version of myself."

Her chair legs scooted over the deck as she slid closer to him. She leaned over the table and used her painted, long fingers to squeeze his arm. "I'm sorry. That was callous of me. I guess, maybe, I'm feeling a little ashamed here, and it's not something I've ever felt before in regards to my sex life. My parents were both atheists. I wasn't taught anything about religion. Never even been to church, unless it was for marrying or burying. So I don't totally get it, but I don't mean to sound like a bitch."

His gaze fell to her elegant fingers on his arm. They looked so odd. All slender and bony with rounded, long tips of nails in a soft pink color. He picked at the bottle's white and yellow label, thinking the premium brand probably cost more than he'd spend on dinner. "It's not shame. It's just not how I want to live anymore."

She nodded, her gaze drifting towards the view over the

fields beside the river, up towards the small town of River's End, and higher to the big, rolling mountains that dissolved into the sky, swallowing the horizon. AJ didn't have a lot of time to gander at the view during daylight hours, but anytime he did, it never ceased to give him pause and pleasure. So much pleasure that he lived there very gratefully. That was his view each time he stepped out of the small trailer behind him. He felt a peace settling over him. God must have had a reason for his previous life, with prison and all, because it led him there.

"My mom taught me that sex and my body were my business and no one else's. It wasn't something to be ashamed of, or hide or act as if I didn't deserve to have sexual pleasure in my life. Lots of women get embarrassed by it, as if they shouldn't feel pleasure. That's more how I look at it, a right to feel good, rather than the religious, taboo factor of right or wrong. I'm sorry. I don't really understand the teachings about it."

"I don't either, to be honest."

"You didn't grow up religious?"

He snorted. "No. I have no idea what my parents were."

"Were?"

He shrugged. "My mom was never part of my life. She ran off long before I could remember her. My dad was around, but only sporadically. He was a gambler."

"Then who raised you?"

"Foster care sometimes. Myself others."

"I didn't know that." Her tone lost the brazen confidence that usually filled it and took on a subtle, subdued gravity he hadn't observed from her.

He waved it off, staring towards the raging river down the valley. "I survived."

"Surviving and getting out unscathed by it are two different things."

99

"Maybe."

"What happened to your dad?"

AJ kept his gaze on the river. Stony faced. He hated thinking about his father. "Last I saw him, I was sixteen. He'd just pulled some damn scam on an unsuspecting couple. They found out and chased us out of their place with guns, literally shooting at us. I decided I was done with him then. That made my father done with me. We parted ways and I never heard from him again."

Silence ended his statement. Finally, she asked, "What did you do?"

"I made do."

"At sixteen?"

"I was strong. I could always do the physical work of one-and-a-half men. Plus, I had a history of bull riding, no fear, and could get plenty of ranch work all over the Dakotas and Montana. I learned how to ride. I didn't have a lot of expenses. Food. A few incidentals. I had a single duffel bag of stuff to my name. I made do."

"How'd you end up in Washington?"

"Decided to get a clean start after my parole was up and I was free to travel. I needed to go somewhere no one knew my old man's name or mine. I needed to get out of the rodeo circuit and all that went with it. I started in Montana, traveled to Idaho, and eventually ran across an ad Jack placed in the local paper for ranch hands."

He drank liberally from the lemonade and set the bottle back down. "So you see, Kate, though you're enjoying your vacation here, this is my life. This isn't a joke or a lark to me, it's all I've ever had. I am an ex-con without even a high school education. This is the end of the road for me, and the thing is, it's the best dang road I've ever been on. While you are on vacation, I must be a novelty to you. I believe if we met up in Seattle, you'd have little or no interest in me. You don't want to sit down and have a stimulatin' conversation with me. You see me as a big hunk of muscles that you can liberally enjoy. And while, years ago, that would have pleased me too and been enough, I don't want to be like that anymore."

Quiet followed his proclamation. He didn't even glance her way, but crossed his arms over his chest and kept glaring out towards the view. She finally leaned her elbows on the table and tapped her pink fingernails. "You're wrong. You're actually quite stimulating to have conversations with. But you're right that this is limited for me. Vacation. But I didn't mean to give you some kind of crisis of conscience. I was thinking, I don't care if you try to deny it, we have a physical attraction to each other. Am I wrong?"

He sighed. The woman was relentless, and completely didn't know the meaning of shy or embarrassed or just leaving something alone. "I suppose not."

He didn't glance her way, but he sensed she smirked when he caught the shaking of her head. "Oh, for God's sake, AJ, you can't deny that you check me out."

"I don't deny it."

"But I didn't mean to come across as if I were using you. I don't think I see you as just a giant hunk I want to touch and fuck."

He sighed. She was not one to mince words. "Where are you going with this?"

She shifted, leaning forward, and her hand came nearer to his. He stared down at it. She stretched it towards him as if to shake his. "Hello, my name is Kate Morgan."

He finally met her gaze. She smiled, raising her eyebrows as if in challenge. Then she nodded towards his hand near hers. "Now you."

He rolled his eyes, looking confused, but eventually he

touched her hand with his, and the zing of her touch jolted up his arm.

She shook his hand. "It's very nice to meet you. I was wondering if you'd like to have dinner with me."

His head jerked up. *What the hell?* "What?"

"I was wondering if you'd like to be my date for dinner? You know, like you're not just a piece of meat that I think can't speak or have an intelligent conversation. You already have, just now, several times, in fact. So I'd really enjoy your company at dinner. My treat."

His astonishment left his mouth hanging open. He expected any number of reactions from her. Never to look or speak towards him again. Pack up and leave. Try it all again. Because she was right, the sex was mind-blowing. And now, almost hesitantly asking him on a… a date? He'd never been on a date before. Not really.

"AJ? Please? It's the least I can do. Just dinner."

"I'm not supposed to date the guests."

She cocked her head. "The no-fraternizing thing? I think we did all kinds of fraternizing last night. Come off it, AJ, that ship has already sailed."

She was right, and the thought of it was so tempting, his heart began thumping loudly in his chest. Anticipation? Desire to do that? Maybe. It wasn't something he felt very often in his life. Simple pleasure to do something? Was he pleased she asked?

"What do you have in mind?" He wanted to take his fist and punch his own jaw. All he had to do was say no and lay low for a few days until Kate Morgan drove that fancy little sports car of hers down the road, and hit the highway, never to look back again. She'd be gone soon enough. A figment of his imagination. Another woman he screwed and forgot and never knew. But no, he let her almost convince him.

"I am a surprisingly decent cook. Only a few basic dishes, but anyway, have dinner with me."

"Where?"

"My cabin?" Her face scrunched up like she had no idea why his tone sounded so fishy.

"I can't go inside those."

"Oh, for God's sake, AJ. You're the Rydells' employee. You can enter their freaking guest cabins if you're invited by the guest. It's just dinner. Jack Rydell can kiss my white ass if he thinks he can dictate whom I choose to have my dinners with." Her teeth grinding and her neck muscles straining, she thumped the table with her fist.

AJ finally had to smile. She was unlike any woman he'd ever spent time with. Not that there were many. She was all fire and opinions and confidence. And very attractive in her fierceness.

She closed her eyes and took a deep breath. "Please, AJ? I feel guilty. It's not a feeling I'm used to enduring and I'd like it to go away now. Appease me. Let me make last night up to you."

When did anyone ever care about how he felt? Let alone try to make something up to him? Perhaps her caring about his opinion was the aphrodisiac he couldn't refuse. He finally nodded his head.

She smiled and ignored his hands-off signals by sliding her chair back, jumping up and wrapping her arms around his shoulders. She kissed his cheek before he could duck; then she let him go, suddenly standing on the edge of his deck. He barely blinked in the time she accomplished all that. She was a firecracker, sparkling everywhere she went. "Tomorrow night, at say, seven? Sneak on down and come inside my... cabin. Be the bad-boy ranch hand I know you are."

He rolled his eyes and she smirked and laughed out loud

as she waved, her grin growing huge when she gave him an exaggerated, lurid wink and raised one eyebrow. She was so lively and engaging, it was almost impossible not to respond to her or try to resist her charm. Her confidence was enticing to him, and yes, she was pretty dang likeable.

CHAPTER 7

A SOFT TAP ALERTED Kate. She peeked over the loft railing and immediately spotted AJ. He stood at cabin number eight's back deck, her cabin for now, and had just tapped using only his fingertips on the glass to alert her he was there. She felt like he was trying to be a ghost, he was so silent. Perhaps he was hoping she wouldn't hear him? Of course, she knew his participation in coming tonight was hesitant, at best. The door was wide open, with the screen shut and her music playing loudly. The sun beat down on his back. He held his hat in his hand and shuffled around in nervous circles. Kate's heart did a weird little skip. There was something oddly endearing about the big, beefy cowboy. He was so cautious and unsure of himself, yet his huge, bold, strong physique broadcasted confidence, self-reliance, and a loud, commanding presence. It surprised her how nervous she made him. She didn't intentionally do it, but there was something inside her that melted in response to his anxiety around her. And when did any man ever make her feel all melting and gooey inside?

Never.

She shook it off and quickly descended the stairs, going barefoot in shorts and a tank top. Smiling, she approached the screen door. He was turned halfway around from her, perusing the new landscape he'd been installing all day. It was a bit disconcerting. He spent the entire day working below her cabin. Now, he was planting a riot of colorful flowers, adding compost and sprinkling water on them before finishing off with beauty bark.

She almost spent the day out sunbathing in her bikini just to flirt with AJ. She normally would have lapped up a man's attention. But with AJ? She figured out it would merely embarrass him. Now, she was starting to realize she didn't want to do that. He didn't take her flirting lightly at all; he took it seriously. She chose to hide in the cabin to avoid upsetting him in public or drawing undue attention to them as a couple. He appeared distinctly uncomfortable as she slid the screen door open, and almost jumped at the sight of her.

She smiled and motioned for him to come in. He stepped over the threshold, both hands clinging to his hat. His hair was damp still, and the blond strands were loosely shoved off his forehead. He had shaved too and his chin was smooth. He wore a clean shirt and jeans. Glancing down, he asked, "Should I take my boots off?"

His voice was so unsure. He fidgeted some more before looking up at her and her heart melted. Okay, the big, tough man had no idea what to do with her. She had all the control, but instead of flaunting it like she usually did, she wanted to soothe and comfort him, if only to convince him she wasn't any better than he was, or more important. He didn't have to be any better than he already was. But his anxiety and unsureness with her remained.

"Only because it's hot. It might feel good. But just make yourself comfortable."

He stepped off to the side and slipped them off. "I should. They're dirty from—"

"Planting flowers? Making an honest living? I know, I watched you most of the afternoon while I was in here working." She motioned toward the coffee table where she stacked her laptop and files. He eyed the pile, and a flash of surprise appeared on his face. "I make an honest living too. I slacked off too much last week, and have a lot to catch up on."

He glanced around the cabin. Unease showed in the way his worry lines bracketed his mouth. "AJ? Why don't you sit down? Can I get you a drink?"

He sat as quickly as she suggested it, perching on the edge of the lone chair across from the couch. "Sure. Water would be fine."

She bit her lip. She felt as if they were on a bad blind date. He was so nervous, she'd have sworn his face was turning paler. Was she that hard to be around? Or was disobeying one of Jack Rydell's rules really that big of a deal? Did AJ actually fear getting fired? Just for being inside the cabin with a guest? The thought again ignited her blood until it was burning through her veins.

She put more ice in a glass, filling it with water from a pitcher in the fridge, and poured a glass of wine for herself. She brought both beverages to the living room.

With anyone else but AJ, she might've suggested they sit on the deck and enjoy the dipping sun as it set over the horizon. It streamed through the sliding window as brightly as if they were outside. The rushing river echoed from further down the gully. "Do you mind if I have some wine? My brain hurts and I feel like relaxing." She motioned toward the pile of paperwork.

"What is it you do again?" His face remained down, but he was staring at the paperwork.

"I run a consulting business. Other businesses hire us to examine how they run their company, from their financials, to internal operations, to how they determine their target customers for marketing."

"You said you owned it?"

"I did? Yes, I do, I mean…" She tucked her legs up under her, settling into the couch, and sipping the wine. "I've owned it for about five years. It was my father's, full disclosure. When he retired, I took over."

"What are you doing with that?" He indicated the stack before her.

She smiled, swirling the liquid around the wide-mouthed glass. "Well, for example in this firm's case they wanted us to focus in on their advertising efforts, so we are presently studying this client's marketing strategies. So I'll evaluate and then design a campaign around what their needs are. Whom are they targeting? What age group? What income level? Whom do they want their customers to be? I'm designing and recommending new advertising to best reach their target customers. We also design the pertinent ads to go with the advertising, whether they be billboards, commercials, radio, TV or internet. Maybe include some travel sites and social media. Anyway, that's a brief overview of what I worked on today."

"You must have had a lot of schooling to understand and provide that service."

"Yes, I got my master's degree from UW."

"You really own your own business? How many employees work for you?"

"Currently? Twenty." He shifted around, clearly becoming more uncomfortable. She sighed, leaning forward and setting her glass on the paperwork. She rubbed her hands together. "I work in a high-rise in downtown Seattle, and live in a twenty-story building in a condo. I've never lived anyplace where I had a patch of grass or even enough room for a potted plant. I don't know anything about growing stuff or farm animals, and this is the longest I've ever been away from the city for my entire life. I understand we are quite different. I also understand how uncomfortable you are just being here because of Jack Rydell's rules concerning you and me as employee and guest. But AJ? We crossed that line pretty hard the other night. So now? We could just hang out together, learn something more about each other, and our different lifestyles, and chalk it up to a good experience to expand our horizons. What do you say?"

He lifted his head. "I feel inadequate, you know, culture-wise, education-wise, and career-wise. I don't see any benefit or value you could get from speaking to me. Other than showing you how to get on a horse, what could I possibly offer someone like you? Except of course..."

She bit her lip. He could barely say the word. Oh, big stud muffin wasn't really all that studly or a muffin. She sighed and shook her head. "I made an erroneous assumption about that subject. I won't do it again. I'm looking right at your face, not your..." *Dick? Penis? Manhood?* All the options filtered through her brain and made her internally grin while picturing his blushing reaction to what she was about to say. Instead, she just grinned widely at his narrowed-eye look. "Your muscles. I'm talking *to you*. Not trying to get something from you."

His mouth twitched. "My muscles?"

"Delicate ears. I understand that now. I may be a teeny, tiny bit crass and casual in the way I talk. I figured with your 'no swearing' policy you wouldn't appreciate it."

He tilted his head, and his cheeks finally relaxed into a smile. His entire body seemed to sag a fraction of an inch, as if he had released the tight rein he had on it. "You do realize I work as a ranch hand, right? Even you can't touch the crassness and rudeness I'm used to."

"Well, yes, I assumed that would be the case, but oddly, with you, I find it's not. You're not crass, rude, or crude. With you, I want to tamper down my naturally sullen mouth and be more polite."

"What? You're protecting my fragile ears?"

She laughed out loud as he lifted his mouth in amusement. "So fragile. I don't want to damage your sensibilities."

He rolled his eyes and shook his head, reaching for the water and letting a quarter of the cup slide down his throat, making his Adam's apple bob up and down. She doubted he realized how much he was turning her on just by the sexy way he drank water. But releasing her runaway attraction to him, she now realized, wasn't welcome. Not like she first guessed he might have embraced her sexual, animalistic magnetism toward him.

But. She kind of liked AJ too.

"So I made pork chops in a sweet and sour pineapple sauce. It goes over rice, and I'm also serving a green salad. Think you'll eat that?"

"Sounds like a treat. I don't know when I've had anyone cook dinner for me. Thank you, Kate."

She smiled, and an odd little thrill traveled down her spine. Was it his unexpected solemnity and manners? Maybe. He was oddly sweet, concerned, punctual, polite, and spiritual. None of the qualities she first thought attracted her to him.

Last week, she might have suggested he have her with whipped cream for dessert. But since she didn't think that was on the table anymore, or would be appreciated, she held her tongue. With a little sigh of disappointment, knowing that would not be the case, she begrudgingly liked the man more now than at her initial introduction.

"So tell me about the bull riding. I honest to God—" She interrupted herself, almost biting her tongue. "Does that offend you? I might say it a lot. Not something I've ever considered excluding from my vocabulary."

He shrugged. "You don't have to censor yourself for me."

"Okay, I honest to *goodness*—" She smiled at the emphasis, and he responded in kind. He had a great smile; it was all sweet with an "ah, shucks" quality. His nose must have been broken at some point and the crooked cleft it left only added character to the rough, weathered planes of his face. "Don't even remotely know how you could voluntarily get on the back of one of those things, and I've only seen it on TV."

He grinned. "Never once scared me. It's just a matter of balance and having no fear. There's technique, of course, and training, but I was a stupid idiot who thought I had the world in my hands. So I just went after it. Easy way to get money, I believed. Until I got hurt."

"What happened?"

"The bull threw me and kicked me in the head. Knocked me out pretty good, too. Anyway, after that, I was advised to stop. Some guys did it for the glory, you know, just to win and make a reputation for themselves. They have this burning passion for it. Not me. I was just trying to make money, and do something honest."

"Get by?"

He nodded. "Yup. To get by."

Something squeezed in her heart. She had a sad, almost disconcerting feeling that was all AJ had ever done in his life. Just get by. All alone. He found solace in the church and a community he wasn't really part of. Like the outsider looking in, he liked what he saw inside and quietly observed. It shamed her to realize she had so clumsily missed that quirk about him, and it only took two seconds of actually listening to him, beyond her assumptions, before she managed to understand him. She would have given anything now to go back two nights ago and not do what she'd done.

It was a selfish pleasure and usually appreciated. This time, however, it almost kept her from seeing his deeper personality inside. Yet, he could mount a thousand-pound bull and literally command it. Juxtaposed between a total macho man and a lost, unsure, almost sensitive boy, he only intrigued her more.

"What's it like?"

He smiled. "It's the wildest ride you'll ever take. I liked doing it for the crowds. That part was fun. People were always amazed, and when they cheered, it was a rush. So I guess I did appreciate some parts of it."

"Were you disappointed you couldn't continue with it?"

He shrugged. "Not sure I thought much about it at the time. Just couldn't do it anymore, so I started looking for the next job I *could* do."

The timer on the oven dinged. Kate rose to her feet and nodded toward the table she set. "It should be only a few minutes. Go ahead and sit down."

He walked over to the table setting, and took the chair out. She could almost smell his awkwardness in her presence. She pulled out the pork chops and dished up the rice and pineapple sauce, along with the green salad before bringing the two plates over. He waited a minute for her to sit, but she waved at the food. "Just go for it. We don't need to be all mannerly."

He dug in. And ate and ate and ate. She refilled his plate three times when his eyes lit up so happily each time she asked if he wanted more. She was flattered by his eagerness and delighted to see the visible satisfaction it gave him.

"You don't eat like this often, do you? No way you'd hold on to that physique if you did," she teased, sipping her wine, and pushing about a quarter of her uneaten food to the side.

"Well, I usually just make a sandwich. I don't cook. But I suppose I do eat a lot of calories."

She sighed. "A girl could dream of that. Anyway, glad you enjoyed it."

Twilight beckoned her through the windows. "I don't suppose you'd dare risk taking a walk? It's such a gorgeous evening out."

"Taking a walk?" he repeated, his face almost blank. "Uh, sure?" His voice almost went higher, like it was a question.

"You don't do that very often?"

"No. I mean, it's where I work, I guess, so I don't ever think to stroll around when I don't have to."

She grinned as she grabbed some sandals and slipped her feet into them. He started to grab the dishes, but she waved him off. "Leave them. I'll get them later."

He nodded, grabbing his boots before he stuck his hat on his head and waited off to the side while she went ahead of him. She'd give him that, he always took his lead from her. She hit the ground off the stairs and remarked, "The flowers are lovely."

"City people need to pretend they're part of nature. They really are not. But they're pretty, I suppose."

"You don't like them?"

"Just about a hundred other things I'd rather do than plant flowers."

They fell into step. Nearer the river, the trail dropped from the view of the cabins and the main ranch, which was farther down the way. They were essentially alone. She nearly shocked him when she took his arm in hers, leaning her head against his shoulder as they walked, practically entwined with him. He didn't know what to make of it; she could tell by the stiffening of his body parts. "What things? What things do you like to do?"

He hesitated, but didn't shake her off. "I like to take care of the orchard probably most of all. I like growing stuff. Ian's the one who planted it. He knows a lot about farming practices and the latest techniques. When he's around, he takes a lot of interest in it. He answers my questions, even if it bothers him sometimes. Probably after that, I like doing anything alongside Jack. His skills with the horses are unparalleled to anyone I've ever witnessed. I learn a lot from him too. They're both so intelligent. It's something I admire."

She bit her tongue to avoid saying that AJ seemed hungry for knowledge and know-how. He didn't have to ask or express any interest in the other men's knowledge. The reverent way he talked about the Rydells made her want to point out to him that the Rydell men had a family and a ranch as a starting point in life. In other words, they were more privileged than most and that was the only thing that separated them from AJ.

She wondered if anyone had actually raised him, or answered his questions, or showed him a skill or trade that might have landed AJ Reed a whole other career in life. Still, she was beginning to realize it wouldn't be *barely surviving* to skimp by and live on someone else's ranch.

"But work is work. I'm happy to do it. So flowers it is. Not my favorite."

He was humble. Grateful. A sense of shame filled her. She made so many false assumptions about him. She sensed that was the story of AJ's life. Tenderness filled her usually crusty heart. She stopped, and together, they stared at the river. She sighed and leaned her head on his shoulder, her hands rubbing his arm.

"What's *your* favorite thing to do? With your job, I mean?" he suddenly asked.

"I like to make up the ads. That's the creative part. That's always been my preferred talent. That's what drew me to it in the first place. And…"

"And what?"

She sighed. "Bossing the employees around. I'm a control freak; and I really like having all the say-so, which is a terrible thing to enjoy. I'm not as bitchy as you might imagine. I'm actually pretty generous as a boss, but I really enjoy being the one holding the reins."

A laugh rumbled from his chest. She lifted her head, startled. "I didn't expect you to admit that."

She shrugged. "I know, you'll probably hate me now. The arrogance. The—"

"I like it that you're so honest. Never met anyone who speaks their mind like you do."

She smiled and strangely, a blush of pleasure at his praise filled her cheeks. She realized his praise meant more to her than anyone else's she'd ever received, besides maybe her parents'. Which was odd. There were so few people she fully respected, but she definitely respected AJ. The realization of it was startling. An ex-con and uneducated ranch hand turned out to finally win more respect than all the men she'd ever known? That thought was sobering.

"You seemed a bit unsure about my honesty the other night. And particularly shocked at the speed in which I took you inside my mouth. I was simply being honest about what I wanted."

He blushed. She shook her head and laughed, enjoying his expression. "I don't expect you to blush, but anytime sex comes up..."

His gaze didn't meet hers, but when he finally spoke, his tone was so soft, she almost missed it. "I particularly did enjoy that honesty. Even if I shouldn't have."

She slid her hand from his elbow down to his hand and clasped it. "AJ Reed, we are two seriously mismatched people." His eyes dropped to their joined hands and she lifted hers to study his face. "Tell me then why it feels so nice?"

"I don't know," he answered, without the usual shyness.

"You think it does feel nice too, then?"

"Being with you? Yes."

"Would you take me to try shooting a gun? I was thinking I might like to try that."

"Yes, I'll take you. Tomorrow night? Around eight? I promised Jack I'd finish up the roofing on Joey's house that I didn't get done yesterday."

"You worked yesterday? On Sunday?"

"Yes, I didn't get it done on Saturday... so..."

"You work the weekends and the evenings?"

"Sometimes. But if you want to, we would still have a few hours of daylight."

They sauntered back towards the cabins. She sighed, knowing he most likely wouldn't be coming back in. She wanted to push him further. Her body was strumming, thinking about him near her, inside her, touching her... but she shook it off. AJ wasn't about that.

"So, tomorrow. I'll wait by your trailer."

"Okay."

She still clasped his hand as she turned towards him and raised up a fraction of an inch on her tiptoes so her lips could brush over his.

He remained stock-still. His hat brim touched the top of her head. She leaned up further, adding just a bit more pressure. Suddenly, his arms swooped around her waist and his mouth opened to hers. Her hands were trapped between them, pressed against the wall of his chest. His tongue touched hers and she felt the ensuing jolt clear down to her toes. It was their first kiss. The one they skipped before their first sexual encounter. The one she now kind of wished she had started with.

He lifted his head from hers, dropping his hands. She wondered if he were about to apologize. She smiled and touched his cheek. "We might have started backwards, kissing the wrong ends and all first, but I enjoyed tonight more than almost any date I can remember."

His smile was tinged with chagrin as he shook his head. "The things you say…"

She sighed, dropping her shoulders. "I don't mean to… I'm just… so…"

"Honest?" he supplied.

"We'll go with that."

He smiled one last time before turning and slipping into the shadows. He was taking the beach route, she realized, probably to avoid prying eyes and the views from the ranch house. She glared up towards it, cursing Jack Rydell for making a fine man like AJ Reed sneak around as if he were a dirty criminal. Meanwhile, she was starting to wonder if he might be one of the most upstanding men she'd ever met, despite his stint in prison.

CHAPTER 8

*K*ATE WAS WAITING ON AJ's deck when he walked up. She was dressed in her pink boots, shorts, and tank top, and smiling a huge grin when she spotted him coming up the walkway. She was sprawled out, with her feet resting on the table, and her head bent backwards over the chair. He was filthy from the work he just finished. Dust coated him from head to toe and sweat stained his shirt in giant rings that began at his hairline. He cringed as he came closer to her cool, beautiful face and carefree sophistication.

"Hey there, cowboy," she said with the exaggerated drawl she often used. "Looks like you were doing more than planting flowers today."

"Plowing one of the pastures. Dust is a foot thick since it hasn't been watered." He kept his eyes lowered, staring at her feet, almost ashamed of the way he appeared to her.

Lowering her feet, she pushed the chair nearer to her out. "Here, sit. You look tired."

He dropped into the chair and ran his hands over his jean-clad legs, suddenly noticing how black his hands were.

She startled him when she silently crawled onto his lap and pushed her hands into his hair until his hat fell off with a soft thump. He jerked back. "Kate, I'm filthy."

She answered by placing her mouth over his, and slipping her tongue inside. "I know." She grinned and took his hands from the chair handles he was gripping fiercely, placing them on her waist. His blackened hands smudged her shirt and he jerked back.

"I don't care." Her mouth returned to his. Her lips were outlined in pink and tasted like Vaseline. He groaned at the slickness of it. She leaned back and asked, "Better?"

Puzzled, his now overheated brain and receptive body didn't know what she meant. "Better?"

"Not so tired? Not so awkward. You looked freaked out to find me here, so I thought I'd remind you why I came. Chemistry."

"Better, then." And worse too, for now, he was turned on. He gritted his teeth in annoyance that he so easily responded to her. She glanced down.

"I can help you with that…"

He shook his head, rising to his feet, and gently setting her off to the side and onto her own feet. "Let me go change, at least."

She sighed. "Oh, my straight-laced, celibate cowboy, the things you're missing out on…" She smiled wickedly, tracing her tongue between her lips in exaggerated slurps.

He finally smiled and pushed at her shoulder gently. "You're just a giant, over-aged brat, aren't you?"

She squealed in delight. "Now you're catching on. See? Not too scary or intimidating a city girl, am I?"

No, strangely enough, she wasn't. He opened the door to the trailer and she followed behind him, glancing around as he started up the two stairs to the small bedroom at the front of the trailer.

"Never been in one of these before."

"One of what?"

"A trailer." She was spinning in a circle as he stared at her. They might as well have been from opposite poles of the earth.

"It's about all I've ever lived in." His quiet tone made her carefree spinning stop dead. Sunlight streamed through the windows, highlighting lazy dust motes that floated over her head. His statement sobered her.

"It's not a reason we can't enjoy each other's company, is it?"

He sighed. An answer for everything, Kate. "No. S'pose not." He grabbed a towel and ducked into the bathroom, quickly starting the shower. His shoulders almost didn't fit inside the small, mini-shower of the RV, but the cool water and some hard scrubbing managed to wash off most of the dust, sweat, and grime. He didn't usually dry off in the bathroom, but no way would he dare to do it out in the bedroom. Not with man-eating Kate. Or so *she* proclaimed. When he was dry enough, he wrapped the towel around his waist and slipped out of the bathroom. Kate sat on the couch and her eyes shot up to look at him. He turned his back and headed for the bedroom.

Shutting the small divider, which was just a plastic, accordion door, she again surprised him. Damn her. She went behind him, wrapping her hands around him as her breasts smashed deliciously against his bare back. She was so slim in contrast to his broad width. Her slimness beside his bulkiness was sexier than any aphrodisiac. Her body felt like the perfect temperature pressed against his dampness. The water droplets from his hair beaded over his back and chest.

He shut his eyes, letting her softness surround him, and her warmth filled his heart. *Sex.* It was all just sex with Kate, wasn't it?

Her lips touched his shoulder, then dropped near his arm, then drew closer and closer to his neck. He tilted his neck to give her soft, tender lips more access to his skin. So rarely had he ever been touched with so much softness or care. Never. Not even as a child. The times when he had sex in the past never involved caring from his partners or him.

She stretched higher on her tiptoes until her mouth reached his neck and ear. Swirling her tongue inside it, his entire body jerked in reaction. He encouraged her, turning his neck in a weird position to get closer as her tongue sweetly bathed his ear.

She moved her flat palms to the wall of his stomach, going up and down his abs and pecs. She stroked him with her palms and the backs of her fingers, creating friction as she longed to explore every inch and feel the texture of his skin.

Her mouth moved from his ear to his jaw, dropping her hands lower, until she gripped the towel in her hands. "Can I?" she whispered into his ear, her tone husky and sensuous. He nearly gulped at the heady feel of her hands combined with the anticipation of what she was asking. His shock overcame him. He nodded.

She undid the towel and it fell to his feet. He jutted forward, ready and willing, no matter what kind of dedication he claimed to have in his beliefs. Her lips were still on his skin, kissing his neck and traveling down the center of his back. Goosebumps broke out all over him when her hands oh-so-gently slid down his back, and over his bare butt.

She followed the indentation of his cheeks, moving in and out, pausing, then rubbing him to let him know how much she liked the contour of his ass. He closed his eyes, his body completely hers now, strumming, and primed to come.

She was so amazing and incredible. Her touch was powerful.

But she didn't touch him anymore. She lifted her hands off him and he felt her shuffling around behind him. Glancing over his shoulder, he watched her drop her shorts, kicking off her boots and socks while working on her t-shirt and bra.

He turned to face her fully. She noticed his interest and instantly encircled the cups of her breasts with her hands, rubbing up and down over the clinging fabric that barely contained her nipples. He swallowed, riveting his gaze on her nails, which were red today. She squeezed her nipples between her thumbs and index fingers, rubbing them sensuously and fluttering her eyes at the contact. With a smile, she finally dropped the frail material, flinging the bra to the floor and stepping forward. He fell back onto the bed and she walked forward until she could straddle him. He inhaled and buried his face in the cleavage of her round, white globes. She had a tan on her arms, neck, and elsewhere, but the white patches over her breasts only highlighted their allure and volume.

"Do you like them?"

"How could you even ask that?"

"Some men don't like fake boobs."

He glanced up and raised his eyebrows in surprise. She tilted her head back with a laugh. "No woman's breasts are this perky on their own. Especially at my age. You really couldn't tell?"

"It was dark last time, and I didn't do much of an examination. It was all, 'Hurry, AJ, oh, touch me there, do that harder...' It was a lot of pressure, I didn't have time to study all the goods."

Her laugh was husky in response. "I did so do that. I told

you I liked to be the boss, always in control. I didn't know you could tease and joke about such a sacred act."

He surprised her when he suddenly grabbed her in his arms and flipped her under him, pinning her to the bed with his hands holding her wrists. "First off, I can control you too. This isn't all your show; and second, there's nothing wrong with wanting sex to be more than just a cheap thrill. You don't have to mock my desire that it mean something. Not much has meant anything to me in my life."

Releasing her breath, her eyes grew huge. "Okay, cowboy. You're never what I expected. At all," she said almost breathlessly. Then she grinned. "And these aren't what you call 'goods.'"

He leaned down to nuzzle her breasts, which were pointing toward the sky. Now that she mentioned it, they weren't as flat as one might expect. His lips circled one and tasted it and then the other. Raising her legs on either side of him, she lifted her knees until her feet came off the bed, and curled her toes. "They are good though."

Sighing contentedly, she threaded her fingers through his hair. "They were the first frivolous thing I ever bought."

He paused, amazed she paused long enough to speak again. Once she got started, Kate seemed to go on and on. But he waited, and she nodded at him before she continued. "I got my condo, started my retirement savings, bought a new car, and still had cash in reserve. So I decided, why not? I hated my body before."

He leaned further back, almost onto his heels, as his gaze scoured her long, naked, horizontal body beneath his. "How do you figure you could hate this? Big breasts or not?"

"I'm broad shouldered and with thick hips. I used to have A-cup breasts. So I looked unbalanced. My mom was so mad at me for doing this."

He didn't remount her. Their conversation wasn't about

breasts. It took him a moment to realize it. They were *conversing* now, of all times... Well, Kate wasn't totally there for his dick. AJ was just starting to realize that.

"Why? Why was she mad? Because it's about sex?"

She laughed outright. "It wasn't about sex, AJ. I wouldn't go under the knife for some guy. I didn't even have a boyfriend at the time. Just pangs of self-consciousness. I felt unbalanced. Notice they aren't triple D's or something equally as ridiculous. They just balance me out, you know, top and bottom. I'm tall for a woman. It's awesome now, as a thirty-plus adult boss of a business usually dominated by men. But being in seventh grade and this tall? Yeah, I felt that I looked like a giraffe, and then, no breasts. They never developed; but oh, my hips did. I promised myself when I was in high school if I could ever afford to, I'd fix them."

"It's impossible to imagine Kate Morgan feeling embarrassed about herself."

"Years of practice. I was always the largest and tallest girl in a classroom, then the office. I learned to embrace it and later flaunt it. I was never a skilled athlete, and no basketball to give me a 'place.'"

"So it helped you?" He nodded towards her breasts. "Those were about you becoming you?"

"Yes, low and behold, I was twenty-eight before I had enough cash for a decent down payment. My mom was furious. She thought any risk of going under the knife was ludicrous, especially for something as cosmetic and vain as fake boobs. Biggest joke in the world, right? But it really wasn't any joke to me. My dad pretended I didn't do it. But my mom actually came to the clinic and was there for me in the end. Even though she lectured me for weeks beforehand and all the way there. But once it was over, and I came out, all groggy and bandaged and a mess, she never said another word. She even babied me and fussed over me. But the first time I put on a shirt, it felt like it tipped the scales from my lower half, and I couldn't stop smiling in the mirror. I'm sure I stand up taller because it was the best confidence boost I've ever had. I was finally... me. I mean, at last, I could reveal how I felt inside."

He waited. Her gaze remained on the window. "Anyway, that's the story of my fake boobs."

Leaning forward, he placed his lips on one leg, and then on her other one. She sighed and her eyes fluttered shut as her thighs separated eagerly. She was waxed or shaven, leaving only a thin strip of hair. He cupped his hand over her and her entire back flew off the mattress with surprise at his contact. He smiled. "My way this time."

He trailed kisses up her thigh, her stomach and the tip of her proud, erect nipple. His hand cupped her and she lifted her hips upwards to encourage him further, but he ignored her. He wasn't hurrying this time. He kissed her breasts and her neck, then her collarbone and her mouth. She moaned into his mouth and her hand pressed his face against hers harder. He finally took her wrist in his hand and held it down. She shifted, elevating her torso towards his mouth more effectively. He smiled. She really couldn't just have him. He kissed and licked and sucked his way lower until he brushed his fingertips over her wet lips. Gasping, she dug her heels into the bed and unashamedly raised her hips more urgently toward his hand. There was nothing subtle about Kate.

He ignored her again and slipped both hands around her, cupping her bottom in his palms. She moaned and squirmed, grinding her juicy flesh into his fingertips. He returned her pressure before lowering his face further. He'd never been with a woman so well-groomed down there. He touched his tongue on her and she, as he expected, nearly melted. Her legs spread-eagled and he could completely slip his tongue inside her as he pushed her closer to his face. She moaned as her torso shifted up and back, and seemed confused over how to control her body.

"AJ—oh, my GOD. You can't... I can't... oh, GOD..." Her pitch grew higher before fading off into a deep groan. Her head twisted back and forth; she shut her eyes and suddenly lifted her entire butt up into his face.

Grabbing the pillow over her head, she brought it over her mouth and nearly screamed with delight into it. Startled, he lifted his mouth off her. She had some pretty incredible reactions. He couldn't remember being with any woman who came like Kate.

Resting his hand on her stomach, he leaned down to kiss her mouth. She shoved the pillow away and grabbed the back of his neck, bringing his mouth to hers and moaning into it. She made love to his mouth with as much energy as she did everything else. He fell against her.

She finally slowed the kiss by gripping his cheeks in her hands. She held his face right over hers, staring up into his eyes. "It means something."

He stilled. Their gazes were locked and her usual smile didn't appear. He had no idea what it meant, but he felt her statement all the way into the pit of his stomach, and the ends of his toes. Nodding, he rested his forehead on hers. He kissed the end of her nose, between her eyes, and her eyelids after they fluttered shut. "This? Us? You think it means something?"

"I've just done this often enough to know the difference."

He didn't ask why or how, but dropped his lips onto hers. She kissed him back, but more gently now. He withdrew briefly to grab a condom from the cupboard that conveniently sat right over their heads. She laughed, breaking the strange mood that engulfed them only a moment before.

"Handy. But why does a celibate cowboy have condoms stashed there?"

"Well... you know, just in case."

"They aren't like years old, are they? Check the date. No risking any accidents."

He glanced at the box. "We're good."

She closed her eyes and sighed with relief. "Thank you, Jesus. Not sure I could handle it if they weren't."

He groaned, "Kate..."

"Oh, sorry, thank you..." She suddenly lifted her head up to whisper into his ear, "Whom should I thank instead?"

He shook his head and smiled at her audacity, her quick wit, and how she made it feel like he'd known her far longer than he did. His being there like that became less awkward and strange around her. Her humor leveled the playing field between their odd coupling and different statuses.

"Maybe me. Thank me, I'm the one who did it for you."

She spoke primly and smiled, as if behaving like a good little student, "Thank you, AJ."

He leaned over her and their mouths met, the heat just simmering now. He allowed her to slip the condom on while their mouths stayed joined together. It was so easy. Her legs parted and he lowered himself inside her, but everything was easy and gentle this time. He pushed inside her and their mouths separated, yet their eyes remained fastened on one another. This time, sex was completely different. He wrapped her in his arms with an almost gentle undulation of their hips together. There was no hurry, no disconnection, and no regrets. They were there together in the same moment as their bodies reciprocated the pleasure. Each stimulated all the right nerve endings and ignited and fulfilled the other.

It was like she put him on fire and doused the very flames she started until he exploded. In the end, they stomped out the flames together before clinging to each other, fulfilled in every way. They were closer now than when it all started, and more than just physically.

~

HE FELT HER WAKING UP. She was startling and then falling flat and relaxing her muscles. She turned towards him, reaching her hands out to touch his chest. Lying there, she gently rubbed back and forth over his stomach. He caught her hand in his to stop his growing reaction to her. She sighed. "Tell me what you dream about?"

"Dream about? Like at night?"

"No. Like if you could do anything, that kind of dream."

"Oh. I don't know. Not sure I really ever do that."

"There has to be something you'd want if you could have it."

"Well, a horse, I guess."

"A horse? That's it? If you were granted anything in the whole world, that's it?"

"Well, a horse needs land and food and care. So if I could own a horse, that would mean I had all those things too, wouldn't it? A horse and the space, time and means to care for it. There's this piece of land, right across from the front gate of the ranch. Been for sale for years. Stuff don't sell too easy around here. Anyway, it's just raw land. Sagebrush and the mountain straight up behind it. I imagine it...well, you know, planted in grass, and maybe a few trees for shade. You'd be shocked what a little water can do to make the land more appealing around here. Maybe put a little cabin on it or a mobile home... and it's got enough room for a horse, or even two. I guess I've always thought it was a nice spot."

Kate was very quiet for a long moment. He immediately felt stupid and hick-like. What a thoughtless answer. As if an empty lot full of sagebrush was her idea of a dream. But then, her hand squeezed his and her mouth kissed his shoulder as she replied, "That's a lovely dream."

"What do you dream about?"

"If only I could bring my mother back." Her answer was immediate and her tone seemed impassioned.

He turned his head to catch her eye. "She died?"

"Forty-two days ago."

His mouth popped open. "Forty-two days ago? Kate, I had no idea. I'm so sorry."

"That's what I'm doing here. It all has to do with her. I just, I miss her so damn much. Usually, I try not to feel it. Like I can banish it from my mind, you know? Kick the grief in the teeth, until suddenly, it comes out of nowhere and bites me in the ass. It just did that. I dreamt about her."

"Even you, my mighty Kate, can't kick grief away. What did she die of?"

"Heart attack. So maybe you thought the other night was wrong. And tonight too, since we're still strangers, kind of, and having sex. But it made me feel... alive. Connected again. I like being near you. It doesn't feel wrong to me."

"Maybe now, it doesn't feel wrong. I just assumed that first night, that's all you were about. With me, I mean. I obviously knew there was more to you. But I didn't think you'd be back to see me beyond that one reason."

"Well, I think I do. We do."

He didn't add *for the few days remaining of your vacation*. So that's all Kate was doing here with him. Forgetting. Vacationing. He held that thought in his head, drilling it in there, lest he fail to remember it.

"I have to get up soon. Go to work. Some of us aren't lazing the days away on vacation."

Kate eventually slipped from the bed and hopped into his shower, commenting on how she didn't see how he managed to fit inside it. She came out wearing one of his shirts and went down to the small kitchen and rifled around. She reappeared back in the opening of the room. He glanced up from where he lay on the bed, contented somehow, just to listen to her shuffling around, and chatting all the while.

"You have like three loaves of bread, cheese, lunchmeat, and instant coffee."

"I told you, I eat sandwiches."

"Three meals a day?"

"Well, no, but two."

She shuddered. "Dear Go—goodness, you need some help with that. I have no idea how you maintain that physique on white bread and baloney. All right, instant it is. I'll boil up the water." She disappeared again.

A laugh rumbled from his chest as a weird, levity filled his heart. Kate, meanwhile, muttered away about his lack of groceries in between her complaints about the instant coffee.

Still, she brought a cup to him in bed, claiming it wasn't really coffee, even if it were all he ever drank. He enjoyed it along with the toasted white bread and margarine she spread on it. He sat against the small headboard. The bed was too small for both of them. Their feet hung over the end. But AJ couldn't remember ever having a better morning or feeling so dang content.

He munched on the warm toast and washed his bites down with the strong coffee while watching the prettiest woman in the world. She perched on the edge of the bed, explaining the cancer-inhibiting factors in fruit and vegetables and the importance of consuming real protein, not the fake, processed baloney he ate. Shuddering at times, on and on she talked. He only half listened as he glanced at the alarm clock. It was nearing seven and he needed to get going.

"How about we go shooting tonight?" she asked as he set the plate and empty cup aside and stretched his huge body out of the bed. He grabbed his underwear and slipped them on, keeping his back to her. Her hand stroked the back of his thigh as he tugged up his jeans.

Standing at full height, his head almost hit the top of the ceiling. "Sure. I have to finish Joey's roof, but after that..."

"How many hours do you work a day?"

"I dunno. Ten or eleven."

"It was twelve yesterday."

"Okay, twelve."

"That seems illegal," she grumbled.

He turned, sliding the t-shirt over his head before he kissed her pouting mouth. "It's money I need. Try again for seven tonight? And please try not to come near me until after we go, okay?"

That request made her wide mouth slip into a smile. "Maybe. All right. See you then."

He opened the trailer door, quickly slamming it shut and stepping into the cool morning. The sun was still hidden by the mountain above the main ranch house. He loved the crisp morning scents, pockets of warm air and the lazy, sizzling sound of the sprinklers. Horses neighed to him, lifting their pretty heads. And a beautiful woman had just sent him off to work. What a fantasy. But still... At least, for one day, he could enjoy it.

Turned out to be five full days that he enjoyed it. When he got back to the trailer after working on Joey's roof, she was there waiting with a decent meal all ready for him. No more sandwiches. She brought the groceries in and didn't ask his permission. Nor did she ask if she could stay. She simply did both; and seemed oddly at home in his trailer. She brought in her girlie combs, makeup, and a whole duffel bag of her essentials. It was as much as he possessed in the entire world. She was there when he left for work and there when he got back. She was often waiting on the deck, all stretched out, "enjoying the view," or so she claimed. Dinner was something new and different each time.

He kept his promise and took her target shooting as she desired.

Driving to a remote, nearly abandoned road, he set up an old box in a safe shooting area. He showed her the basics of the gun and safety procedures. After loading it, he snapped the stock and barrel back together, raised it, checked the sight, and gently squeezed the trigger. The box's center exploded as gunshot sprayed right where he was aiming. Kate let out a squeal, sounding all girlie-like. "You got it." He lowered the gun, glancing at her as he pumped the empty shell out.

"You wanna try it?"

She nodded, coming forward. Holding the weapon, it drooped strangely in her arms, like it was much too heavy for her. Her lack of confidence at the novelty resulted in her fear of it. "Look here, it's not loaded."

She nervously bit her lip in concentration as he loaded it. He stood behind her, ready to shift her arms around to the right position. Placing the stock against her shoulder nice and tight, he parted her legs, and she shifted her weight. He showed her where to sight the gun with relation to the target, and how to release the safety before massaging the trigger with a gentle squeeze.

She was not to use a quick pull. Standing there for a good three minutes while she adjusted her position, her arms started to shake before she finally pulled the trigger. She jumped as if she were the target she just shot at. And missed. Letting the gun drop in defeat, AJ caught it before it hit the ground as Kate rubbed her sore shoulder.

"That was not what I expected. It was loud and it hurt me when it kicked."

"It shouldn't hurt. Maybe you weren't holding it tightly enough. Want to try again?"

"No. But I'll watch you."

He shot a few more rounds to please her before sitting down on the tailgate beside her. First, he carefully unloaded the weapon and stowed it in its case at the back of the truck. He put the ammunition in his glove box, keeping the two separated. The doors were open on his pickup and the lazy strum of country music and nasal twang filled the air.

Kate's gaze wandered over the shadows made by the pines surrounding them and further beyond into the mountains as the sun sank lower. "It's really raw country up here."

"Yeah."

"God, guns, and country, huh? Around here. No wonder you fit in so well."

"Well, yes, it is."

She leaned back, placing an arm over her forehead. "It's hard to picture we're both from the same state."

"That's why it turned out to be a good vacation spot for all you coasties."

She smiled, turning her head, and squinting against the setting sun. "Do you guys really call us that?"

"Yup, we really do."

"I never knew until I came here that I belonged to a special group."

"It's not a compliment." He grinned, leaning back against the side of the pick-up, and letting his legs stretch out before him. She moved her legs to entangle his and pretended to kick him.

"Yes, so I gathered."

"How come you wanted to shoot a gun?"

She shrugged, gazing up at the sky. "I don't know. Never did it before. They kind of intimidate me, in all honesty. I don't like to be scared of things I know nothing about. So I thought I'd face off against it, and I think it won. I just really do not feel comfortable around them."

"Hard to picture you being scared of anything," he commented.

"More than you'd think," she muttered. She twisted, rolling onto her side and setting her hand under head. "In my meanderings around the ranch, I happened to notice the littlest Rydell, Charlie, isn't that his name? I noticed that he often follows you all around."

"Your meanderings? I guess you go anywhere and everywhere you want. Shane mentioned seeing you to me. He was wondering what your deal was with the bikini."

She smiled, her eyebrows wagging. "You, cowboy. That was entirely about my effort to get your attention."

"You only needed a brown paper bag over your head and you had it."

"Well, you were obtuse about it. Why? Shane didn't wonder if I wanted him, did he? I talk to him quite a bit. He's a chatty guy. But it wasn't him I was interested in."

"No. I've heard more than once and from different sources that the guest Kate is overly curious. I try to pretend that it's only about me, but sometimes, I'm not so sure it is."

Her smile didn't reveal anything. "Anyway, back to my question, why does he hang around you so much?"

AJ leaned his head back on the rim of the truck bed. "He fancies himself going into bull riding someday. Jack would never allow it. Charlie tries to pick my brain about it. He wants to find out how I trained for it and what I did. He's hungry for any story I tell him about those days. I always try to shoo him away because I know where Jack stands on the matter."

"Jack again! He sure likes being the boss and telling everyone what to do and think."

"It's his son. I wouldn't want Charlie to consider it seriously either. It isn't exactly golf."

She flipped over and slid up onto her knees before walking forward on her knees. "I've never done it in the bed of a pick-up before."

Arms crossed over his chest, AJ shook his head, although a small smile showed on his lips. He opened his arms, reaching over and sweeping his hand through the cap of hair on her head. "You're impossible."

"Just trying to forget my pain. Help me to do it. That's what this trip is about for me. Think of it like charity... Isn't that your Christian duty?"

He let her crawl closer until she was near enough to draw her arms around his neck. She dropped her lips onto his. As their mouths touched, he said, "I don't think this is exactly what they meant."

She lifted her face barely off his, her wide eyes brightly staring into his. "It actually does help me, AJ. I wasn't being all that funny."

He closed his eyes at the startling beauty of her keen, intelligent eyes. He honestly could not believe she even looked at him twice, let alone seemed so attracted to him. He let her kiss him as he fell back on the bed of the pick-up. This time, he got all the little bits of gravel, dirt, wood chips, and branches scratching up his back. Sex in a pick-up was highly overrated in his estimation, but not this time. Not with Kate. It was worth every single prick and scrape he endured.

CHAPTER 9

*K*ATE WAS NO CLOSER to why she came to River's End in the first place. It certainly wasn't to start a strange, newfangled relationship with a farm hand. Despite all she learned about the Rydells, she still didn't know Jack. And still hadn't found the smoking gun to prove why her mother would so completely have turned her back on her only son. Her firstborn. Her child. Kate's *brother.*

What did it mean? The same words often traveled through her brain. Listening to AJ, so alone with no family in the world to his name, was like déjà vu when she realized she was almost as alone as him. She had no parents now either. She was an orphan.

But she did have a brother.

The days became a bit of a routine for her. She woke at AJ's and slept at AJ's. Then she unhurriedly wandered to her cabin to get cleaned up, put in a few hours of work, only handling the most urgent and timely correspondences as well as the current campaigns that were in progress.

Sometimes, late in the afternoons, she strolled over to the ranch. She figured out where Jack and Erin lived; and spoke almost daily with Shane every time she passed his shop. He was often in there, working away on a seriously evil-looking, uncomfortable chopper. She also spent some time in the afternoons with Erin, who was happy to see her when Kate began watching her from the fence as she worked out the horses one at a time. She answered Kate's questions, which usually started out with an inquiry about whatever Erin was doing.

From there, Kate's questions grew more personal, and included the Rydells. Eventually, Kate navigated the conversation to glean something about Jack. But usually, Erin seemed to sense Kate's insatiable hunger for information about her husband. She, consequently, turned tight-lipped about him. Kate gathered that Erin wasn't sure what to think of her; while Erin was wary of Kate and didn't trust her.

However, since there was nothing specific to accuse Kate of, Erin held her tongue. No doubt she was trying to patiently bide the two weeks until Kate was scheduled to leave. Other than crossing the guest boundaries, Kate didn't really violate any rules. She just had an unquenchable interest in the man who owned it.

Erin prepared to put the little horse away. Kate wasn't sure if she should call it a foal or a mare or a mustang. She had no idea what it was properly called. Having so many names for a horse easily confused her. To Kate's surprise, Erin mentioned she was thirsty and wanted to get a drink; did Kate want to join her?

Kate did. Progress. Any hospitality from Erin was encouraging. They settled on the stairs of the porch after Erin brought out two glasses of lemonade with ice and sprigs of mint. "We don't live here anymore, but we always try to keep lunch stuff and other refreshments around so we don't have to go all the way home on our breaks."

"When did you move?"

Erin sipped her drink. "Oh, almost a year ago now."

"Why? This house is so incredible."

"It belongs to Jack's family. Ergo, the four brothers were always coming and going. And who ended up with it? Us. Why not Shane or Joey? I wish I knew. We didn't know how to divvy it up fairly, not that anyone would have contested it. But to be honest? Jack lived here with his parents, who died, and then his first wife..."

"Who died too. I get it. Bad mojo."

"Yeah, sometimes. And most of all for me. Jack moved from here so I could have my own house, you know, one that wasn't theirs or Lily's; she was Jack's first wife."

Kate put a mental tally point in the plus column for Jack. Not too many there yet, but her opinion was open for any positive input. "What made you turn the ranch into a resort?"

"It was Ian's idea, originally, but he was right. It was kind of like us dividing up the house. I mean, how could we allocate the ranch into four parts? Not to mention Ben and Charlie. Come to think of it, they're really could be six or ten or more kids, depending on what Ian, Shane and Joey do. It seemed like the right time to branch out, while trying to be more diverse and fair to everyone. Until that time, it was only Jack running the ranch and raising the boys. Occasionally, he enlisted Shane and Ian's help. Now? There're less kids to raise and more brothers to share it all."

"Oh, so you two didn't necessarily want the cabins? I don't get the feeling Jack likes them at all."

"No, if it were just us, probably not. I don't mind them. But Jack does..."

"So you must too," Kate mumbled under her breath so Erin didn't hear her. "Speaking of the resort, which I assume you all agreed on eventually, I wanted to throw in a few ideas. You can refuse me with no hard feelings if you're not interested. I won't take any offense. Kinda like you seeing a horse being trained the wrong way and it makes you want to jump in and help? Well, I know how to market ideas successfully, and honestly? You all aren't doing much of anything. You have a ton of possibilities here, a potential gold mine, if you market it right. I actually put some ideas together, and I wanted you to look at them first, before I even mentioned it to Jack or any of the other brothers. I feel like you have a far better pulse on reality. You're not as 'crazy protective' over its authenticity and simplicity, and you're nicer too. You should be the face of the Rydell River Resort, not Jack or Shane. I don't know the other two brothers yet, but since they aren't around, I assume they probably aren't that interested."

From the messenger bag over her shoulder, Kate withdrew the stapled proposal she had compiled on a whim, during the last few days, when she had some spare time. Her real work was finished and she tried to ignore the urge, knowing Jack would bristle at the suggestion, which was all she'd managed to garner about Jack. He resisted change, and resented the resort. The ranch was all he cared about. To the extent of crazy. But after seeing how they ran the resort, it was nearly killing Kate to keep her constructive suggestions to herself. She saw how easily she could streamline the business. All they needed were a few fairly cheap attractions, like a swimming pool, and more aggressive advertising. There was almost none being done. Kate was nearly salivating at the prospect of digging into it. She regarded Erin as the most receptive of the Rydells and her best chance for a positive outcome. The Rydell brothers seemed as rigid as a tree trunk when it came to any changes. Kate held the tidy packet of typewritten pages on her knees before handing them out to Erin.

"I run a consulting firm," she explained to Erin. "We offer recommendations on how to streamline and/or improve businesses, thereby securing their market niche. I'm sorry, but you guys could use a lot of recommendations. This place is brilliant. Ian was right; this makes a great resort. But there are a few things you should add. A pool, for one. I know there's the river, but during seasons like now, when it's hot every day, the river is too dangerous and dirty to swim in, so it isn't part of the package. A pool is the first bit of advice right off. And... well, I have some more listed as well. Would you browse through them briefly and just see if it's something Jack or Shane would even consider? I don't want to waste anyone's time, especially my own."

Erin's gaze was riveted on the papers Kate held out to her and she didn't move. Then she almost stopped breathing. Her chest rose and fell suddenly as her eyes shot up to Kate. "Oh, I—I don't know. I mean, you should discuss any of that with Jack. He handles that side of our business. I wouldn't know. He—my opinion is irrelevant." She hastily shoved the paperwork away from her, almost panicking as if Kate were releasing a live tarantula in her hand.

Then, Erin jumped to her feet. Kate stared down at the unexamined papers in her hands, disappointed, to say the least. When she looked up again, Erin's face was completely pale and her eyes grew huge. Was she afraid of the innocuous suggestions? Kate slowly rose to her feet. Was her brother so much of a tyrant that he wouldn't even allow Erin to review potential improvements to the operation?

Kate swallowed the knot of anger lodged in her throat, and her reply to Erin, which was, *Run girl, run!* Away from this place, this town and mostly, that horrible man. Instead, she said gently, "I just wanted your opinion, Erin, before I showed it to Jack. I wouldn't tell him that you saw them first. Please?"

Erin shook her head more vigorously, leaning back into the railing of the stairs as if Kate were threatening her with a knife. "I—I really just can't, Kate. Please don't ask me to do that again. Jack wouldn't like it."

"Why do you care so much if Jack would like it or not?" The concern on Kate's face was evident. "Are you afraid of him? I mean…"

"No. I'm not afraid of Jack. God! Just drop it. Please. It's none of your damn business." Erin shoved her way past Kate and stomped across the yard. A stunned Kate followed her.

"Erin. Wait. Please! You shouldn't be afraid of your own husband. What is it? Why are you so scared of him? And his opinion? Can I help you?" Real fear for Erin clutched Kate's heart. The ever-controlling Jack, the old-school "man" of the ranch and Erin was the "little woman";or at least, that seemed to be their dynamic.

Seeing Erin's strong resistance, all Kate could imagine was that Jack had to be much worse in his private life with Erin. There had to be more to it.

Erin stopped dead, whipping around so fast, Kate stumbled and almost ran in to her. "I'm not afraid of my own husband. I don't know what your damn obsession or problem is with him, but I want you to leave our house, our land, and our fucking resort!"

Erin kicked the dust and a plume of it swirled around Kate's shin. All Kate could see, however, was Erin's extreme defensiveness. She was trying to get Kate away from learning something she shouldn't, but was way too hot on the trail of to stop now. Apparently, it was something that Erin wanted to conceal at all costs.

"What does he do to you? Why can't you even read a simple advice proposal, Erin? I think you need to—"

"Kate. Enough."

His deep voice snarled behind her. *AJ*. Although where he came from, and how he managed to sneak up without alerting them, baffled Kate.

She glanced over her shoulder at AJ, knowing he'd protect Jack, the employer he so revered. AJ didn't see the telltale signs she witnessed or a woman so desperate for Kate to leave. And so strangely upset about a pretty casual topic. It only further hinted at the pervasive control wielded by Jack Rydell. Her brother. The brother her mother chose to forsake. Kate again clung to "there had to be a valid reason why my mother did that."

"I'm sorry, but I can't," she answered AJ, leaving her gaze locked on Erin. Color now infused her skin in anger, flooding the previous pallor.

Erin rolled her eyes, placing her hands on her hips. "Oh, for God's sake! What?! Do you think Jack beats me or something? Just leave, Kate. Now. I'm sick of your prancing around, and breaking all our rules with your inappropriate questions. What is your obsession with him? Do you fancy yourself with him or something? I thought that's what it was, to be honest. I decided to grind my teeth and bear it because you paid us a shitload of money to come here. So for two weeks, I figured I could deal with you. But—"

Kate shuddered. "I don't want Jack! Ick! No." Her gaze skittered up to find Jack standing in the opening of the barn. He had been drawn outside by their screaming.

Taking only about a second to observe them, he started running towards them, his eyes blazing. He came up behind Erin, touching her lower back and letting her know he was there. Sweet. Maybe it would have been if Kate hadn't known Erin was hiding something from Jack, namely Kate's suggestions for profitable improvement.

She wondered if Jack was close enough to hear the disgust in her voice.

He glared at her. "That's a relief, because you aren't wanted here. Get off my land."

"I still think you want Jack," Erin persisted.

Kate rolled her eyes. "I've been sleeping with AJ for two weeks, no offense, and I have no reason to want anyone else." Especially Jack! The blustering, overbearing ass. Kate stood taller, bracing her stance. "And I won't leave here until you tell me why she's so afraid of some stupid ideas I had for your resort. Mostly in regards to how you market it. Why is she so afraid to tell you about them, Jack?" She flung out his name, *Jack*, as disgustedly as possible.

"What the hell do you want from us? Erin isn't afraid of me. And besides, it's none of your damn business."

AJ came up closer. All eyes shifted to him. His low-brimmed hat kept his eyes hidden but his jaw was clenched. Kate had a feeling she'd worn out her welcome anyway, both with the Rydells as well as AJ. She didn't mean to be so critical, but when she got mad, harsh words sometimes escaped her.

"Oh? Let's talk about business. What about you not 'allowing' your employees to associate with your guests? It's like a punishable offense around here. Who does that? Who controls their employees' personal lives? What is this? All I see is that you decide what everyone should or should not do. Including whether or not your wife can judge something for herself. But rest assured, I don't want anything from *you*."

AJ leaned closer and pushed his hat back. His eyes were blazing as he said, "Enough. You need to stop now, Kate."

"I don't need to do anything because he said so. Believe me, this is my last day here."

"Good. Because I can't figure out what you were doing here to begin with," Jack said, glaring at Kate darkly with his fists clenched.

"Then let me enlighten you. I came here because, by some miracle of biology, we are fucking related, Jack Rydell. I came because I wanted to see if my mother was an awful worm of humanity for abandoning you, or if she were simply saving me from you. At last, I can see it was the latter."

Everyone went silent, including Kate. Her eyes widened as she glanced around and realized what she screamed out by losing her temper. She dropped her head and unclenched her fists. She had a bad habit: she tended to go off half-cocked, saying anything and everything that came to her mind when she was mad. Whether it were true or false, once provoked, she spewed whatever vile thought crossed her mind. It rarely happened, which is probably why she really lost her shit that time.

Her temper blew, like a dirty bomb detonating in a crowd. No one was safe. Not AJ. Not Erin. Not Jack, even if he deserved it. And worst of all, not herself. She finally revealed her connection to Jack. The one fact she preferred to conceal. She totally planned to disappear from the premises with the knowledge. Now, her head bowed under the weight of her confession.

"What?" Jack finally asked, his tone sounding as dumbfounded as she felt.

"I wasn't snooping around to come after you; you're my half brother. I was trying to figure out why my mother never told me about you. I thought you had some fatal flaw that would let her off the hook for doing something so horrible."

Erin's gaze felt hot on her. "I can't read. Or at least, I can't read a document like the one you tried to give me. I get particularly embarrassed about it around strangers, especially someone like you, a woman my age, who is obviously successful, and smart. My only fear was your scorn, not my husband's wrath."

Kate shut her eyes and her shoulders stooped down.

Jack's hand was on Erin's shoulder. "You thought I could actually beat my wife? That's what you were hoping to discover?"

"No. I just saw her reacting with fear and I leapt to a conclusion. Obviously, the wrong conclusion. I'm sorry, Erin, for... putting you in such a position. I honestly had no idea. So when he butts in to help you, it's simply because..."

"I can't read. Yes. It's him supporting me, not abusing me, Kate. He knows how much it embarrasses me and he's just trying to protect me. He's the most kind, generous, loyal, and protective man I've ever known. And you are not our friend. I don't know what game you're running by coming here. But I..."

"Aliza Tribony. That was my mother's maiden name. She married Henry Jack Rydell. Then she walked away from the ranch when you were two years, two months and four days old. She never contacted you again. She... she was my mother too."

Jack's entire body stiffened and he withdrew his hand from Erin as his gaze met Kate's and he squinted at her. "How do you know that?"

Kate's shoulders slumped further. "I told you, she's my mother too."

Jack shook his head. "Why couldn't you just have introduced yourself? Why all the shenanigans? Staying at our resort? Talking to my boys? My brothers? Cornering Erin for information? What did you hope to gain?"

"Gain? Oh, for Christ's sake, Jack, nothing. I could buy and sell you if I chose to. Okay? This isn't about money. I pulled in the first day and went to the house there. I didn't even know about the resort. I ran into AJ, who unknowingly assumed I was a guest. I decided to lay low and find out what you were like. I was about fifty percent sure I wasn't going to ever tell you who I was. So I—"

"That was you lying low? Stalking my family? Seducing my foreman? What can I do for you, Kate?"

Kate glanced to the side. AJ was as stiff and blank-faced as the rest of them. "I didn't seduce AJ. I wasn't stalking anyone. It had nothing to do with you actually. More specifically, I was trying to understand how the mother I knew, loved, and adored could abandon her firstborn child. I desperately wanted to find a good reason for it. Because if there were a good reason, then it meant my mom was the woman whom I loved and believed in for my entire life. But if there weren't a good reason, as it now appears... then it means my mother was wrong. She was evil. I don't quite know how to handle that."

"Ask her those questions yourself. I have no desire to know her."

Kate's voice lowered, bereft of all heat and anger now. She stared at her fingers, and linked them together in front of her stomach. "I would love to, but she's dead. I found out about you after she died. It was while I was examining her private things. So, you can celebrate her demise, Jack, she's very dead."

Silence, then Jack asked, in a tone a bit less volatile, "When? When did she die?"

"April."

"This last April?"

"Yes."

There was a long sigh. "I'm sorry about that, Kate. Really, I am. I understand now how that would propel you here. Both Erin and I lost our mothers. We understand the kind of grief you must be enduring, and why you might not have been yourself in handling this. Perhaps it was not how you should have done it. But understand this: she never meant anything to me. I don't even remember her. I don't even have a picture of us together. I hardly knew her name or the bare bones facts of her life. She means nothing to me. I don't really want to open any doors to her. My mother was Donna

Rydell. I already suffered the devastating experience of grieving for my mother after her premature death."

Tears burned hot and achy in Kate's eyes at hearing Jack's softly issued confession. He was far less rude and abrasive than he had been to date. She was surprised by the positive change, and nodded her head sympathetically in response.

She replied, "I understand too."

Spinning on her heel, before the tears fell, Kate could not bear for any of them to see her break down. The talk of her mother soon became too much for her. It was still impossible for Kate to see her mom as the villain in this scenario, but apparently, she was. She was the woman Jack couldn't even remember. She was his mother and yet, she had cold-bloodedly abandoned him. And worse still? Kate would never know the reason *why*. How could her mom do such a thing?

AJ stepped back and headed off in the opposite direction. Her heart swelled until it hurt her chest. He'd never forgive her. She had revealed their affair, knowing how important it was to AJ that she keep it quiet. Not only that, but she also violated the stupid rules laid down by Jack. Somehow, she knew the revelation that she was Jack's sister wouldn't allay anything, but only make it worse.

She clutched the bag with the infamous papers around her shoulder. That's what started it all. Erin couldn't read? How could Kate have ever guessed that was the cause of her odd behavior? And why couldn't she? It was so surprising. Why didn't Jack just teach Erin to read? Or pay a tutor to teach her?

She kicked a loose rock near her foot and started down the trail towards the cabins. Entering hers with a heavy heart, she began gathering her stuff and setting it all inside her trunk. She glanced around one last time with unmasked disappointment before shutting the door, with the keys in her hand. She walked to the check-out office. Jocelyn was there as usual.

"I'm checking out."

"How was your stay? Will you be coming back?"

"It was... informative. I doubt I'll be back though. But the resort? Pretty amazing."

She walked to her car, opened the driver's door and stared off towards the river. She could see AJ's trailer, but only as a smudge, it was so far down the way. She slammed her car door. She wasn't running away from him. She had to talk to him. She'd say goodbye, sorry, see you in the next life... or something.

Walking down the ranch road, Kate was scanning for AJ's broad back or the telltale white hat. Finally, she found him beside the river. They were working on a pipe that ran into the water. She waved. He noticed her, but quickly turned away. She thought he was ignoring her until he said something to Caleb before turning and approaching her. He stopped a few feet back, putting his hands on his hips.

"I'm packed. I just thought..."

"Goodbye, Kate."

He was so cold. Especially after all the warmth she uncovered beneath his shyness. That's it? Her heart felt like it melted into a puddle of disappointment. That was all he had to say to her? About them?

"I hope what I said won't jeopardize anything for you with Jack."

His hard gaze at her was emphasized by his tight-lipped mouth and frown of disapproval. "Which part? Ignoring Jack's rules? Or because you're his sister?"

"A sister he wants nothing to do with. I'm sorry. How could I tell you that? I wasn't even planning on telling him."

"Oh? But you did tell him, didn't you? As epically as you

tell everyone anything you think. You vomit whatever is in your head in spurts and all others be damned."

She dropped her gaze to her toes, now properly shamed. "I admit I have a bad temper..."

"From the moment I met you, you say and do anything you please. No cause for concern about anyone but yourself. Or anyone else's beliefs or lifestyles. I bet your whole life is filled with a wake of people just like me. You plow over, through, and under them, doing whatever suits you, and then when your needs are met, you move on. Done. Forgotten. Just like Greg. Just like what you just did up there to Jack and Erin."

Kate flinched. "I truly had no idea Erin was illiterate."

"You practically accused Jack of beating her. There was no indication of that. I would have told you about Erin if I thought it was any of your business. Or if I suspected you'd go after her so ruthlessly. They don't broadcast their flaws to strangers, they are discreet. But it's not a secret. It's about respect. However, I have a feeling there are very few things you respect in life. You're too busy always being right."

AJ turned and darted away. Kate opened her mouth to yell after him, but let her words wither in her chest. There was no use. Not if the set of his shoulders were any indication. She stepped back. Shocked at mild-mannered AJ's verbal attack on her, she bit her lip. She went too far. Heat and shame filled her, remembering how doggedly she'd gone after Erin, and accused Jack, and now... what? She lost any chance of being welcome here. Even if she no longer knew if she wanted that.

She was done. She would leave River's End and go back to Seattle where she freaking belonged. The strange thing was, her heart felt so heavy that it seemed to sink further in her chest than before. She had a hard time recalling her condo. Or even remembering what living there was like. She would go to work, dressed so much more appropriately and stylish than her pink boots and the jean shorts she wore this week. She would not have had sex with a man who lived in a trailer and ate baloney sandwiches for all his daily calories. Or prayed for his soul after she defiled it.

River's End sounded awful.

And it was. Worst of all? Leaving AJ so disgusted by her actions. She would be the girl he regretted for the rest of his life. The one who used and abused him, coaxing him to abandon his morality and clean living by breaking his celibacy. Perhaps, if she hadn't ruined it, he might have concluded it wasn't such a terrible thing. But after she so thoroughly corrupted that memory, he would always hate her.

She almost couldn't stand the stab of regret and sharp pain she suffered at that knowledge.

Turning slowly, she trudged back to her car. She got in, started the ignition and watched the resort fade into a blur in her rearview mirror.

CHAPTER 10

*K*ATE SQUINTED HER EYES and set her foot on the brake. The damn gate was shut! The main gate to the resort road was shut and chained with a padlock. Incredulously, she got out of her car and stomped towards it, jerking on the chain. No shit. They locked it. What the hell? Why? They must have thought she'd already left and wanted to lock her out. Bit excessive, wasn't it? It had to be some kind of fire hazard to lock in their other guests. Sighing, she dropped the lock and glanced around. Then, she spotted a figure walking, except it was more like jogging, from the main ranch house.

Erin. Erin was sprinting towards her. Kate crossed her arms over chest, waiting.

"You locked me in, or perhaps you intended to lock me out?" she called as Erin got closer.

Erin finally slowed up, brushing her hair back from her face. "Hey, Kate. I locked you in." Erin removed a key from her pocket and undid the padlock, releasing the chain and swinging the gate open.

Kate's jaw dropped in disbelief. "You really locked me in?"

"I figured you probably went off to talk to AJ before storming out of here. I wanted to make sure I caught you. Otherwise..." She shrugged.

Kate squinted skeptically at Erin. "That mild-mannered thing you do isn't real, is it? I thought this place was all under Jack's control, but you're the one in the driver's seat, aren't you?"

Erin smiled as she finished latching the gate to a hook in the ground. "Kate, withdraw the claws. I apologize for how I reacted earlier. You caught me in a moment. I was embarrassed by my inability to read the proposal, and everything else became secondary to my need to hide that from you. So I missed your whole intention. You weren't trying to bully me, but you must've guessed I had a secret, one that I was protecting; the wrong secret, yes, but a secret all the same, and you were just trying to help me. You didn't turn your back on me and ignore it, or chalk it up to being *our business*, when you sensed I could be in a violent situation. Thinking more rationally about it later, I realized yeah, it wasn't that far of a stretch. And I also admire the guts it took to go up against us when you believed you were doing so for my safety. Unfortunately for you, I go ballistic when strangers get the faintest inkling that I can't read."

Erin's hands were now on her waist. She was a small woman, and several inches shorter than Kate. Her hair ruffled in the afternoon breeze.

"How come you can't read?"

"I'm dyslexic. Shane's wife, Allison, is a school teacher and now she's a certified dyslexic specialist. She tutors me. I've actually started to learn to read, but there is no way I could have read the stuff you handed me. I'm usually just dealing with the guests here, and the horses, of course, and I'm mostly outside, so it rarely ever comes up. Both times when it happened with you surprised me. Again, I lose my mind while trying to conceal it. Jack knows that and he just wants to protect me."

"I'm sorry. I had no idea."

A small smile lifted Erin's lips. "Most people don't. I lived here for months before Jack figured it out. Speaking of my reception here... Well, I think you need to come into the house and have a civilized talk with us. If you're Jack's sister, you can't leave, not with things the way they are."

"So you're the one who locked me in?"

She grinned. "I did. I figured you were doing damage control with AJ."

"He's pretty mad."

"He's not the only one."

"Jack doesn't know you stopped me?"

"Not yet." She grinned wider.

"You're not afraid of him at all?"

Erin burst out laughing. "No, not hardly." She tilted her head. "You know, his temper is a bit like yours. When he goes off, look out. But otherwise, he's generally rational and wonderful. Anyway, what do you say? You're here. It would be completely stupid for you to leave now, not like this. Your secret was revealed at the wrong time and in the wrong way; so now, let's all be adults about it and work out what we should do next."

Kate nodded. "I could probably be a whole lot more adult."

"Good. Pull your car over and park, and come back with me."

Kate followed Erin until they entered the main yard of the ranch and she saw Jack walking out from the barn. He was frowning as he wiped his hands on a rag. "What's going on?" His tone was calmer than before, and his statement was directed at Erin.

"Let's meet your sister. She's agreed to be adult about the

subject, so we're going inside to discuss it and see if we can figure it out."

Jack threw the rag behind him on a fence post. "All right. I suppose we should."

Kate didn't meet Jack's gaze. Her cheeks burned just from listening to them. Realizing that Erin had more control than Jack in their relationship, there was no doubt how wrong she was. She glanced down at the little woman before her. Interesting. She was as petite as a child, yet seemed to rule the whole place with an iron fist.

Meanwhile, Jack was her brother. The knowledge made her completely uncomfortable. She wasn't sure she wanted a brother. She'd always been an only child. This pursuit answered part of her question, but now she had to deal with her mother's inexcusable actions.

She followed them to the porch of the main house. Entering, she looked around and was visibly impressed. The fireplace was two stories tall and the stairs had a balcony that overlooked the entire first floor. It was huge and elegantly furnished.

"Go ahead and sit down, Kate. Can I get you another lemonade? Shall we try this again?" Erin offered.

Kate nodded, sitting at the kitchen table and resting her arms before her. She nervously linked and unlinked her fingers as she stared at them. Jack sat across from her in a chair. Erin came back with the ice-cold drinks, and Kate gripped hers as if it were the Holy Grail. She cleared her throat and reached into her messenger bag where she had crammed all her paperwork while vacating the cabin, and extracted the proof of who she was. She slid the folder to Jack, saying, "My birth certificate, and my mother's, along with her marriage license."

Jack took it. His demeanor wasn't half as confident or macho as it had been earlier. He didn't meet her gaze and she twitched and hesitated, but he finally opened the folder and perused it. Minutes ticked by before his hand lay flat on the paperwork and he softly sighed, lifting his eyes to hers.

"So you *are* my sister."

Kate pressed her lips together. "Seems so."

He stared at her forehead and his eyes descended, pausing briefly on her face. He was looking for any resemblance. Kate knew instantly. She'd done the same thing to Jack when he wasn't aware of it.

"I wondered why you kept staring at me over the last few weeks. I thought perhaps you were…" He trailed off and nearly shuddered, clearing his throat. "I thought you might be interested, but you were actually looking for any signs of a family resemblance."

"Yes. I was. I was also trying to determine if getting to know you was even worth my time."

"And?"

"And I think you are. Or at least, I like the woman you married and that reflects well on you."

Jack's smile was swift. He grabbed Erin's hand and held it. "I do have good taste."

Erin rolled her eyes. "So… Kate, you were saying, all this turmoil came about because you are really a consulting executive?"

Kate nodded, her tone and demeanor now more subtle and subdued, like Jack was. She described her job, along with her living circumstances in Seattle. Jack nodded at her bag. "Do you still have those suggestions with you?"

Kate slipped them out and set them before him. Jack scanned them briefly and asked, "Do you mind if I take few days to review them?"

"No, you can keep them."

They started conversing, although it was slow and awkward. It didn't flow immediately or take off, but at least, it remained calm and they did learn a few facts about each other. Jack cleared his throat. "So you've met my boys?"

"Yes, Ben is engaged to his high school sweetheart and Charlie is nagging AJ to become a bull rider. He's very shy with me. But Ben is very polite. He looks so much like you."

Jack's smile was genuine and it grew wider as he replied, "Yes. So does that make you their aunt?"

"I guess so. I've never been an aunt before."

"They've had only Allison for the last year. So…"

Erin leaned back in her chair. She was much more at ease than either Jack or Kate. "Look, Kate, why don't you stay for a while? Now that we know who and what you are to us, it could be a totally different experience. We have this huge house, sitting here all empty. You can stay here as long as you want. There is a home office with all the equipment you could possibly need. You mentioned you were catching up on some work from here, so why not continue to? Stay as long as you like. I don't see how we'll ever get to know each other otherwise. You'll go home and I don't foresee you ever coming back. Not based on this one conversation. It's nice we all aren't yelling anymore or trying to second guess each other. Now that I'm not being beaten by my husband, and Kate isn't after Jack, what does it mean? Nothing yet."

Kate jolted straight up, never having expected the invitation. She glanced at Jack for his reaction and their gazes collided. Jack shrugged, clearing his throat. "It's true, the house is empty. You wouldn't have to put up with anyone else and you'd have a lot more space than you do in the cabin." He eyed her up and down. "And it's true, I don't foresee us coming to Seattle, not with my boys and Erin and all… but you're already here. If you leave now, nothing will come of this event."

Kate stared at her fingernails, clicking the ends together

nervously. "Do you want it to? I mean, do I want something to come from this?"

His mouth opened and then closed, and he shook his head. "I've known the truth for about two hours. I can't answer that yet, Kate. I don't know what I want. But I guess the whole sister thing is big. And I don't know what it means, but maybe it means something."

Something. What did he mean? To her life? To theirs? It reminded her of AJ. She remembered what he was searching for in his life and from the people in it. Her heart squeezed, and she rose with renewed optimism. Maybe she could ask him to forgive her. Or at least, not hate her. And not remember her with a bad taste in his mouth. Even if she already felt that way about herself.

"I could stay for a few weeks. Why else be the boss, right?"

"Right." Jack smiled, and so did Erin.

So that was it. She was now an officially invited guest of her brother. She didn't expect that to be the result of the day that went so wrong, so fast, and was mostly doomed because of her own doing. But now? She had a brother and a sister-in-law and a nice place to stay.

Erin sipped her drink before setting it down with a sigh. "When I showed up at this ranch, I was searching for my brother after my mother killed herself. I was very sad and feeling lost. Strangely, you came here for the same reasons. I think there must be something to that." She shook her head, and a self-deprecating smile appeared on her face. "Of course, you're a successful business woman. I was a homeless illiterate without a cent or any prospects to my name. I got stranded here whereas you came here as a guest, and are now *our* guest. My point is, I understand the pain of losing a mother. And your brother is a lot nicer than the one I came here looking for. I hope you give Jack a chance, Kate. As well as this place. There is something special about it. I wasn't born and raised here, but it is the only place that I ever felt like I belonged."

Erin rolled her eyes and wiped them, laughing softly in obvious embarrassment at making such a tender speech. Jack nodded. "Her brother was horrible. He stole all her money, along with her luggage and car, leaving her all alone here with nothing to her name. I can't be that bad, comparatively speaking." He shrugged, and a little smile curled his lips.

Kate glanced at their linked hands. "I'm afraid I could be. Are you sure you want me to stay?"

"Well, we won't know unless we try, will we? And if Erin approves, then she knows better than me. I don't read people as clearly as she does."

Kate sat back, letting out a sigh, and finally relaxing. "You won't punish AJ for my involvement with him, will you?"

Jack shuddered. "I don't need to know anything more about it. I have no comment."

Erin glanced at Jack. "Yes, I was going to have a little discussion about that. Did you forbid the ranch hands from associating with the guests?"

Jack shifted his butt around, and ducked his head down. "Well, no, not like that. I didn't want a bunch of complaints from any heartbroken single women, or men whose wives were cheating, or young daughters being taken advantage of, or whatever the word is. We have a good-looking crew of men, and I just wanted to avoid any drama or lawsuits. Or fist fights. It's not like they aren't good enough. Crap! I like them far better than anyone staying here," he added, shifting his glance to Kate. "No offense. But I just thought it would be better to have a 'no sex with guests' as our unwritten policy."

Erin rolled her eyes. "I didn't know about that rule. Yeah, Jack, we can't be limiting people's interactions or controlling their personal lives." She nodded towards Kate. "No, Jack will tell AJ himself that it isn't any of our business, is it?"

Kate had to press her lips together to keep her grin concealed. Jack nearly ducked down in his chair in shame at Erin's scolding. He frowned. "I can't talk about that with AJ! You have to do it."

Erin glared at him. "First off, AJ will probably wet his pants if I start talking about his sex life. Don't you know him at all? He's extremely discreet, not to mention shy, and he would find it thoroughly inappropriate to discuss his love life with me, of all people. And besides, it was *your* stupid rule."

"I don't think you'll have to worry. He won't talk to me again after today... but I don't want that restriction to affect his life here," Kate interjected.

"It won't. Jack will fix it." Erin smiled sweetly, sliding her chair back. And that seemed to be that. Jack glanced Kate's way.

"Uh, there are towels and basic food supplies in there. The master bedroom is right through that door. You're welcome to use it. The only bedroom off limits is the third door from the stairs. That's Joey's. He still lives here whenever he's back in town. Jocelyn, whom you probably met already, cleans the house once a week. So anything you need to have done you can let her know. Or me, or Erin, of course."

Kate put her hand out. "Thank you, Jack."

He glanced down before taking her hand. "I'm glad we worked this out."

"Yeah, me too."

"Okay, well, I'll get to work. I'll review these suggestions and let you know what I think."

She waved them off and watched them leave together, letting out a slow breath. Eventually, she drove her car to the front and hauled her stuff inside to begin settling in.

~

AJ FINISHED the watering and walked to his trailer. Despondent, he dropped onto one of the patio chairs and stared out listlessly at the view. He knew she'd leave. He knew it from the very start. He didn't, however, expect it to end like that. He had nothing but total disgust and disappointment in whom she turned out to be. Feeling empty and hollow without her now, he missed seeing her. She was usually waiting there with her pink boots up on the table and her head tilted back, enjoying the sun's warm rays.

He sniffed himself, and recoiled at the odor of sweat, covered by dust, and decided he sorely needed a shower. After bathing it occurred to AJ a beer would have been perfect right then. He frowned. Where did that thought come from? He hadn't had a beer in years. Things would get better tomorrow. He'd sleep on it, go to work, return to normal and it would all become a distant memory, eventually forgotten.

It sure as heck could not be any worse tomorrow.

He groaned internally, thinking he should touch base with Jack, just to make sure he was still welcome there. Heaving himself to his feet, he dejectedly started towards the barn office where he usually found Jack at this time of day, finishing up. He waved at Charlie, who was drawing with a stick in the sandy floor of the horse arena. "Hey, AJ!"

"Hey, Charlie." He entered Jack's office with a brief knock. "Have a minute?"

"AJ, sure. Come in. We need to talk. I was heading out to feed. Would you walk with me?"

Jack always fed his own private horses. They had more than a dozen that were for their family use. He rarely asked any of his hired help to do it. That's another reason why AJ respected him. Jack put in the hard work too. AJ's stomach churned at the thought that Jack needed to talk to him.

He steeled his spine. He was used to it by now. The regular departures. The wandering. The new places, jobs and people. He'd been doing it his whole life and was stupid to have gotten so comfortable there. The temptation of stability. And besides, he knew the rules so the result was his own doing. He wouldn't beg or plead with Jack to forgive him or give him another chance; he knew he was in the wrong. He'd take Jack's words at face value and respectfully clear out.

Jack entered the barn and headed for the tack room to mix up the evening portions of feed for the horses.

"So you and my sister, huh?"

AJ's eyes jerked up to Jack's face and his mouth twisted in shock. When Jack suddenly burst out laughing, AJ was puzzled. "I don't care, AJ. She wasn't my sister until about four hours ago. So… it's none of my business. Erin pointed out I had no right making that kind of a rule between you guys and the guests. So as long as you're not mad that I did that, we're still good; at least, as far I'm concerned."

AJ swallowed. Shocked was putting it mildly. "I shouldn't have disobeyed your wishes; it's your place, after all."

Jack cleared his throat, and paused from pulling the oats out of a bag. "Uh, AJ, to put this delicately, I don't know too many men who could have not succumbed to her ministrations. I didn't know who Kate was, I just knew someone interesting was here. So… yeah, I get it. I'm just glad it turned out to be you and not me."

"Well, it's all over now. I still apologize for going behind your back. It won't happen again."

Jack scooped the grain out and dumped it into a big bowl before bringing hot water out of a hose specially plumbed and dedicated for that purpose. He let it soak into the mixture until it was mushy. "She's still here. Erin locked her inside the resort. Literally locking the resort gate to make sure she would talk to us before she left. They resolved all their differences by the time she dragged me into it and I talked to Kate. She agreed to stay in the main house. So… yeah, whatever you want to do about that. Again, none of my business and my opinion is irrelevant from now on. Just let me wish you good luck, man. She's no shrinking violet."

AJ's ears rang and his stomach tightened. Was it relief? Anger? Disgust? Regret? Happiness? He wasn't sure. But something in his chest swelled at learning she wasn't gone. She was still there. He left the barn and glanced up toward the house. Sure enough, her silver sports car was parked there and lights blazed from the house's windows. He gulped. Worried that his job and stability were almost snatched from him, he took a step back, and then another and another before spinning around and hurrying off to escape into his trailer. He already had too much Kate today. But he wondered what tomorrow would bring for Kate and him.

CHAPTER 11

*K*ATE FINISHED HER REPORTS for work, as well as the other pressing matters Greg had brought her. Stretching out, she took her coffee cup to the porch. It was about a hundred feet long and overlooked the entire ranch. She felt like a king surveying his kingdom. *Pretty breathtaking place to live,* she conceded. Learning that Jack gave it up for the much smaller, simpler house down by the river said something about him, didn't it?

Her mother once slept there. It was a surreal thought. Had her mom really done this? Fallen for a cowboy and moved to River's End? Did her mother also try to turn her fantasy affair, like the one Kate was having, into a real relationship? Here? On this ranch? It blew Kate's mind to think that her mother had lived there for almost two full years. Her mother also enjoyed this same view. Possibly, her mother even touched this porch column. Did she drink her morning coffee while watching the sun filter its rays over the land?

Did her mother also realize it was many miles from anywhere and anything and anyone else? Especially back then, when they had no internet? Her mother must have felt very cut off. Remembering her chic, Seattle-loving mother was such a contrast; especially when Kate imagined her mother in her prim, pastel-colored suits and pearls...here? It didn't compute at all. Was she trapped in a sex haze before she realized she was residing with stinky farm animals and enduring long days from dawn to dusk?

The sweaty, dusty men probably became gross at the end of the day and maybe the allure of all that dirt eventually wore off. Kate wanted her mother's ghost or spirit or karmic voice to channel through her. She wanted her mother to answer her questions. To teach her. Why? Why did her mother run off?

Was Kate doomed to re-enact her mother's mistakes?

Kate imagined getting pregnant and becoming a house-wife there. *Never.* She'd just hire help. She wasn't her mother. Kate was dependent on no one and self-supporting, where her mother had needed constant care until the day she died. Perhaps that's why Kate strove to become the complete opposite. She was autonomous to the extreme, and some-times needed to prove herself too often.

Kate straightened off the porch rail when she spotted AJ crossing the yard. His arms swung at his sides and his stride was purposeful. He was headed straight for her. Was he pissed? She wasn't sure because his hat, as always, hid his facial expression. Swallowing the last gulp of coffee, she grimaced when she tasted the grounds. Kate watched AJ until he reached the bottom of the porch steps, resting his boot on it as he grasped the railing.

"So it wasn't really goodbye." Kate retorted as she raised her lip, eyebrow and shoulders all in a *Gee, isn't that funny?* kind of expression.

"No, I guess not."

She set the coffee cup down. "AJ, why don't you come in and we'll talk like adults? You know, like Erin insisted I do yesterday? I admit I was wrong, okay? About all of it. How I handled them, myself, and mostly, you. I have a flaming temper and I lost it yesterday. But now? I think I'm staying for a while; and if not, I think I'll at least come back."

"Yes, because you're his sister, and not just a guest here on a fun-filled little vacation."

"I never said it was a fun-filled little vacation. I told you I just buried my mother."

"Jack's mother too. You failed to mention that."

She swept her hand, motioning him forward, "Please, let's go inside and talk about it. We could stand here trading insults, but Jack is over in the barn, and someone I don't recognize is walking along the fence."

AJ stiffened before he approached her. She turned, hoping she had scored a small win. His mood after yesterday suggested he might have been done with her and preferred that she leave.

Taking the hat off his head, AJ stood in the doorway, sweeping his gaze around the inside. Kate also spent quite a while taking it all in last night after Jack and Erin left. The fireplace was the main feature and each individual rock had laboriously been carried from the river and placed there by one of their distant relatives, another Rydell, now long dead. AJ didn't step in any further. Crap. He, no doubt, felt uncomfortable walking in there.

"AJ, come in. They don't care." Kate restrained a sigh. It wasn't owing to Jack and Erin's restrictions anymore, it was AJ's own decision not to go certain places, as if he somehow weren't quite good enough. A second-class citizen. Maybe that was AJ's perception, but no one else's, including Kate's.

Timidly, he ventured two steps inside and twirled his hat. He wasn't about to sit; Kate took his wide-legged stance as a clue.

"I'm very sorry."

"I don't think it matters, Kate. You were leaving, getting out of here. Let's just drop it as that."

Her heart dipped. No. Just… no! That wasn't what she wanted. The strength of her emotions struck her deeply. Even if she were going back home, she didn't want it to be over. She liked AJ, so much. Way too much. And no way was it over… not yet.

"You don't mean that."

"You were only staying for two weeks. From the start, for me, this was two weeks and over. Why do you think I was so unhappy about the first night? I didn't want you, Kate. Not like this. I still don't. But you were leaving. You're not supposed to still be here, much less, be Jack's sister."

"But you were a willing participant. You can't lay all this at my feet. You totally were into every moment we spent together, platonic and otherwise."

"I did. Because it was *two weeks*. After that, I planned to go back to my real life."

"I handled it all wrong. They forgave me. Why can't you even discuss it?"

"Because I think this is the real you. You do and say what you want, regardless of what others may think or feel or request from you. I asked you to stop. Didn't it occur to you for a second that I rarely spoke up to you? Or that I would never knowingly tolerate any woman being hurt, in front of me. You didn't even consider I might know something more about Jack and Erin than you. All you had to do was listen. But you just don't, or you won't. You're sorry because you told Jack I was sleeping with you when you knew pretty clearly I did not want that fact being flung out there like that. If that weren't bad enough, you totally miss the point of why I don't want to be around you."

She closed her eyes, sucking in a breath. "You think I'm that awful? I admit when I know what I want, I go after it.

And when I think something is wrong. Erin was acting strange. It didn't occur to me that the paperwork was causing her anxiety. I thought it was because she dreaded having to tell Jack about it. I should have stopped. But there was more going on there than that. I was thinking about him as my brother and it all played into it. I overreacted. But I am sorry. I do listen, AJ. To you especially."

We had sex because what I did felt good to you. There was not a single protest from you. And when you did express some doubts, I invited you to dinner because I felt guilty. But after that? You were a major part of the entire experience. I might've pushed things forward faster, and I did not listen to you yesterday. But that isn't indicative of my entire personality. I didn't listen in that one, isolated instance. Other times? I listened to you. You just can't admit that you wanted to have sex with me, and once you did, nothing could've stopped you. So quit blaming me for that. You have your commitments and beliefs, but AJ, you're the one who broke them a few times over, not me. Quit blaming me for that."

He squinted at her, still scowling, but finally sucked in a breath. Shaking his head, he sighed in resignation. "I thought you'd be gone, so I could just go back to how I was living before you."

Hope stirred in her chest. Was he mad because he really wanted her there? He wanted her still? Is that the reason for all his blustering and blame? "Please accept my apology for the way I acted yesterday."

He nodded. "Okay."

"I will seriously attempt to avoid being a controlling, crazy-sounding jerk again. I will try to listen better to you, and respect what you say. I do respect you, AJ. Everyone here does. They all talk about you as one of them. I talk about and think of you more than any man I've ever dated or had sex with. You think I saw you as some kind of cowboy novelty I was just flirting around with? It may have started out that way, but it quickly changed. If I could replay how I first approached you, I would. I worry you don't believe I take this… us… you, seriously. But remember: I knew there was a distinct chance I'd come back here, so I do take it all seriously. Yesterday was about Jack, not you."

"I have to get back to work."

She restrained a sigh, doubting anyone kept track of AJ's hours. Besides, he rarely took any breaks or even ate lunch. They could finish this discussion, and no one would care. But she understood him better now; he gave his word to Jack on the first day he started there and that was that. The day was dedicated to work. AJ was inflexible in that. "Just one more minute. You think I don't respect you. I'd like to change that. We could do this differently. Make it more real. More proper. Like two people who are not on vacation."

He tilted his head in consideration of her comment. "I don't understand."

She smiled, and strange nerves bubbled away in her stomach. She wrung her hands together. "Like, you know, we could date. Maybe like that night we had dinner. The way you would have liked it from the start. You know, we could get to know each other better. Talk some more. Figure out who we are. No sex."

His eyebrows shot up. "No sex?"

"Well, isn't that a source of the issue for you? From the start, you indicated it was."

"Yeah. But…" AJ's face became a puzzled scowl.

She waited, now confused. "What?"

"You're here to stay, at least, for now, and you don't want to have sex? But you do want to hang out? Does that sum it up?"

"It does."

"You think we can avoid having sex?"

She bristled. "Of course. *I* can."

"It's not as easy as you think," he mumbled, putting his hat on as he threw up his hands. "Fine. Whatever. What do you have in mind?"

"Why don't we go to out tonight? On a date?"

"Working on Joey's roof."

"Oh, right. Well, how about sometime this week?"

He shrugged. "I'll get back to you."

"Right," she mumbled to his back. Had she just been sidelined? AJ seemed kind of cold, like any normal asshole guy. Did she now just wait for him to include her in his plans and somehow fit her in? She sighed because it was the first time in her dating life the man had the control and all she could do was... wait.

CHAPTER 12

*A*J CALLED ON KATE a few days later. She was trying to catch up on her work. She had been neglecting most of it, but with the home office now and AJ always so busy, she had a lot more time to focus on it. Jack and Erin often invited her to dinner, and she gratefully returned the favor. It was still unnatural and strained between Jack so she and Erin usually talked nonstop for hours. She learned most of the relevant information from Erin, and all about Jack.

Sure, it was progress, except they still avoided the real subject matter: their mother. The only time her name came up was when an innocuous question about Kate's life in Seattle was asked before comparing her answer to their lives in River's End.

Her staff was flabbergasted when Kate didn't return. The longest she'd ever been gone from work was when her father died. So after the first two weeks, her unforeseen commitment to staying longer in River's End was pretty unheard of.

During that time, far removed from AJ, she calmed the hell down a bit. It was time to get a grip. They'd fallen into a short-term, intense tryst. Whatever one wanted to call it. Fling. Affair. Liaison. However, it felt much deeper than any of those words implied. That was the point; she needed to step back and let it develop more naturally, make it more real. So when he showed up at the front door, asking her to go out the next night, she nodded, but didn't let him in. They didn't kiss. Or touch. Or hardly even talk. Then, he turned around and went home as she firmly shut the door of the house.

They finally went out on a proper date for once: dinner and movie. The movie theatre was a half-hour drive and Kate realized after his complaint about her not listening to him that he was right. She hadn't really listened to him. She simply responded to his body language as he did to hers. She never heard he didn't want a sexual relationship. And though she never dated any man without sex being involved, she was willing to try. She hoped to better understand herself and wanted to do it only after they were a lot more established, if that would even happen. Maybe they'd fizzle out in the next day or week or months... who knew? Maybe without sex they would hate each other, or bore each other, or have nothing to say.

Maybe he'd find her pretentious and she'd consider him an uncultured bore.

That would have made the most sense, to be honest.

The date was beyond awkward at first. She dressed the way she usually did in Seattle and AJ dressed the way he always did. That was the first discrepancy. She offered to drive her car, but he refused, which prompted her to argue the logic that his truck was hard to climb into, especially while wearing a skirt. It was high without running boards and the torn seat stuck to her bare skin.

But oh, no, he insisted on driving his truck, and they spent the first part of the date without talking. He was stone cold, and she was filled with annoyance at his macho-ness. His reason for having to drive his truck was ridiculous, and he accused her of trying to control him.

The movie eventually chilled them both out. They shared popcorn and drinks and went out to dinner at a casual grill. There weren't a lot of choices in the way of restaurants. Not compared to Seattle, which she mentioned. AJ sneered that they probably charged a week's worth of wages for one dinner. Kate rolled her eyes and smiled, sweetly informing him no, at least, not for her.

The ensuing conversation became stilted. After they finally pulled into the ranch, Kate jumped out, smiling and thanking him for dinner. He grumbled his thanks, since she paid for the movie before he could get to the ticket booth.

After that, they shared a few more dinners. Nothing more intimate ever happened. Kate even asked to attend church with him, and had gone twice now. She found, to her surprise, it was mentally stimulating. AJ was right; the pastor was pretty cool. First of all, she was a woman. Second, she was very progressive and awesome. She talked all about God and Jesus, but managed to relate them to the real world.

Kate really liked AJ. She liked his church. She liked his town. She was even starting to kind of like his ranch.

Despite his grumbling, bickering, and general annoyance, she saw someone who could captivate her interest, and match her in debates. It was exhilarating as much as it was surprising.

AJ FELT LIKE ONE GIANT, pulsating gland and it was all Kate Morgan's fault.

Grumpy, annoyed, and downright unpleasant were only a few words to describe his current state of malaise. *Three years.* Maybe it was even longer than that. No sex with anyone. No one. Zilch. Nada. No sex at all. Of any kind. And now? Three freaking weeks, and he could hardly stand his own company. And it was all her fault.

Why would she suggest they date without having sex? She started it, heavily, and expertly. It wasn't like Kate did anything gently or delicately. No, it was always headlong, full tilt, full... well, every thought seemed to turn dirty of late, but full-on Kate. And that's what getting to know each other was based on. Now? Nothing. He could hardly stand being so close to her without touching her. Nothing. Not even a kiss hello. But he didn't press her, or mention that whenever he was within three feet of her, he had to clench his fists to keep from grabbing her, pressing her against him and doing every inappropriate thing she used to invite him to do with that mouth of hers.

When she asked to come to church with him, of all places, he had no idea what to think. It was bad enough that she wore the impossible skirt again. Those things and others... drove him insane. He began picturing the first night with her, her comments about the torn vinyl on his seats made it hard for him to resist the urge to fling her over the bench seat and be done with it, then and there. But now? No touching, and lots of talking. As it turned out, strangely enough, there was rarely a lengthy silence between them anymore. They didn't always agree and Kate, being Kate, never quit an argument, even if it ended in outright bickering.

Somehow instead of frustrating him, AJ found it exhilarating. Like the hottest foreplay he could imagine without touching. Keeping up with that brilliant mind of hers and her even fiercer tongue in an argument stroked his ego and filled him with a certain degree of pride. Not all women could do that.

But his frustration wasn't about arguing or talking or being around Kate. It was about *not* being with her.

She was one kick-in-the-ass personality, whether or not he slept with her. He'd never been around a woman like her before. She could stand toe to toe with him, and be eye to eye. Other than her feminine inferiority in physical strength, she remained fierce and valiant from the tilt of her head, to the flint of her eyes, to the vertically straight line in which she held her posture.

And now, church? He waited in his truck for her to come out the first Sunday, as they had agreed upon. It wasn't a date. No one went to church for a date. She wore an appropriate dress that was knee-length, featuring a floral pattern and a modest neckline. Seeing Kate so prim and proper was as much of a turn-on to AJ as she was the on the first night in her jean skirt and pink boots. He missed the pink boots. Most days, she worked inside the house so she didn't wear them as often.

She sat next to him in the pew, holding her head high and gazing frankly around her as she studied every single person at the altar and the pews. She waited with curiosity for the pastor to come out and speak. When others prayed and closed their eyes, she listened carefully trying to make sense of it.

AJ lowered his head as usual, closing his eyes and mumbling his prayer right along with the congregation, but he felt so proud and tall with Kate beside him. Turning toward her, he noticed her head was up and her eyes were open. Tapping her knee and jerking his neck slightly, he tried to urge her to simply lower her head. She startled and then did so. Head down, with his eyes open, he was unable to quit watching her. Her profile reminded him of a regal queen, her chin firmly up, her eyes wide, her short hair styled just so, and her makeup perfect.

A problem arose as AJ sat in church, where he was supposed to be listening, praying, reflecting and finding some peace. Instead, with Kate next to him, he could not ignore *her*. On the contrary, he became intensely aware of every time she slid her butt or swiped her hand over her skirt to keep it from bunching underneath her.

His entire body responded with a jerk to attention. When her skirt rose up higher over her thighs, although still modest, he couldn't stop staring. He repressed a wild desire to slide his hand up between her slim thighs and find the heat and moisture that he knew was waiting there. He began to think, almost obsessively, about whether or not she was wearing panties this time.

He had to shift around when all his wondering began to make him uncomfortable.

She seemed completely oblivious to his attention as well as the direction of this thoughts.

Going to church became a trial at times. Once, it had been his escape, until she kept coming. Ever so politely, she'd shake the pastor's hand afterwards, even asking a few questions about the day's sermon. She never hesitated to admit she had little exposure to religion before then.

They talked for twenty minutes the first time, thirty the next, and AJ lost track on the third. AJ never said anything more than hello to the pastor. Never mind that the woman had rekindled his faith and brought more comfort in his life than anyone had before. She inspired AJ to change, and find a better path and less rocky road to walk on. For so long before coming to River's End, AJ longed to be different. He was searching without any definable object or goal. He didn't know how to get to where he wanted, since he couldn't say where he wanted to be.

So he drifted, pointlessly, always alone, accountable to no one, and mattering to no one. For years, his life had been that way, so he abused alcohol, drugs, and clung to the adulation of crowds. No matter how many strange women and loud bars he frequented, they could not drown out his reality.

After first entering the quiet, tiny country church one Sunday when he was exceptionally bored and feeling hopeless, he was unsure why he wanted to go in there. The pastor was talking about God and His love, saying that He was with everyone, no matter who they were or what they may have done. AJ sat there, stunned. He had no idea what that felt like before. God? Jesus? Faith? Religion? They were just words to AJ until that moment. With giant question marks after them.

But this pastor had reached something in AJ, and changed the question marks to periods over the course of the next several months. AJ stopped taking refuge in all his old vices and began to realize how his previous unhappiness and anti-social behavior only led him to prison. That's what his faith-less life had been before now. So being there that day in church changed AJ's life. He wanted to clean it all up because he discovered a love for something beyond himself that would never leave or walk away from him.

Not like Kate.

He shook off the thought, but it kept creeping in. And making him angry.

And now? She was all chummy to the pastor who saved his life. He'd been unable to articulate his own experience to the one person responsible for it. He mumbled hello, with his head down, swiftly jamming his hat on his head to slip out as quickly as possible before anyone, the pastor especially, tried to engage him in small talk. He couldn't deal with that. He was never raised or taught how to do it. There were no family get-together or dinners out with friends. He never had any occasion that required him to learn social cues and graces. All through his teens and twenties, he was drunk with rodeo crews in crowded honky-tonks. There was never any need for chit-chat or polite conversation. Look at how he fumbled with Kate.

However, her oddly forward re-introduction to sex gave him back his voice, so he could be around her and still talk. Sex was one hell of an ice breaker, but in retrospect, it literally took that for him to even attempt to talk to her, or anyone.

Not like he wanted to make that his pattern.

Although in his youth, he tried pretty hard.

In all honesty, Kate was the first person with whom he had ever been completely, fully himself... and they actually talked, chatted, and socialized.

With the Rydells, he had no trouble discussing the ranch, the horses, the hay, or the work. He knew what to talk about with them. And he never did unless he had a ready subject. What could he say to Kate? His tongue grew thick when he was with her and no words formed.

Kate easily talked. To anyone and everyone. Never, not once did she seem unsure of what to say. In fact, she was usually overly sure of what to say. She was steadfast in her opinions. She was also friendly, confident, funny, witty, quirky, forward, and frustrating. In a word, she was likeable. And AJ was not.

All he had to offer Kate was sex. And now, that wasn't even part of the equation. So he waited for her, biding his time until she was ready to go, and where did that leave him?

At the church. He would go back to church and the former quiet pleasure of his River Road permanent residence.

For now.

Because nothing was permanent. His future was still contingent on his job and his ability to mesh with the Rydells. They still had the power.

Surprisingly to AJ, Kate found the church invigorating and called it "an intellectual experience."

AJ considered Kate's presence in church a distraction. It took away the entire goal of why he came there: to strive to be clean, sober, and celibate. Kate's long legs kept dangling next to him. Sure, they were crossed properly, but she liked to gracefully slip off her high-heeled shoe, distracting him sometimes to the point of not hearing the service.

The fourth time she went, she had a rather invigorating discussion with the pastor in the foyer of the church. The oppressive outside heat wafted in each time a parishioner came in or went out the door. AJ stood off to the side, clenching his hat in his hands as he waited patiently for Kate. He nodded and smiled periodically at the passing citizens of River's End.

Lots of them stayed afterwards for the brunch and their kids rushed to play on the toys at the side of the church. Women came in and out, carrying all kinds of bowls and trays of food. Most were salads and other side dishes. AJ never stayed for the meal. What would he do there by himself? There was no one to stand beside, and no one he knew except the people on the ranch. None of the ranch workers ever came to church on Sunday, and the Rydells never stayed for brunch.

The pastor asked them both to stay that day. Kate's smile was genuine as she shook the woman's hand. "Oh, we'd love to. I didn't realize there was a brunch afterwards."

"Every week. You're welcome to enjoy it. We just ask for any donation of food or money or drink, whatever you can comfortably give." The pastor nodded at the collection bowl.

Kate opened her purse. "Of course, that's totally under-standable." Kate only had money to give.

AJ grabbed Kate's arm, and leaning closer, he said, "I don't usually stay."

Kate glanced up. "The food is practically free." Then she eagerly followed the pastor out the front doors while AJ stared after her, helpless. He didn't know what to do. He could see the crowd collecting under the majestic old cottonwood trees whose shadows cooled the freshly clipped lawn. Tables overflowed with the usual potluck dishes as the families, couples, teens, and older people milled about.

There weren't many places to spend money, nor much to do in River's End, so church was more of a socializing outlet. Except for AJ. He had no idea how to deal with the occasion. His hands started to grow clammy. Kids screamed and shrieked. A cacophony of voices turned into a blended murmur, and the bees hummed while a neighbor's sprinkler spun in lazy circles. It was idyllic. Lovely. A painting.

A picture AJ would never and had never set foot in.

Kate glanced back and AJ forced himself forward. He pulled his hat lower, grateful for the anonymity it provided as well as a place to hide.

He stepped behind Kate, who was chatting to an older lady, perhaps in her fifties, and serving at the table. Kate already knew her name. She held out her paper plate and received potato salad, quiche, and baked beans. She added some pieces of fried chicken, inhaling the delicious aroma and smiling. Kate talked and babbled with everyone she encountered: the older, matronly women, as well as a hard-of-hearing, balding man who was flattered by her genuine interest.

She sat down at one of the picnic tables, facing the lawn and placing her meal on her lap. AJ followed her like a puppy afraid to lose its mother. He took the same food as she before sitting down right beside her and balancing his plate on his lap. He kept his head down and used his hat to hide from everyone's view.

It did wonders in keeping him from making any eye

contact or having to talk to people. Lacking eye contact, most people weren't too anxious to start gabbing. A facial expression is the first sign of welcome in a conversation, and only a rare person would just start talking to AJ unless they knew him. Very few would ask him questions or try to initiate conversation.

He ate his meal swiftly and kept clean. After dumping his empty plate in the garbage, AJ was ready to be done with it. Meanwhile, Kate, who didn't have any hat to hide under, and didn't want to hide anyway, was intrigued. She had been drawn into several conversations. Most were from passers-by who stopped and wanted to meet her.

She'd become a bit famous in River's End as Jack's long-lost sister. Kate's mother was already notorious. She was the woman who ditched River's End and Henry Rydell. One old lady lit into a small tirade when she remembered Kate's mother. It wasn't the most pleasant conversation, but Kate merely smiled politely and refused to comment.

Finally… it felt like hours, but was barely an hour, Kate was ready to leave. She slipped into AJ's truck and became uncharacteristically quiet.

Pulling into the ranch, AJ glanced at her. "Did the questions about your mom bother you?"

"Honestly? Yes. I forgot actually, that anyone here might've remembered her. Even Jack has no memory of her, so we just talk like she never existed despite the link between us. You know? But realizing my mother lived here, in this very house for a year or so and tried to be part of the community, is like we're talking about someone else. If you'd known my mom, imagining her being married to a rancher is like… like…"

"Anyone who knows you imagining you with a ranch foreman?" AJ supplied, his tone deep and soft.

She glanced over his shoulder sharply. "I was actually

looking for a physical metaphor, like a fish taking residence in a bird's nest, or a bat suddenly clinging to a rock covered in algae. She was the prissiest woman I ever knew. She wore eight rings on her fingers, and a dozen bracelets and necklaces. Her clothes could have funded a small country. Her hairspray alone would have choked you and she singlehandedly could have created the hole in the ozone layer with her product overuse."

AJ clicked his door handle and jumped out. Kate tried to slide out while holding her skirt down. She needed running boards for that. She couldn't comfortably get in or out, especially in a skirt and heels. She finally landed and adjusted her stance to bear her weight, closing her door before walking towards the porch. "You didn't like us staying after church. Why is that? Church seems so important to you that I assumed it would be something you regularly did."

"No."

"The pastor didn't even know your name, AJ," she added softly.

Stepping past her, he walked through the Rydells' front door without knocking or asking for her permission. Sometimes, it still made him pause because it felt so odd and wrong to do. He threw his hat on the table and walked over to the sink, pretending he needed a glass of water instead of going there simply to avoid her probing inquiry.

"I don't talk to her much. I suppose she doesn't."

"But it's so important to you."

He drank. Liberally.

She walked closer, but he didn't turn to look. She stopped behind him. "Why?"

"Why what?"

"Why don't you talk to anyone? You've lived here for three years. You said the permanence of this address was very important to you. Why not try to get to know some of the people who live here?"

"I don't think I'd have much in common with anyone."

"There were all kinds of people at that church potluck. They are not pretentious people. I think you'd fit in better than I do. So… why haven't you?"

He set the glass down, shrugging his shoulders and staring out the window. Far down below his trailer sat. Not his trailer, really.

"AJ?"

He ignored her and rested his hands on the edge of the counter, leaning his weight on them.

"Tell me why you won't even try to make any connections here?"

"Because I don't know how, okay? I don't know how to talk to anyone." Agitated, he walked to the kitchen table and sat on the edge of it. She turned her body angle to follow him.

"You talk to Jack, Shane, Caleb… so that's not true."

"I discuss work. What we're doing. I tell them what Jack wants. I ask Jack what he wants. It's a confined topic. I know what they want out of me. What do I know about those people at church? What should I say? What do they want to talk about? I don't know. I have no idea what they'd want to hear from me. What could I possibly have to say that they'd be interested in? I talk to no one. I do nothing but physical grunt work. I have nothing to say. And no one to say it to. So I don't socialize."

He stared down, crossing his arms over his chest when he could almost *feel* her eyes searching over him. "You have lots to say."

Glancing up for only a brief second, his gaze instantly slid off in the opposite direction. "To you, maybe."

"Well, that started with us being complete strangers."

"Yeah, and you nearly stripped naked before I said hello. We were strangers then. I was just thinking in church, while watching you interacting with everyone, how open and easy you are. You can socialize with everyone, which made our encounter one heck of an ice breaker and if I could do that with everyone..."

"But the point is, once the ice was broken, okay, maybe I was a little too brazen, considering—"

"You weren't."

"What?" she glanced up at his soft interjection.

He sighed and rolled his shoulders. He hated talking like this. "You didn't act too brazenly. In fact, that's what I *liked* about you."

"What? Sex? Well, of course you did, you'd been denying yourself for three years."

"No. I mean, yes, I liked the sex with you. But I meant, I liked knowing what you wanted from me. There was no waffling or obscure signals with you that I was afraid of missing. I wasn't confused about what you were doing, or why you were doing it. So maybe that made it easier to talk to you. You asked me whatever you wanted to know. You showed up where you wanted to be. And when you felt like having sex, we did."

Her head tilted and her eyes softened as she glanced over him. He wished for his hat.

"You're unsure of how to talk to most people? But you're not really shy. That's what I couldn't put my finger on when I first met you. You were there, but you wouldn't engage me. You wouldn't talk to me. Yet I felt your presence, so it wasn't like I thought you were that shy. Is it because you don't know what to say?"

"I never learned, okay? I grew up with no one to teach me. I mean, living in one house or another, full of strangers who didn't give a crap about me, and the one who should have cared only came to get me when he planned to use me in one of his scams to get money from innocent people. He'd tell me what to say and I mimicked it until I got old enough to tell him to screw off. So I never learned any manners. I have no idea what polite society like that church or where you live in Seattle would talk about. I don't know much. I only know cowhands. I know work. Men. We talk when necessary, but we don't *share* anything, not even the weather."

"It's not okay, actually, AJ. It's really screwed up that your father would do that to you." She stepped closer. He wanted her to step further away. He didn't like that. He didn't want her crowding him right now. Not while they were *talking* like this.

"He didn't do anything to me. There was no abuse. Look at me, you think once I got past the age of thirteen anyone would dare mess with me?"

"I think that it didn't just mess with you, it fucked up your whole childhood. And besides, you don't use your strength in ways like that."

He pushed his hand out to stop her from coming closer and stared right into her eyes. "You didn't know me. You have no idea what I'm capable of. I took a bottle, a glass beer bottle, and smashed it over another man's head. Right here." He pointed above his temple. "Do you realize the damage I could have done? I went to prison, Kate. It wasn't detention, or juvie hall, or some white-collar jail, it was a penitentiary for—"

"Violent criminals?" She stepped right between his legs, which he was dangling over the table. She clutched his jaw in her hands. "It was a horrible thing to do to anyone. But I don't, not even for a minute, believe that was *you*."

"It was inside me."

"I don't think it is anymore. What was going on?"

He shrugged, trying to avoid her touch. "What do you mean?"

"What was the man doing? Standing on the street corner and you just casually walked up and cracked a bottle over his head for sheer pleasure?"

He scowled. "No, we were in a bar. Drinking. I was three sheets to the wind. I made a bet of course, on the football game. So often did I do that. Anyway, I won. The guy was being loud and obnoxious about it. He didn't want to pay up. We exchanged words, and fists and then... honestly? It's a little fuzzy, but at some point, I grabbed a bottle and hit him with it. Knocked him out cold."

"So it was a bar fight."

"I consider someone needing stitches a bit more than a bar fight."

"It was a fair fight that got out of hand."

"Not what the court ruled."

She sighed. "Fine, you win on all the facts. My point is your intentions. I don't worry about my safety or anyone else's when I'm around you. I believe your intentions are to avoid hurting anyone. In fact, I think you prefer to stay out of everyone's way."

"Things work out better for all involved when I do, me included."

"Except for with me."

"You were supposed to leave." His arms were still crossed over his chest. He refused to budge. He felt her body tensing against his. He kept his gaze pinned on her elbow, studying the little, floral designs of the dress fabric.

"But I didn't. And that's what you wanted. That's why you got so mad at me."

"It made it easier, I suppose, to do what we did because we knew it wouldn't last. I didn't have to worry past the obvious."

"Sex?"

"Yeah, even if it worried me to do that too, considering my past."

"Except we had lots to talk about."

"No, you did, and you do, Kate. Not me."

He peered at her for a second and caught her biting on her lower lip as if in concentration. "But then I didn't leave and stopped it. I stopped our sex."

"Yeah, I've suffered from that decision."

"But that's what you wanted. Because you thought you could retain control. If we were having sex, then we were just like your wild, misbegotten youth. I was just another woman. Because you understood sex. You don't understand what's going on now, do you? That's what's inside you. I wasn't sure. I thought this would make you happier with me, living by the stuff you believed in from the church. But that wasn't it. You don't have the first clue how to sustain any kind of relationship, do you?"

She was talking to herself. As she stared down, she realized she was explaining AJ to herself.

She shook her head. "But then why would you? No one ever showed you how to."

"I just thought you'd leave. Two weeks. That's all you were supposed to be here."

"And who can get hurt in two weeks?" She lifted her face to his and her nails stroked his cheek. "That's what you counted on. You live your entire life avoiding relationships beyond those directly related to your work because you think that's all you have to offer."

He pushed her hands off his face, combing his hand through his hair and leaning back to avoid her. "Stop it, Kate. The mini psych lesson? I don't need that."

"Am I wrong?"

He grabbed her waist and hauled her against him so she

could feel his immediate erection. "Yes. The hesitancy in church? All I could picture was sliding my hand up your skirt and thinking you'd most likely let me. When I should have been praying, keeping eyes closed, my heart open and all that, I was staring down at the part of your thighs. I didn't want to talk to anyone, I wanted to take you home and mount you."

Her breath caught and slowly released as he shoved his face into hers, letting his tongue delve deeply inside her mouth. Her hands threaded through his hair and pulled back his head, separating their mouths, so their eyes were staring right into each other's. "Except you don't have a home. You don't even know what a home is. Especially this one."

Her words were like a razor threatening his dick. Everything deflated and he quickly released her. "No. I haven't. And it's not."

"But you *can* talk to me, and you like to talk to me. That's what's so different about us, isn't it? You don't know how to talk to anyone else. But you can easily express yourself to me."

"You're spinning circles here. Are you turning me down or not? Insulting me or not?"

"You don't think anywhere is your home, and you think no one wants to talk or interact with you. But you do with me. You have a connection with me. That's what we're talking about. Not just two weeks."

He closed his eyes and had no idea what she saying; much less how to respond. He didn't get it.

But he kind of did.

He opened his eyes.

"I'll be back. When I go home, I plan to come back. That's what you got so mad about. You realized it might mean more than two weeks. You don't know what to do with that."

"Do you?" he countered.

Her lips tipped into a tiny smile. "Touché. Good point. Maybe not. But there is no two-week limit. So I guess we have some figuring out to do. I couldn't get a handle on what you were like at church and afterwards, compared to being here. Then I remembered the first few times I saw you and it was often like that. My first impression of you was that you were shy. But then, no, that doesn't totally fit either. You're quiet. Yes. But then, I think you must have a lot to say."

"And that starts now?" He eyed her and her smile brightened.

"Yes. I think it does. I'd like to understand what church does for you, since you don't say a word to anyone else." He pressed his lips together and dropped his arms before nodding. Then she added a smile. "But tonight? You can come into my bedroom and properly seduce me. And for once, let's make a note that this was *your idea.*"

The smile that spread across his mouth was one only Kate could have drawn so spontaneously from him.

CHAPTER 13

*K*ATE HEARD FOOTSTEPS AND THUDDING. Confused as to what was going on, she slipped out of bed and softly crept towards the kitchen. She stopped dead when a man's form materialized near the refrigerator before he opened it.

"Who are you?" Kate asked nervously.

The man whipped around, a few inches shorter than she, and nearly jumped at the sound of her voice.

"Joey. Who the hell are you? We didn't start renting this place out, or did we?"

"Joey Rydell? Jack's brother?"

His smile was a cocky half grin on a face that could've been featured on a movie screen. "Yeah, again, who are you?"

She smiled back, holding out her hand. "Kate Morgan. Jack's sister."

Joey's smile slowly faded. "Jack's what? What the hell did I miss?"

She laughed and muttered, "A lot. I take it you don't contact home very often."

He shrugged and turned, grabbing a couple of small

glasses from the glass-fronted cabinet, and the neck of a bottle of booze with the other hand. He brought them both to the table with a thud. "This deserves some alcohol. Care to partake with me, Kate, Jack's sister, while you explain to me how my brother could have a sister I've never heard of?"

She nodded in the affirmative and Joey splashed some brown liquid into each glass. Sliding it towards her, he raised his glass in a mock toast before swallowing a large gulp. Kate sipped hers and backed up slightly to lean her hip against the kitchen counter.

He made a face and smacked his lips. "Okay, so Jack's sister, why are you here?"

"I take it no one knows you were coming here today?" Kate replied.

He smiled with great pleasure. "My house, Sister Kate, I come and go as I please. Didn't expect to find a pretty woman sleeping in here though." His eyebrow waggle was predictable and the ensuing wink was insufferable, although she had to laugh out loud.

"Jack's mom, the evil villainess I'm sure you've heard of, who ditched him and River's End, was my mother. I only learned about Jack when she died. I came here to check it out."

"Hmm, and big brother probably didn't take that very well."

"Well, no, because I screamed the truth at him right after I insulted Erin."

Joey cringed, backing up and leaning on the kitchen table before pulling his leg up under him. "Oh, big mistake. Seriously. You never mess with Erin. Why though? What could you say that insulted her?"

"I didn't know she was dyslexic. I handed her something to read and when she refused to take it, I assumed it was because she feared Jack."

Joey choked on the liquor in his throat. "You assumed Jack was beating Erin?"

"That's about the sum of it. Plus, I hung around here, pretending to be a guest for two weeks, so I could poke around anonymously and Erin thought I was after Jack."

Joey threw his head back, laughing, his teeth flashing, and his blond hair seeming even whiter under the lights. "Oh Sister Kate, I wish I'd been here for all that. You are a girl after my own heart. How'd you end up staying after that fiasco? You're lucky you didn't end up with tire tracks on your back."

Kate sipped her drink. "Erin locked the main gate, so I couldn't leave. I had no choice."

"Ah, that girl gots a temper. Gotta love her sometimes. That's why I slept with her." He shook his head with a shit-eating grin. "Well, I don't usually go there much anymore. Erin and I hooked up long before Jack entered the picture. It didn't go over too well, and I almost had tire tracks on my back. But that was years ago, and tons of water has flowed under the bridge since then."

"Wow. You're an interesting addition to the ranch. Are you staying long?"

He lifted his drink to his lips, keeping his gaze solid on hers. "Might just have to now, Sister Kate."

She held his flirtatious, sex-me-up gaze. Yeah, he was pretty. Hot. Handsome. The entire package. But it was a placid observation from Kate's end. Kind of how she evaluated Jack, who was a good-looking guy too. "You already slept with Jack's wife, don't expect to sleep with his sister."

Joey let out a surprised laugh. "You're a bit outspoken like him. I like that."

There was a scuffle behind them. Kate turned and found AJ standing there, scowling at Joey, his arms crossed over his muscle-bound chest, and the tension in his neck muscles visible. He was shirtless, wearing only a pair of jeans to hide his nakedness.

Joey, in the process of pouring more liquor into his glass, dribbled some on the counter when AJ startled him. "Well, well, well, if it isn't AJ Reed." His grin brightened. "In the main house. Never thought I'd see you in here. Jack's sister, huh? Does he know?"

"Hello, Joey," AJ said, his tone low and easy. His hands dropped to his sides, unflexing his fists eventually. AJ used the same respectful tone he always did with any of the Rydells.

"Well, you always claimed to love the Rydell family, so why not the Rydell sister?"

"I'm not a Rydell," Kate jumped in. Joey seemed to miss the odd stance of AJ. He was thinking hard about pouncing on Joey, but the stupid idiot didn't realize it.

Joey resituated himself. "So you finally found a way in. This guy..." Joey waved towards the silent, glowering AJ, "was always so respectful toward Jack. He would have kissed his feet, eh, AJ? Now look at you. Inside Jack's bedroom at long last."

Kate set her glass down on the counter. "Joey Rydell, have you failed to notice this man outweighs you in muscles alone by a good twenty or thirty pounds? And he has was arrested for breaking a beer bottle over another guy's head and sending him to the hospital? Do you really think you ought to stand there ribbing him at two in the morning, especially after propositioning his girlfriend? He's not happy about our little talk just now, in case you couldn't tell by the scowl on his face. But I can. Now be a good little boy, Joey, and toddle off to bed before AJ Reed proves he is more man than three of you and much scarier. I don't know if I'd care if he slammed his fist into those pretty teeth of yours. And right now, I think I am the only voice of reason he'd listen to. So don't insult him again, or talk to him like he's an inferior. He is not a servant for you to kick around for your enjoyment. Just because you're a stupid little shit who comes and goes to his family's rich ranch without any notification, some people aren't so lucky. They work for a living. And AJ is respectful of his employers and his *employer's family* because he has good taste and a proper sense of manners and integrity. None of which you possess. I have a feeling Jack wouldn't stand for your little retort to AJ, so neither will I. Now run along, you idiotic little shit, before you get seriously hurt and find me applauding it."

Joey's mouth half opened at her unexpected speech. She kept her voice even and sweet and her smile remained bright. He swallowed, glancing toward AJ, who stood stock-still, glowering, fisting his hands. Joey's smile instantly vanished and his eyes narrowed before he seemed to reconsider his rudeness toward AJ.

"That's right, little brother, no more treating AJ like that," she added softly.

Joey visibly swallowed before smiling quickly and nervously. Standing up, he collected his bottle of liquor and the two glasses. "Sure, of course. No harm meant, AJ. I am always just kidding around. I won't bother you anymore. I mean it, man. Kate... er, Mrs. Morgan. Good night."

"Goodnight, Joey," she said, biting the inside of her lip as Joey nearly ran off. He was twenty-four years old and still had a lot to learn. A lot to be humble about. No longer would AJ hang around this fucking ranch falling on his knees in gratefulness to be given a job to do.

"You probably shouldn't have done that. Jack is barely your brother and holds no loyalty to us over his own brother. Joey is the brother he raised as his son."

Kate shrugged, pushing off the counter. "Yeah? Well, he could have done a lot better job with his brother-son. Maybe

193

by teaching him the value of those who work for their living, and support their lifestyle. Jack not only should be teaching that, but he needs to demonstrate it too, by his actions."

"He does. But didn't we talk about not interfering in my relationship with the Rydells?" AJ crossed his arms again, one eyebrow rising as if he were the school principal, scolding Kate for writing on the bathroom walls.

"Joey? I'm sure he won't tell anyone about tonight. He comes out looking the ass and besides, he's young enough not to want anyone to know what a sissy he turned out to be. And I know he would not want Jack to hear how he speaks to you. No one ever knew that until now, because you never said anything, did you?"

AJ shook his head. "But it's not right, as Joey correctly pointed out, for me to be sleeping pretty regularly in Jack's bedroom with his sister..."

"Jack could care less. You're the only one who thinks he should care. You're the one who doesn't value yourself highly enough and all the services you provide for Jack, this family, and the entire ranch. You have to realize that you'll keep undervaluing yourself and letting young, entitled shit-asses like Joey insult you. I was once entitled and privileged. All my schooling was paid for. Private school from K through twelve and then it was university all the way. But I never once addressed anyone who was doing work for me or hanging around me like that. I didn't act rude to anyone because I was raised not to be, and neither should Joey."

"You know, I wouldn't actually do anything, no matter what he said or did."

Kate had a secretive little smile as she stepped toward him. "Well, I know that. I'm not so sure he did though."

"And he didn't know about my stint in prison."

"Oh. Maybe. I'm sorry. But it effectively illustrated my point."

"Which was?"

"Not to mess with you. Look, I might have gone a little too far, which I often do, but you shouldn't let anyone talk to you like that. A broken beer bottle to the head might be going a little far, but a stronger tone in your voice is okay to use in situations like that. No one should ever insult you. You don't deserve it. And I don't want you to put up with it."

She stepped closer to him and wrapped her arms around his neck, and he released her from his embrace. "You know you were flirting with him."

She shrugged. "I also do that. I don't believe you find it too shocking. You also know it's completely harmless. Why? Were you actually getting mad about that?"

His shoulders moved up and down under her hands. "I don't know. I mean, I don't enjoy finding you in an eye lock with a guy like Joey. Especially knowing you'd probably have fallen for his brand of charm if you'd met him first."

"First of all," she said, moving her hand to his jaw and making him look at her directly in the eyes. "I might flirt, but I would never cheat. I'd let you know if I wanted to have sex with anyone else. Okay? I do not cheat. Second, I don't fall for any guy's charms. I saw his little act a mile away. I just know how to play him. You know? Like playing along. Men often flirt with me. You might have to restrain your massive arms here and there, or whenever it happens. I don't even notice when I do it. I'm outgoing and sometimes men consider it flirting, but I don't see any harm in it. And last of all, Joey is not my type."

"How can you say that? He seems exactly like your type. He's outgoing, playful, and flirty, and he's much easier to talk to than me. He's all the things you are."

"Yes, and handsome too." AJ scowled and she laughed as she kissed the corner of his mouth. "But, AJ, his ego rivals mine. Can you imagine the two of us together? We'd both be vying for the center of attention! You allow me that. Joey, on the other hand, thrives on having all the attention. We would never work."

AJ's lips slowly tilted up into a smile. "You're something else, Kate."

"I am. But I hope you see that you are too and start acting accordingly. I agree, you probably can't go around intimidating all the jerks whenever you feel like it, but you can stand up for yourself. It's a matter of common decency. Even if I might have had a bit of a fantasy of you going all caveman after me and fighting for my honor. 'Cause you could so take on Joey."

AJ kissed her, nuzzling her neck as he muttered, "I could take on most men, Kate." She giggled at his surprising statement. He rarely admitted how strong and manly he was to her. He lifted his face from her and smiled, "The thing is, so can you. You don't really need me."

Roaring a loud laugh, she wrapped her arms around his neck. She was grinning as broadly as he was. AJ was no big, brash brute when he found her flirting with Joey, even if everything about his appearance said he would be. She loved each layer about AJ that was so the opposite of how that layer appeared. And perhaps why he could hold her attention when no man had ever totally captured it before. Not like AJ Reed had.

THE NEXT DAY, when AJ walked into the kitchen, he was fully dressed. Joey was already there pouring coffee, his hair spiked up, and red sleep circles under his eyes. He was still in his pajama pants. *What a sissy. Wearing pajamas like a girl.* AJ sneered internally. AJ always slept in his fully naked glory. So did Kate. He really loved that about her too.

Sometimes, she walked around in small, silk shorts and something she called a *camisole*. AJ wanted to ask her not to wear it around the house anymore, now that she basically lived with another guy, but he knew better. She'd probably wear it on purpose if he asked her not to.

Joey stopped when he saw AJ and held up a white cup. "You want some coffee, AJ?"

His tone was quiet and kind of subdued. AJ stood up taller. Usually, he hunched his shoulders forward whenever he was in one of the Rydells' presence. But Kate might have been right. AJ was ten times the financial worth of one man in what he produced for their ranch. It was much more than Joey could ever dream of. He, in contrast, was nothing but a drain on the Rydells' finances.

"Thanks, Joey." AJ nodded, taking the cup of coffee.

Joey poured himself some more and sat down. "Do you, uh, live here now?"

"No. I still have the trailer." AJ leaned back against the counter.

"Well, I, ah was planning on staying awhile this time."

"It's your home. I'm sure Jack will be glad to hear it."

Joey glanced behind AJ, towards the closed door where Kate still slept.

"She lives here now. That means we will be living here, together."

"I think she made herself perfectly clear last night. As far as I'm concerned, we're good."

Joey's shoulders slumped. Relief? AJ had to conceal a grin of satisfaction. Who knew he could intimidate Joey? Joey had spent most of his vacations at home making AJ feel inferior or stupid, like he was an indulged pet whenever he was in Joey's proximity. Joey set his coffee cup down, grabbing his temple. "You're more man than me, AJ. She's got a sharp temper."

AJ chuckled, finishing off the coffee. Time to get to it. "She sure does. Don't mess with it."

He was at the front door when Joey called his name and he glanced back. Joey shifted his butt around. "I'm sorry. You know, for being such a dick to you. Jack was always comparing me to you. I didn't do this or that as well as you did. It used to piss me off, so I acted like a shit towards you. But you've always been solid to me, AJ, and everyone else here."

AJ's eyebrows lowered and his mouth dropped open. He could only nod, he was so unsure of what to say. Finally, he waved Joey off. "I appreciate it. But I might have let you off too easily. Be forewarned, Joey, I won't do it again. As I said before, we're good as far as I'm concerned."

Joey nodded.

AJ walked out into the morning light, feeling a few inches taller. He stuck his hat on, marveling at the mysterious woman who went to bat for him when he'd never done so for himself. Maybe it was time to realize his own value. If someone like Kate could find so much potential in him, then who was he to argue? The small smile on his lips stayed with him as he started the tractor up and headed out towards the orchards. It was the *Kate effect,* he was starting to realize.

JACK ASKED Pedro to call AJ up to his office. AJ stepped into the barn and stopped dead. A well-dressed woman turned towards him, which was totally incongruent to find in the barn, even more so than seeing Kate there when she first arrived.

Wearing a severe navy blue skirt and jacket, the woman's white blouse looked crisp and fresh against the deeper colors. Perhaps forty, she was quite stunning, as tall as Kate and striking enough to draw all the air towards her. At least, that's what it felt like.

"Mr. Reed?" she asked at his appearance.

She had a cool tone. Jack was standing a few steps back. He gave a small shrug of his shoulders to AJ, letting him know he had no idea who she was or what she wanted. AJ wished he were wearing another t-shirt and clean jeans. He was sweaty and dirty as usual. Except this woman wasn't Kate, who always appreciated it and assured him he should stay that way rather than clean up.

"Yes, ma'am, can I help you?" *Prison? Parole? Lawsuit?* All those words filtered through his brain and instantly made his stomach cramp. Had he missed something? Had he been released prematurely? Or broken some law he wasn't aware of? A wave of apprehension shuddered through him.

"You are not an easy man to find out here."

Probably not. He had moved all his life. Never owned anything major to speak of and had no credit cards. Unless she was from the Department of Corrections, he might have been very hard to find. "Why, ah, were you looking for me?" AJ's gaze skittered to Jack, and his nerves made his words waver, making him sound almost guilty.

The woman cleared her throat. "Perhaps we could go somewhere that we could talk more privately?"

"Um, well..." *His trailer?* Except this woman seemed above that. Which was odd because he never felt that way with Kate, but this woman wasn't Kate.

"You can use the house, AJ," Jack offered and AJ nodded his appreciation. Jack might also have known AJ had at least one clean shirt at the house. How did one face an unknown stranger so poorly dressed?

"This way, ma'am."

"Nicola Ragenou."

"Uh, Mrs. Ragenou, it's nice to meet you." Was her name supposed to mean something to him? Because it didn't.

AJ went in first, holding the front door open for her. She entered, and her gaze beheld the impressive room. AJ still marveled at it too, but he simply walked in now as if he owned the damn castle. Half the weight of his muscles lifted when Kate, hearing them enter, appeared in an open doorway. She was in the downstairs room that served as the Rydells' home office, but of late, it was hers. She glanced at him, puzzled by his appearance, until she saw the strange woman behind him.

"Hello," she said, moving forward. She offered her hand when she got close enough. "I'm Kate Morgan."

The woman put her hand in Kate's. "Hi, I'm Nicola Ragenou." Still no title or reason for why she was there. AJ lifted his shoulders in a half shrug, answering Kate's silent inquiry that he had no idea what she was about. Kate smiled. "While AJ grabs a shirt, would you like some coffee or lemonade, or maybe some ice water?"

He smiled his relief at Kate, first because she gave him a task to do; and second, it was also the chance to cover his bare chest. "Excuse me," he mumbled to the stranger. "I was working and it gets hot sometimes—"

"I'm sure Mrs. Ragenou understands it's the middle of your workday, AJ, and the kind of physical work you do makes you sweat. Now what would you like to drink?"

AJ could have kissed Kate. She never let anyone or anything make her feel inferior, and strangely, she extended that gift to him too.

He rushed into the bathroom and quickly ran the cool water over his hands, face and torso, drying off with a towel. All he had were t-shirts in Kate's room so he returned feeling severely underdressed next to Mrs. Ragenou and even beside Kate. Kate set the woman up at the kitchen table with a glass of lemonade, and was talking amiably with her. Thank God, she came out and took control as she was wont to do. He needed her meddling this time.

He slipped into a chair and Kate smiled as she pushed a glass of lemonade toward him. He eagerly gripped it, grateful for a place to put his hands. "Why were you looking for me, Mrs. Ragenou?"

"Nicola, please." She dug into the brown leather bag she had set beside her and pulled out a file filled with paperwork. "I work for the Department of Social and Health Services." AJ glanced at the card she offered him. Sure enough, there were her name and credentials. Which still meant nothing to him. She glanced at Kate. "Perhaps we could have some more privacy?"

"Uh, no. Kate can stay." AJ could not handle this unscheduled meeting without Kate's confidence and easy rapport. His tongue already felt challenged. She smiled and reached over to discreetly link her fingers with his. He grasped them as if she were a lifeline, rescuing him from a sinking ship.

"Okay. Well, then, I am here about Parker Sanchez. Do you know her?"

AJ sat up straighter. Talk about a name from the past. From more than a decade ago. From when he rode bulls in the rodeos. She often hung around them. But what the hell did she have to do with *anything*?

"I know her," AJ answered, keeping his tone respectful. "She was a close friend when I was younger."

"I'm sorry to inform you, but she is deceased."

Deceased? She wasn't even thirty. And younger than him by two years. A pang of regret stabbed his heart. She was pretty deep into the partying. Last time he saw her... hell, when was that? Must have been before he got arrested probably. He was genuinely sorry to hear of her demise.

"I'm real sorry to hear that. She was a nice girl." If anyone had ever given her two licks of attention, maybe she'd have had a better shot in life. Still, why would her untimely death bring this lady to him? Did Parker remember him in her will? Seemed like a huge stretch of the imagination to foresee her having anything to leave in a will.

"Yes, well, she also left behind a young child. A child whom she listed you as being the father of. I don't know if you just left her and never went back, or perhaps you never knew, but I'm here to inform you, AJ Reed, that you have a thirteen-year-old daughter."

CHAPTER 14

COMPLETE NUMBNESS FILLED AJ. And the words the stranger had just uttered didn't totally register. *Dead. Child. You.* White noise filled up his head. He didn't know what to do. He sat on the wooden chair, his hand now going slack in Kate's while the other tried to grip the cold, moist cup that perspired.

"Mr. Reed? I take it by the shock on your face it must be a case of not knowing. She listed you as the father on the birth certificate. That is all we had to go from. Your DNA is on file with the state databases after being imprisoned for a felony. We did a paternity test with the girl's and it's a match."

"Th-that's impossible. We were... I was seventeen. She was barely fifteen. I mean..." AJ's brain seemed to be short circuiting as if an essential wire just snapped in half. His breathing escalated.

"I realize this is a lot to take in all at once; and there might be strong feelings..."

Strong feelings? The lady had just detonated his own personal dirty bomb.

"But she is currently a ward of the state and I'm trying to

find her emergency housing. She's been placed in temporary guardianship, but it isn't going well. She needs a more permanent home almost immediately."

Those familiar words. Images from his childhood spun all around his head. Temporary guardianship. Foster care. Not going well. Placement.

He stood up, sliding the chair out so fast, it almost hit the kitchen cabinets. His breathing was so fast, it began to hurt. Sweat broke out over his skin. "Excuse me," he mumbled before nearly racing off to the bathroom. He stopped before the sink, running the water and splashing it over his head as he stared into the drain.

Daughter. Parker. Dead. Daughter. His child. Paternity. Permanent placement. The words made no sense to him. They didn't relate to his life. He cupped more water and splashed it over his head. Running both hands through his hair, he stood up, using his fingers to spike up the strands. What had he done now?

She didn't knock, but simply appeared. He should have known she'd follow him. Kate swung the door open and stepped inside, locking eyes with him in the mirror. Her eyes were wide with wonder, but seemed resolute. Nodding her head slightly, her cool, soft touch fell on his shoulder. "You need to come back and hear her out."

"I can't. I can't have a—"

"It sounds like you do, AJ."

Of course, fearless Kate could in minutes, or maybe even seconds, wrap her head around this latest revelation and remain grounded enough to deal with it. "This is…"

"A game changer? Yes, it is."

He leaned harder on his hands, still staring down into the sink. "I didn't father any child."

"Is it possible in your teens you weren't as careful?"

He shuddered. Of course it was. It was very possible. Kate

gently rubbed his shoulder and his upper arm. "Who was she?"

"A girl. Just a little girl, looking back on it. But she was a lot like me, a forgotten kid no one gave a shit about. She was molested by a creep in the house where she lived, some old, perverted jerk. The guy's wife kicked her out when she tried to report him. She could ride too. We shared that. We were just friends, or survivors. I didn't know…"

"What happened to her?"

He shrugged, shaking his head. "I left. Moved. Drifted. Whatever. I disappeared, or she did. I honestly can't say. I never heard from her again. I didn't know. I didn't know."

"Well, you know now. Camilla. She named her Camilla Smith Reed. Cami, for short. Nicola says she goes by Cami."

Cami Reed? She used his last name? No one he knew had his last name, which was disconcerting. A daughter. A girl. A teenager. What the hell was he supposed to do with her? What could he do?

"You need to come back and hear her out."

He nodded, still so blind to what his eyes were seeing.

He pushed off from the sink and Kate nodded her encouragement. Her mouth was tight, but he sensed real sympathy in her eyes. She went first, and AJ held the door as she passed through before returning to hear his fate.

Nicola waited primly with her legs crossed at the ankles while she sipped her lemonade. She nodded as he sat down, mumbling an apology. Continuing as if he never left, she said, "So, Mr. Reed…"

"Please, call me AJ."

"Antwon Jester, isn't that your given name?" Kate's gaze flitted to his. AJ shrugged with a small smile. She had never asked him what AJ stood for, and it sure fit him better than that mouthful.

"Yes."

"You spent time in the system too, I see, before you fell off the radar."

"Yes. It wasn't a good experience for me. I left as soon as I could."

"Is this your permanent residence?"

"No. Not even close. It belongs to the family who owns this land. They employ me."

On and on, Nicola asked all the questions that outlined his life. The woman finally sighed, saying, "You are Cami's father. You have every legal right to her custody. In fact, she has nowhere else to go. She'll be shuffled around the foster care system. Older kids like her are rarely adopted. You already know the drill, it sounds like. I'd like to place her with you, AJ. You simply have to apply for temporary emergency guardianship. There are also some legal channels to cover, but since your DNA matches, I foresee no huge hurdles. But right now, she needs a place to live. And that place is with you."

Nicola then listed the procedure for obtaining temporary emergency custody while AJ's head spun and his hands sweated.

He really had a daughter?

He was a father. The words were English, but they sounded so foreign to him. They sounded downright wrong when applied to him.

In a daze, he acknowledged Nicola's departure. After some platitudes, and a brief reiteration of the instructions, Nicola assured AJ she'd bring Cami there tomorrow. It seemed Cami had been brought to Nicola from Idaho where she had been living. So Cami was within driving distance of River's End. *Tomorrow.* Kate shut the door and turned towards him. The ensuing silence was palpable. He slid his chair back with a loud scrape and stood up slowly.

He couldn't do it. Any of it. He couldn't even get the

ominous words to stick in his head. He wasn't like Kate. He wasn't capable or ready for such a life-changing event and didn't know how to handle it. Rising, he simply walked past Kate, going out the front door and beyond.

~

AJ SAT DOWN, staring at the river, but the gorgeous scenery was completely lost on him. His head was everywhere but in the reality of the rocky beach he sat upon. All his thoughts were about his daughter. The physical shock almost made him wonder if he were having a stroke.

A scrape of shoes walking over the rocks alerted him someone was there. Assuming it was Kate, he couldn't muster the courage, and failed to have the interest to turn and see. So weary and exhausted, he never remembered feeling so weak in his life. Digging back into the miserable heap of crap his adolescence had been, he was ashamed to realize how it affected Parker so badly. She had his baby while she was still just a child.

His child. How could Parker not have told him? What would he have done if he'd known? That was the sadder part, he wasn't sure he'd have stuck around back then to face it.

"Not now, Kate."

A figure squatted beside him and he jumped when he realized it was Jack. Nodding, AJ rose to his feet. *Crap!* He forgot to go back to work. That never happened before. No. He never spaced out on work before. He never failed to show up on time either, not that he could think of.

"Sorry, Jack. I..." He dared not say *I forgot*, and snapped his mouth shut. "I'll get back to the orchard now..."

But Jack pushed his shoulder down. "I know about Cami. Kate already told me. Relax. I certainly don't expect you to be working right now. I'd be freaking out." Jack slid onto his ass, drawing his legs up before him..

"Yeah. That's about the sum of it. I didn't know about her."

"I believe you. I don't think I made it clear to you, as Kate just pointed out to me. I consider you an equal around here. Your integrity and intelligence are unanimously valued and appreciated."

"I know. I know how well you pay me, compared to other ranch foremen. And Kate needs to stay out of it," AJ grumbled.

"I think we can both agree that in the short time we've known my industrious sister, she doesn't stay out of anything she thinks she has a right to meddle in." Jack glanced at the river, throwing a small pebble. "Anyway, so your daughter will soon be coming to live here."

"I don't know. I don't know. I can't..." It sounded so wrong. AJ pushed his hands against his aching, ringing head. She wasn't his. Not his kid. Not his daughter. He didn't even know what she looked like. He wanted to scream and protest, "She can't be mine."

"Well, DNA is pretty conclusive, so, she'll be coming here. We need to talk about that. Make new arrangements. A young girl can't be stuck out in a trailer with a stranger."

"I don't expect you to do anything. I'll figure it out."

"By tomorrow?" Jack's tone sounded skeptical.

Tomorrow. How could this be his new reality?

"I guess. I have no idea."

"You're going to have to accept some help from us. And since a child is involved, if your stubborn pride acts up, always remember you're doing it for a bigger and better cause than yourself. She's just a kid. Imagine Charlie all alone without anyone. I can't... so really, we need to do right by this young girl."

AJ opened his mouth to argue, but nodded his head and promptly closed it. "Thank you, Jack."

"Come up to the house. We can all talk in there."

AJ started to rise, wiping the loose sand off his butt. With a sigh, he followed Jack.

Inside the living room were Erin and Kate. Kate had apparently wasted no time in setting off all the alarms. AJ resented her taking control, but then, he thought about tomorrow. That was something he could not look forward to.

There were all kinds of murmurs of appreciation despite his situation. Shell-shocked and numb, he sat down.

"She'll need to stay here, inside the main house."

That comment finally cut through the haze. "No. I can't do that. I have the trailer. I can't…"

"A young girl can't live in a one-room trailer with a man she doesn't even know, AJ. It would be embarrassing, awful, and awkward for both of you… and really inappropriate. She's a young girl. Thirteen. She needs privacy and room. Space. Especially with her father, even if she doesn't know you yet. How can you change clothes in that trailer? Think about it. For now, this is the best solution. There is plenty of room in the main house and Kate's here. It's a good arrangement," Erin said in her gentlest tone.

AJ rubbed his face anxiously, saying, "I can't believe this."

"I know."

CAMI REED WAS A TEENY, tiny girl, petite from her height to her width. She looked more like a young child than a teen. AJ nearly gulped when he saw her. She barely reached his elbow. He appeared like a huge, overgrown buffoon next to her, and would've probably scared the living bejesus out of her. When she got out of the back seat of the car, AJ was sure his eyes revealed his astonishment no matter how much he tried to remain neutral.

She wore a hooded, dark sweatshirt that she had pulled up over her hair, which was dyed a terrible black and had bleached streaks running all through it. The ratted, messy hair skimmed her shoulders. Fully goth, she had black eyes, eyelids, eyelashes, and at least an inch of black liner under her eyes in dark circles. Her lips were also black. Her small face and features were overwhelmed by so much darkness. AJ blinked, curious what she looked like under the mask of black paint. The huge pants she wore dripped off her waist. Black and gnarly too, they were all ripped up, like her shirt and sweatshirt. The hems dragged over her shoes so the ends were soiled dark brown and also tattered. She scowled at AJ as she glanced around. Ear buds dangled from her ears. Nothing. Not a flinch of her mouth or a squint of her eye.

AJ stepped forward. Should he put his hand out? That seemed stupid to shake hands with a girl who looked like that. But then again, she was his freaking daughter. He was supposed to feel... something, right? He didn't, however. He felt nothing except an intense urge to pass around her and keep walking towards the fields. He wished he had nothing more to do than go twiddle around in the pastures, work on the buildings, feed the livestock, or do anything but this. Anything was better than standing there and staring at this churlish girl.

"I'm AJ," he said finally when they stared at each other for far too long. It was uncomfortable and awkward for both parties. She lifted her eyes up, and up and up until she finally met his gaze.

She shrugged, saying, "Cami."

"So... I guess we could go inside?"

"That your house?" She nodded to the impressive log

house behind her. Most onlookers took a second glance or gasped even, it was so visually impressive. But Cami? Raising one eyebrow in disdain, she couldn't have shown less interest.

"No. My employer. I live here now though and you can stay here also."

Shrugging, she lifted an earphone and nestled it inside her ear, hiking her bag up onto her shoulder, and passing him without another word as she entered the house. He stared after her, far beyond astonished. Holy crap! After all his stress and worry, wondering with anxiety how to handle her, and that was her?

Nicola patted AJ's arm, reassuring him she was normal. Cami was still traumatized by her mother's death and just needed time...

All AJ could hear was the white noise filling up his head. How could he, of all men, offer Cami what she needed? He didn't even know her. And vice versa. How should they start up any kind of relationship? AJ's first relationship of any real substance was with Jack Rydell as his employer, and until recently, he had no other relationships in his life. Now there was Kate and a *daughter*? He ran his hands through his hair and rubbed the back of his neck before finally following her into the house.

Kate was in there, but no Cami.

Kate's face melted into sympathy when she saw him. She stepped forward and wrapped her arms around him. "I told her my name, and she asked where her room was. I pointed it out and she went in there, slamming the door shut. She's scared. Confused. She doesn't trust us, of course. So it went about as well as I think it could have."

"I told her, 'my name is AJ.' That's it. That was my huge welcome for my long lost daughter that I never knew about. It was so stupid. Like something you'd say to a convenience store attendant. I mean"—he threw his hands up—"Crap! I told her my name. I don't know what else to say. I don't know how to even reach her, let alone... whatever else I should do. She's screwed. Her life sounds like it's been hell already, and this is the solution? Me? You've heard me talk, you know I can't be a father. What good am I at that?"

Kate squeezed him tighter to her. "You're here, AJ, that's good for her. You won't run. You won't abandon her. You'll deal with her no matter how hard it might be, and how little you know about what you're doing."

"How do you know that?"

"Because I'm never wrong." Kate smiled quickly, but AJ saw a sad, deeper gleam in her eye. "I'm not wrong about you, AJ."

He closed his eyes and drew in a breath, grateful for her steady faith in him. Physical faith was what she invested in him, not like the faith he found through God. It was different to have someone right there, touching him, talking to him, encouraging him, and believing in him. Especially when it was someone you trusted, admired and respected most in the world.

"What do I do?"

"Go to work. I doubt she'll be out for a while. Be patient. She'll need to eat at some point. Or she'll get bored and come looking for something to do. There's no TV, computer or anything else in her room. I'll be working in here, and I'll be sure to get you if she comes out."

"I didn't expect... anything."

"How would thirteen-year-old AJ have reacted, AJ?"

He nodded. "Not so well. I was always wary of the next home, and person, or whatever. To me they were all full of crap. I knew I was nothing to them too. A temporary layover to whatever happened next. It's hard when you don't belong anywhere, and no one is looking out for you. No kid—"

He shook his head, throwing his hands over his face, and shuddering as he remembered. No one gave a shit about him and there was always the fear of the next day. And the next stranger. The next... unknown. It was never good. "No kid of mine should have ever known what it was like. If I'd just been informed of her. If Parker had at any point reached out to me... I would have done anything to find her, and change her life, and protect her."

"Then you'll have to do that now. It's too late to cry over what was. What counts is what happens now. The damage is done. I think we already understand that. You can't reverse it, or stop it, but you can find a way to undo some of it. For today? She's here. She knows your name. That's enough of a start." Kate smiled and made a face as she said "name."

He accepted her hug, her smile, her advice, and her loving face. He turned to head out, gladder, and almost ecstatic to escape. He paused. "Are you sure?"

"I'm sure."

Nodding, he pressed his lips together, "Thank you, Kate. Not sure how I'd—"

"Maybe something was at work here, you know? Here I am, and just in time. Isn't that how it goes? You believe everything always happens for a reason, His reason, right?"

"I used to. But I don't know what reason God would have for a girl to be all alone in the world... but you being here? Maybe, yeah."

IT WAS NEARLY eight o'clock before Cami finally came out. AJ was planted on the couch, staring at the giant TV, and Kate was reading next to him. They had already eaten dinner, and talked in low tones about what to do, but eventually decided nothing. Finally, the door to Cami's room opened.

She slipped out and stood at the top of the stairs. AJ jumped up, quickly moving to the bottom of the stairs and their gazes met. Cami simply stared blank-faced at him.

"Are you hungry?" AJ asked.

"Yeah."

She descended the staircase, her gaze drilling him with an almost evil scowl. The goth makeup was enough to make him step back. *Fierce. Zombie. Scary* were just some of the words he could think to use as adjectives. She purposely put more space between them in her stride.

"We had spaghetti for dinner. Would you like some?"

"Whatevs."

Yeah, whatevs. He took in a breath to stabilize his nerves. He was trying very hard with her, but felt completely unqualified. Kate sat quietly listening. Her small smile was her tacit encouragement to keep *trying*.

Following Cami, AJ noticed a gothic cross tattooed on her neck with blood drops that disappeared under the collar of her shirt. She was only thirteen. It stunned AJ.

Jocelyn had tattoos all over, but she wasn't *thirteen*. He really liked the hard talking, hard living Jocelyn with her spiked-up short hair, swaggering walk, and tough ways. She danced hip-hop and was always jumping around with her earphones in both ears. She'd suddenly appear to jump or twist or kick off buildings or rocks before doing difficult aerial gymnastics. Jocelyn was awesome. But she wasn't thirteen and she didn't look like that.

He dished up the meal on a plate and microwaved it. Waiting, he busied himself by pouring her a glass of milk. Seemed like something a kid would need.

She sat at the table and stared down at her fingernails. Yup, also black. The girl loved black. He sighed and jumped when the microwave dinged before grabbing the plate and setting it down before her. She didn't look up. No thank-you either. Without a word, she started shoveling the food into her mouth. AJ stepped back.

When she finally glanced up, she said, "Do you mind not watching me?" Then, dropping her head and looking down, she mumbled, "Pervert."

"Uh, sure."

AJ gleefully escaped to the couch, almost skipping, he was so eager to get away from her. Every move he made was wrong. He wanted to be reassuring and accessible to her by giving her plenty of space and not pressuring her. Instead, he creeped her out? He sat down on the couch, shaking his head at Kate's sympathetic gaze. She squeezed his arm in support and he shrugged.

Cami ate her dinner and left with her dishes still on the table.

Days passed of the same ilk. She practically hibernated in the bedroom. Jack, Shane and even Joey asked about her, saying they'd yet to see any glimpse of her. No. Nope. She seemed to be unwilling to show her face during the daylight hours. AJ was never so mixed up before. He had no idea what to do with her. She ate the meals. That's all he knew about her.

Joey lived in the same house and never saw her. It was an odd situation. She was like a mean little ghost squatting upstairs.

Cami always sneered, scowled, and rolled her eyes at AJ. He was the dirt, bacteria, and shit under her feet. She was more than clear about that. Kate was in the house every day so she kept track of her, but there was rarely any interaction between them.

"She'll come around," Kate kept saying. But AJ could see she was just as unsure as he of what to do. They were the adults, but Cami had all the control.

She mumbled *pervert* at him on the few times he

attempted to engage her or just talk to her, so he backed off, feeling totally confused. He did not know how to approach her. What if she accused him of being a pervert to Nicola? The threat of the state coming after him, assuming he was a child molester or worse, had him dismayed. What the hell was he supposed to do? She could accuse him of things... and what if someone believed her?

Kate insisted he could not let her continue controlling him as she was. Kate would vouch for his innocence. No one would believe he was a pervert. But hell, the thought of it made his stomach churn. By keeping his distance, he figured she had nothing to complain about. He wasn't being a creep by showing too much interest in her.

Shit! Even his internal language changed. All the peace he found during the last few years here in River's End was starting to slowly erode. He began to wish Cami would disappear so he could go back to his life from a few months ago. Even the changes Kate required of him were things he'd never done for anyone else. Now his daughter seemed hell-bent on despising him. Every time he said, hi, hello, good morning, or good evening, she called him a pervert.

Finally, one day she didn't come out at all. AJ knocked on the door, asking her if she wanted to eat. She claimed it was her time of the month and she was in too much pain to walk.

He removed his hand from her door and swiftly fled out into the fields. Gross! He didn't need to know about... that. It made him cringe and he died a little inside his head that day. He really didn't know if this teenage daughter thing was for him. Though no one was asking. Which was perhaps the hardest part of it all.

KATE WAS NEARLY at the end of her tether. For the first few days, she understood, and her sympathy poured from her heart towards the little, lost, freaky gothic-princess, potential serial-killer, strange girl who was living in the room upstairs. It must have been very confusing to Cami, being there all alone, so young and immature amongst complete strangers. Her pain and fear must have been overwhelming.

But when she started calling AJ a creep and a pervert over and over again, Kate watched their interactions more closely. She knew Cami was watching AJ discreetly and how violently AJ reacted when he was called those awful names. So far, he just backed away from her, nearly tongue-tied and flushed with bright colors. He retreated as far as the room would allow from her. Oh, she was a masterful manipulator. She never spoke even a hundred words to anyone living there. And usually she punctuated her statements by muttering some rude name at them.

They kept in touch regularly with Nicola. Kate fully supported and backed up AJ, and Nicola assured them that no one believed anything sordid or inappropriate was going on. AJ didn't even sleep inside the house any longer. He and Kate had not had sex since Cami's arrival.

Cami liked to pretend her period kept her bedridden. AJ even provided her meals by leaving them at her door. Kate got so mad, she thought her head might finally explode. She patiently held her tongue, remaining quiet, although her patience as well as her tolerance were nearly at an end. The arrangement definitely wasn't working for her and Kate was fully prepared to explain to AJ why.

Kate didn't want to lose AJ over this latest situation. Not yet. She spoke the truth when she said it was a game changer, but she hadn't yet decided if it changed the game for her. One thing she knew for sure: her decision would not be determined by the thirteen-year-old flaming mess who was living upstairs.

In the almost eight weeks since Kate's arrival there, she tried to go home every week for a night. Leaving at dawn, she spent the entire day in her office, going back to her condo exhausted at night, only to wipe the mildew off her toilets. Once in a while, she swiped the dust that was always collecting. Then she'd gather whatever clothes she might need, and work the next day in Seattle before driving all the way back to the Rydell River Resort. What she liked most from these trips was the kiss AJ always gave her the night she returned. There were no words, and he didn't whine or complain. He didn't even express how much he missed her. He didn't say one word. But the kiss? That said everything.

During those two months, she and Jack engaged in some real conversations too. It started off slowly as a passing encounter or bumping into him at the beach. He politely inquired how she was enjoying her walk or horse ride or whatever, which often led to more chit-chat. She found he was far more composed than she first believed. But once Cami came into the picture, Kate's regard for her stranger-brother soared, and it changed into a mutual respect as a kind of rhythm seemed to exist between them.

Joey lived in the house with Kate, but they observed a cool, hands-off policy in their dealings with each other. Kate felt like she kind of ruled the Rydell River Ranch main house. So huge and luxurious, she knew she should not become so comfortable with the Rydell hospitality, but she did nevertheless.

And it happened by accident, which Kate also appreciated. Her only complaint was, Cami had intruded on her kingdom. She really didn't like the way Cami was treating the prince of Kate's little scenario either. Never before had there been a prince in Kate's scenario, so she felt more than protective toward him.

Okay, she might have fallen a little more in lust... or like... oh, hell! Pretty soon, she'd have to start calling it *love*. She watched how sweetly her big, brawny, kind, shy, considerate, clueless, and sometimes lost cowboy tried so hard to do the right thing with the venomous critter that was so rudely inserted into their perfect world.

Then, one night, Kate awoke to a voice screaming. Only it wasn't a woman's scream, it was a manly yell and he was swearing. Hearing lots more swearing, Kate jumped out of her bed to investigate. She grabbed a robe, but only out of consideration for AJ's senses. He handled Joey's presence in the same house at night pretty well, but she didn't see any reason to risk making him jealous. AJ was attentive enough to her, and she had no desire for contrived interest.

Plus, he trusted her. If he didn't, she would have probably worn her bra and panties around Joey, just to prove to AJ that she *could*, despite what he said. *No one owned her*, no matter what their relationship with her. Luckily for AJ, he wasn't unreasonable, so instead of having to proclaim her independence to him, Kate needed only to respect his wishes.

As she came into the living room, she found Joey rushing down the stairs. He wore pajama bottoms and a t-shirt, since he too did not care to antagonize AJ. It cheered her slightly. He'd been such a shit about AJ, she was glad he seemed to now consider AJ a sleeping tiger. As long he didn't provoke him, he was safe. *But!* And that was the silent threat. Never mind that Kate knew there wasn't any real threat, since AJ would never do anything to harm anyone. Especially one of the Rydells.

Joey was muttering, shaking his head, and running his hands through his hair when he spotted her. "Fuck. Shit. Damn. Hell. I didn't do anything, Kate. You've got to vouch for me. I didn't ask her to be upstairs. And I was there first. I didn't do anything. You have got to tell him that."

At the top of the stairs, as Kate suspected, stood Cami Reed.

She wore nothing but a bra and panties. Her ratty hair hung around her face. For the first time, it was scrubbed free and all the excessive black she ringed around every feature of her face was gone. Kate looked closely at her for what felt like the first time. She had a small, button-like nose, and large, narrowly-set eyes. Her forehead was low and her cheeks were hollow. Pretty? Yes. If someone showed her how to properly wear makeup, she could have been adorable. But that wasn't the look Cami went for, even if her pixie height, delicate body structure, and facial features insisted it was.

Joey glanced up and quickly threw his hand over his eyes before he faced Kate. Gritting his teeth, he said firmly, "She," as he waved up towards Cami without looking back, "climbed into my bed, and got on top of me, and started to kiss me. I was in a dead-ass sleep, Kate. I swear to God! I opened my eyes and immediately threw her off me. I would've hurled her across the room except I didn't want to hurt her." He kept running his hands through his hair and shuddered dramatically from his shoulders down to his feet. "Fuck. That's so gross. Oh, my God!" He tilted his head back. "She's fucking thirteen." He made choking sounds.

Kate might have grinned at his comical, shocked expression if not for the gravity of the situation. "It's okay, Joey, I know you didn't do anything here."

"Yes, but will *he*? He's going to fucking kill me." Joey's hands were behind his neck now, and his elbows pointed out in serious distress.

"He, being AJ? He'll understand. Really, don't worry. I'll talk to him, and *her*." She shot a glare up the stairs at the stony-faced girl watching them.

"I'm outta here. I'll be staying at Jack and Erin's from now on. No way am I up for this shit. I'll be back in the daylight for my clothes and stuff," Joey announced. He didn't glance back, but walked right out the front door. Kate stared after the shut door and slowly turned around. Cami raised her eyebrows and held Kate in a long eye-lock, her nonverbal challenge to Kate. Kate suddenly started up the stairs after the girl, startling her with her sudden assault.

Visibly surprised, the widening of Cami's eyes was a belated reaction before she hastily started down the hallway. Kate grabbed the strap on her bra and pulled it hard enough that it could have snapped. Grasping her by it, Kate managed to reach her bicep and she dragged her unceremoniously as they started down the stairs.

"Hey, bitch! Let me go!" Cami screamed as Kate strong-armed her down the stairs. She had about ten inches on the girl and outweighed her considerably. Those were the most words Cami had ever spoken to Kate. Kate smiled in grim, resolute satisfaction. Finally, her hundred and fifty pounds proved an advantage. This little waif could not begin to resist her. Kate would merely sit on her. She'd had *enough*.

After being thrown onto the couch by Kate, Cami landed with one knee on the cushion as her back was shoved down. She whipped her head around. "You can't do that to me!"

"Oh? We're just beginning all the things I can do to you. Sit your scrawny little ass down. Or I swear to God, I'll sit on you. And my fat ass will flatten you like a pancake."

"Real nice, bitch. Who are you to manhandle me like that? I'll turn you in to the Child Protective Services. They'll come after you. They'll punish you for abusing me. I have the bruises to prove it."

"You'll have my handprint squarely on your ass in a spanking too if you don't shut up, right now!"

As she screeched at Cami right in her face, Cami lifted

her hand as if preparing to slap Kate. Kate caught her hand and they had another staring contest. Then, the front door burst open and AJ stumbled in, wearing jeans and a t-shirt.

"Kate!" He rushed forward, his eyes huge with shock. "Take your hands off her!" he ordered, addressing Kate.

Kate rolled her eyes and pushed Cami back onto the couch.

"How did you know?"

"Jack called and said something was going on up at the house. Joey woke them up and wouldn't say why, but he refused to come back here."

"Well, should we ask her? Mmm? Why don't you explain why a thirteen-year-old climbs on a sleeping man who is at least a decade older than her, wearing only her bra and panties, and starts to molest him? Please explain that, Cami."

"You what?" AJ's shocked glance skittered over to Cami, when he realized she wasn't wearing any clothes. He whipped around, placing his hand over his eyes as comically as Joey had done. He disappeared into her room and came back with a shirt, which he shoved to Kate before turning away. Kate rolled her eyes and handed the shirt to Cami, who snatched it from Kate and slipped it on.

"I don't have to explain anything to you."

"You will. I'm so sick of your shit." Kate marched up the stairs. Before she came back down, she threw Cami's bag of stuff all the way down the flight of stairs with several armfuls of miscellaneous items that were strewn all over her room.

AJ watched her, completely lost. His face was perplexed, confused, and heartbroken. He had no idea what to do. Kate usually did, but she was tired of the whole thing too. She eventually emerged from the bedroom and kicked aside some of the clothing as she calmly walked down the stairs. "You no longer have a bedroom. You will sleep on that couch. Until you show some respect to those around you, there will be no more hiding in your room. And no more avoidance of decent conversations. Every morning, you will get your lazy, useless ass out of bed and start interacting with the people around you like a normal person. You'll eat meals with us. And you'll do the chores that I tell you to. In short, you'll act like a fucking human being!"

"I won't do anything you tell me to," Cami screamed, jumping to her feet. "Who are you? No one. Just some old, fat bitch who can't control me."

Kate smiled a pleasant, sugary-sweet smile and her voice remained as even and calm. "Oh? I can't, huh? You don't like it? There's the door. Go find yourself another family to abuse. Oh, wait, that's right, you don't have anyone else, do you? No else wants you. You were dropped on our doorstep. No one else's."

"I'll just run away," Cami said, puffing up her chest and fisting her hands at her sides.

"'Course you can take off, but do you realize we're about fifteen miles from the nearest town? You could hitch a ride. Go for it. All kinds of good freaks are somewhere out there. But that's if you can even find another person. You see the dark, right? It's endless. And snakes, bears, bats and cougars are all roaming out there. But by all means, go ahead, and do it all alone. By yourself. A little ninety-pound nothing like you? And I swear to God, I'll take you up to the end of the road and leave you there myself if something doesn't change right now. "

Cami's gaze skittered to the windows. The lack of window treatments only made the outside darkness look like a thick, impenetrable wall. Cami swallowed visibly, her bravado wavering for a moment. "You can't do that."

Kate leaned down, putting her nose right in Cami's face. "Try me," she whispered softly as a smile stretched her face. It was nasty, mean smile.

"Who the fuck are you? AJ won't let you."

"Me?" She smiled even more snidely, leaning closer. "I'm your wicked, fucking, soon-to-be-stepmother. So you wanna bet? I don't see AJ stopping me."

Cami's face fell and she stepped back. AJ would have stopped Kate, she knew, if he weren't rooted to the spot, frozen in shock. His eyes were huge, and staring at her with a trace of almost fear. Kate had to work quickly while his senses were too overloaded to react.

Once he did, he'd freak the hell out, and blame her if she didn't already have Cami under control by then. But to Kate's way of thinking, nice people and plenty of personal space weren't working. She was calling this potential juvenile delinquent's bluff, now before she caused more damage later.

Of course, she was nowhere near to becoming this girl's stepmother. AJ didn't even call her his girlfriend. But Cami didn't know that. And AJ was too stunned at the moment to clarify it. So off Kate went.

"Now, what you did was completely inappropriate."

"I do that all the time."

She eyed the girl. "Bullshit. No more. You're too young and it's not allowed here. Neither are drugs, alcohol, gang paraphernalia or swearing. Your father gets offended by it, so we need to stop that right now." Kate took her hand, grabbing the girl's arm and swiping at her tattoos. "And wipe off all these too. You just look stupid. You don't have the personality to pull the look off."

Cami snatched her hand back, cradling her arm to her chest. AJ's eyebrows furrowed. Poor guy, he could not understand any of this. Kate smiled at AJ, explaining, "They're just temporary henna-inspired tattoos. She puts them on with a wet rag and they last a few days. She keeps applying them. That's probably what she does while holed up in her room."

"Now, Cami, I'd like you to meet your father, AJ Reed. He

is a very nice man who doesn't require much from you except simple, basic decency. Let's start with you ceasing to accuse him of being a pervert whenever he feeds you dinner or attempts to clean up after you. From now on, you will clean up after your goddamned self. Oops! You got my tongue spewing filth now, listen to all my profanity. This time, I want you to say hello to your father, Cami."

Kate stepped forward when Cami didn't do anything. "Do it, or get the fuck out of this house and see where you end up. Drugs? Prostitution? A broken, little, used runaway. Sounds pretty awful to me. Or you could simply say hello to the man who just discovered you even existed and would like to provide you with a clean, safe home and food, clothing and other essentials. He wants you to be where no one will hurt you, abuse you or bother you." She smiled again. "Except for me, maybe."

Cami stared at Kate and they exchanged a long, heated eye lock for many seconds; almost a minute ticked by. Kate had her fingers mentally crossed. Did she go too far? Would that work? She had no intention of kicking the lost little waif out, of course, but she had to appear bold and forceful to regain control with this kid. And if it didn't work, AJ may never have spoken to her again.

"Hi, AJ," Cami finally said before dropping her gaze onto her feet.

AJ's jaw dropped open in silent disbelief. Kate's bold action took the words right out of his mouth. Kate exhaled a deep breath. "Well then, I'm going back to bed. You can talk. We'll figure out the chores and other things for you to do tomorrow. Hell, it may sound crazy maybe, but you could go outside before your skin becomes transparent from lack of sunlight. There's lots to see and do out here. Goodnight. And stay away from strange men. Seems like you should already know that."

Kate turned and fell against her closed bedroom door. The tremors started the minute she was alone. She could not believe what she did. Her hands were trembling and her stomach fluttering. Her head suddenly ached with the stab of deep pressure. Holy crap! That could have gone so wrong. She hoped AJ understood what she was trying to do, and would still talk to her.

Did he hear her referring to herself as his fiancée?

CHAPTER 15

"*S*HE'S CRAZY. I HOPE you realize that," Cami muttered after Kate slammed her bedroom door, trapping AJ with his daughter. At least, his daughter was finally speaking, although her profanity towards them left much to be desired.

"She's not. She's just excitable. You set her off."

Cami looked different, and AJ finally noticed. Her face was bare. No makeup. He finally got to see the face of the girl he called his daughter, and she was quite pretty.

"You look like her." The comment slipped out of his mouth before he thought it over.

"Who?"

"Your mother. You look like her, I mean, when she was at your age."

"You knew her then?"

He nodded. He didn't explain to Cami about the mixed up, drug addict who was her mother. "Yes, I knew her. We were both foster brats. I met her while I was riding in the rodeo, and we hung out together."

"She's dead now. But, whatever," Cami retorted. AJ didn't

believe her indifference. Judging by the stiff way she held her body and the anger in her voice that nearly trembled, AJ recognized the little girl's cry of pain. All at once, he felt something. Maybe he saw Parker's face in hers. Or maybe it was because he realized Kate flipped the dynamics in the house. He was the adult. He had the power now, not Cami, and it was time he used it. It no longer mattered if she didn't like it.

Maybe in the end, it would save her life. Maybe she'd learn it wasn't wise to climb on top of an older man. Thank God it was Joey Rydell. AJ knew Joey wasn't a predator despite how much he irritated him in general. But lots of men would have responded to a girl like Cami and not stopped or vacated the premises.

"I'm sorry about that, Cami."

Cami shrugged. Kneeling down, she started grabbing her items, stuffing them into her bag. It was just a backpack, but it held all she had in the world. Same as AJ's duffel bag. The pathetic thought struck AJ straight through the heart.

How was it possible his daughter, separated from him for thirteen years, was managing to lead the same life that he had? He fisted his hands. It was so wrong. Both of them were so lost and alone as little kids with only a damn duffel bag and backpack to their names. She might have tried to look threatening, but she was just a little girl. He sighed heavily. The immense responsibility of her well-being was just beginning to settle over his shoulders and the weight of it seemed to push down onto his shoulder blades.

"Why did you do that tonight?"

Cami wouldn't look up, but seemed to concentrate solely on pushing her clothing and odd trinkets into her backpack. "Didn't think you all would freak out like you did."

AJ sighed audibly and sat down on one of the recliners. "When I was your age, my dad, who was in and out of my life for years, would periodically show up and take me with him. He was bad news. The only reason he got me out of foster care was to use me in his stupid scams. I hated it, but it was better than being left behind, you know? So, one of the times he left me again, I went to this family who had several other foster kids. I stole money from them often. Just small amounts that were mostly unnoticed. Looking back, I can't understand what I was doing or why. Did I want to act out to that family? I didn't care about them, not even enough to bother them. And I didn't know why I did that, no matter how many times they asked me. Turns out, looking back, I think it was to punish my dad for leaving me again. Technically speaking, my actions and emotions didn't correlate, but in a twisted way, they did. Have you ever gotten that feeling?" AJ asked Cami in an unthreatening tone. It was just a mildly curious question. He thought he might have captured Cami's attention. Her shoulders went still, and her arms quit searching for more stuff to put away, although she stayed kneeling on the floor, facing down and seemed to still avoid him. Her silence spoke to AJ and he felt he understood her finally.

Maybe, in a strange way, all his terrible experiences and mistakes could help Cami avoid making them. Kate was saying earlier that God always had a reason for things that happened, so perhaps his whole life's purpose was to bring him here. Maybe he could actually help his lost little girl, he more than anyone else.

Cami shrugged. She did lots of shrugging. When she finished stuffing her possessions away, she stood up. She didn't even glance at him as she walked towards the couch, but mumbled, "Maybe."

He understood. Maybe she knew the reasons for tonight, and it wasn't because of any of them or Joey or sex. It was because her mother left her alone in the world with a strange man. AJ being the stranger. And if Parker had just told him about Cami, everything would be different—

No, that anger would eat away at AJ gradually, and Cami didn't need any more fuel for her obvious rage at her situation. *Their* situation. But AJ realized as he stared at her when she flopped dejectedly onto the couch, her hair hanging in her face, that she was so young, and his child. He was the damn adult. The situation was on him. *He* had to make it better, not her.

Maybe she needed him. "I think I'll move in here."

Her gaze flickered to him. "Why don't you live with that woman?"

"Kate? Because we're not married. But I think I should be here. You know, where you are."

"Whatevs. You're not going to really make me stay on the couch."

He bit his lip. "Um, maybe for tonight. It's late. We'll figure things out tomorrow. But that has to start with you interacting and talking to us. So maybe Kate's right about that."

"She's crazy."

"She's got a pretty explosive temper."

Cami finally, and for the first time it seemed, raised her eyes to AJ and actually looked at him. "You don't?"

He shifted forward, trying to sag his shoulders down, and fold up some of his bulk so as not to appear so huge. "Actually, no. I don't."

"And you like her doing that? You don't mind her short temper?"

"I like her passion about things. About right and wrong. She knows it's wrong for a young lady like you to do what you did tonight."

"I don't like short tempers. You can't predict them."

AJ nodded. "I agree. I didn't like her short temper the first time I witnessed it, but later, I started to see hers was only agitated when she was trying to help people, not hurt them. Makes all the difference, knowing that. You understand?"

"I understand," Cami whispered.

AJ cleared his throat. "Well, you should get some sleep." He got up and went into the spare bedroom to find some bedding, which he brought out to his daughter. The realization of his fatherhood still made him feel dizzy. "Good night."

"Whatevs."

He turned on his heel. He was done with trying to figure her out. He opened Kate's door and found her in bed. She jerked upright. He put his finger to his lips, slipping his hat and shirt off as he kicked off his boots and slid down his jeans. He slipped into bed beside her and wrapped his arms around her. She lay on her back, nestled in his arms, her arms and hands resting over his. "I was afraid I went too far."

He kissed her head on her hair. "You did."

"Do you hate me? She was insufferable. She didn't even care what she'd done. I just—"

"Needed to do something. And I stood back and didn't do anything. So it's going to be you, I see, between *us* that does things. Maybe someday, you'll learn *not* to go quite so far with whatever you're doing. I think that's something you could learn from me. "

"I thought perhaps you might not come near me again."

"I did though."

"Is she okay?"

"No, not even close. She thinks you're crazy, but she actually strung more than two words together with me just now and none of them were *creep* or *pervert*. So it worked, Kate."

Releasing her breath, she nearly flabbergasted AJ when she started to cry in his arms. She turned towards him, her chest tucking into his, wrapping her arms around his neck and shoulders. Tears streamed down her face and a series of shudders wracked her body. "I was so mad. I was so scared. But once I started, there was no turning back. I just—" A sob filled her mouth and her body shook. "I could have ruined it for you. What if she had walked right out of here? What if I made her do that? What if I'd driven away a thirteen-year-old little girl? Oh, God, she's so young."

"I would have followed her and carried her back in here. She's thirteen and we are all she has now." AJ pressed his lips into her hair, shushing her.

Kate's body stilled and her face jerked up towards his. He had to lean back to see her. "We?"

He shrugged, his hand still on her shoulders. "For now. Yes, we. She needs all of us. Safety. A place to live. A father. A woman in her life who can tell me that she's playing me and that having a period doesn't actually incapacitate her."

Kate closed her eyes and her lashes fluttered over the wet pools of her eyelids. "I didn't want you to hate me, AJ."

"I think I might have realized that when you told my daughter you were her wicked, effing soon-to-be-step-mother. I started to get an idea of where your thoughts were headed." He kissed her again. "Why did you say that?"

"For the fuller, more dramatic effect; it was better than muttering, 'I am the woman who seduced your father, then weaseled my way into living with my long-lost brother and I'm still seeing your dad.' That doesn't have quite the intended impact."

A weary smile curled his lips. "You, Kate Morgan, always manage to make an impact."

"I'm sorry." She buried her face against his chest.

He sighed and rubbed the back of her head in repeated strokes. "I don't think I am, Kate. I don't think I'm sorry."

~

KATE GOT up and dressed quickly, keeping quiet while Cami slept. She made coffee, eggs, and toast. Finally, Cami lifted her head off the couch and eyed Kate. Kate responded to her with a great big welcoming smile as she held up her plate. "Can I get you some food?"

Cami just stared silently. Then she nodded. Wandering over, her feet were swimming in socks that were too big as were her sweats. Her hair were all twisted up and her eyes showed only fatigue. Did the girl sleep? Do drugs? Who knew?

Kate dished her up a plate and set it before her. Cami briefly leaned over it before she started wolfing it down.

"So I hear you think I'm crazy?" Kate remarked.

Cami whipped her head up, and stopped chewing. "Uh," she gulped. "Well, yeah."

Kate smiled as she leaned over and touched the girl's hand. "Just don't forget that, and we should get along just fine. Now, how about I show you around this place? It's really pretty wonderful. And today, it's supposed to be close to a hundred degrees; so it's high time you came out of the air conditioning and experienced some of it."

Cami rolled her eyes. "Whatevs."

Kate leaned back, crossing her arms over her chest. At least Cami didn't call her a *pervert* or a *bitch*. Kate won the first battle last night, and the second one just now? Also Kate. She was on a roll.

AJ came out then all dressed. After another round of polite good-mornings, AJ glanced at Kate with his eyebrows raised. Then he smiled at Cami. She replied with a smile. Huh. Big improvement now that they weren't being called *perverts*.

"AJ, why don't you take today off and show Cami around?"

His head whipped up, and a shocked expression froze his face. "Well… uh… I…"

"People take personal days, sick days, vacation days. It's fine. Ask Jack. Jeez! He's not a workaholic like I first thought. You're the one who can't stop working. All the overtime and extra jobs you do for him? Believe me, Jack doesn't care."

AJ shook his shoulders out, trying to loosen them. All these new rules. New things. New People. New women. He wasn't used to any of it, but he politely nodded. "Uh, yes, if it's okay with Jack, Cami, I could show you around the place."

"Whatevs." Cami's gaze alternated between AJ and Kate as they discussed their plans for the day. Kate didn't think Cami missed much between them, or anything around her. That was probably how she survived.

AJ glanced at Kate and a small smile brightened his face. Her heart expanded. That was something.

AJ ate so quickly that Kate truly wondered how he had managed to survive until then on nothing but white bread and baloney. He thanked her, like he always did whenever she cooked, which was often, and kissed her cheek as he glanced at Cami. "I'll go check with Jack, I should be back in a half hour. Be ready." Sticking his hat on his head, he stepped outside. Kate nodded her satisfaction. He'd finally taken her not-so-subtle hints to man up with Cami. Too much private space and ongoing sympathy had her not only walking all over them, but also manipulating them. Cami was too screwed up and naïve to be allowed to make her own decisions.

Kate stayed in her office until AJ returned. When Cami and AJ disappeared out the front door, Kate peeked out the window, watching them. They made an incongruent couple as father and daughter. AJ was a mammoth beside the little bird-like figure of Cami. AJ wore his work clothes and looked like a rural country-hero come to life, while Cami was back in her full goth makeup, like she just stepped out of a horror movie.

But none of that mattered now; Cami was out of the house.

Kate wandered back into the kitchen. She glanced around the now quiet house and leaned on the counter, drinking some coffee. What the hell was she doing? Playing house with a man she had just started dating and his severely troubled daughter. They needed time together, lots and lots of time to figure each other out, and what to do with themselves and each other. Kate knew she didn't fit into the scenario, and she shouldn't have. She didn't want to. She was signing up to become the future stepmother to a horrible teenager. Especially *here*, at her half-brother's ranch.

Except... she stayed. It was a joke to say she was only there for her brother. Her brother and she surprisingly, despite the initial flare of drama, managed to settle in pretty well with each other. They got along swimmingly. It was an amicable relationship that built gradually, and their bond grew stronger each time they talked.

It was good for Kate actually. If she visited them every few months, Kate predicted they'd develop some real feelings for each other. Jack was respectful, and she could see that improving. He was easy to like, and seemed to feel the same about her. They sat down together a few weeks back and he listened to her ideas about streamlining the resort. He even asked her to write it up as a formal proposal so he could meet with his brothers and discuss it. He told her they'd like to move forward with some of her suggestions. She could continue to build her relationship with Jack from Seattle via the phone, text, email, and visiting.

So what the hell was she doing living in his freaking house?

Because of AJ.

She finally knew she had to admit that to herself.

Was it real? She had no idea. Her heart was clearly aching still from the loss of her mother, whose memory felt tainted now at the realization she really did abandon her son. Jack Rydell was a good man, and Kate didn't believe that as a boy, her mother had any justification for leaving him. So she didn't want that life or the ranch, which was something fixable, but why would she abandon her child? Kate couldn't make that right in her head no matter how many times she tried. It tainted her mother's memory, along with her entire childhood, and the trusting relationship she had shared with her mother as an adult.

Suddenly, Seattle was not so attractive to her. She didn't know why exactly. Or if she was running away from her pain, her mother, and her former beliefs about life. She couldn't decide if AJ were just a distraction, or if she stayed on *because* of him. She honestly couldn't say for sure, so she continued to stay there.

And now there was a young girl involved. Kate's stomach twisted. It wasn't right anymore. To be here and so involved. What Kate did last night wasn't the right thing to do, even though she'd done it knowingly.

Sighing, she returned to her work. Working from the ranch was actually turning out just fine. Her staff was stellar, and she got more tasks done in less time due to the fewer distractions.

Later, cracking her back as she stood up, Kate walked out of the office she commanded and entered the kitchen after hearing AJ's voice. It surprised her when Cami responded.

AJ glanced up at Kate's entrance. He smiled and her heart lifted. She was tired for no real reason, just a hard day's work and crouching over her computer. The bills had to be paid as well as the other administrative tasks connected to her business. Seeing AJ's smile, however, at the end of a long day, was something she never ceased to enjoy and look forward to.

Shaking her head at the thought, she straightened up and smiled back. No. All that domestic stuff wasn't her. Neither was taking on a man so different from her personality. AJ was so incongruent to *her* life, let alone that daughter of his.

But there they were. Cami didn't smile at Kate. Her excessive makeup made her eyes resemble a raccoon's and she blinked at Kate, but said nothing.

Kate didn't care; at least Cami had ventured outside.

That was a huge accomplishment. Which hit her sharply in the gut how much she cared about what happened to Cami and AJ.

THE DAY WAS TOO HOT. The temperatures were already in the nineties by noon and heading even hotter as the blistering white heat baked everything.

The entire family picked Saturday to go to the beach, and had already arrived by the time Kate got there. This time, however, she wasn't a guest, crashing their sanctuary. She understood why they refused to sacrifice the rare stretch of white, sandy beach and the deep, placid swimming hole. Otherwise, it was mostly a white-water river flowing beside a steep cliff with large river rocks and tiny patches of sand occasionally. Theirs might have been the best beach on the entire river.

Halfway to the beach, Kate bumped into Jack and Erin, obviously surprising them. Jack had Erin pressed against the trunk of a large tree, shielding them from the rest of the crowd at the beach. His head was down and they were in a tight, long, lip-lock. Erin was perched up on her tiptoes, meeting his lips while her hands nearly clung to his neck.

One of his hands was snarled in her hair and the other was down her back.

Kate didn't expect such a demonstration of passion from her modest, composed, or so it seemed, always correct brother. She smiled to herself. They certainly never expected to see her either. She called out, "Afternoon, brother. Enjoying yourself?"

Jack immediately dropped Erin as they both whipped around. He grinned when he spotted her waving at them as she passed. She smiled and waggled her eyebrows at him. Erin groaned in mock embarrassment and hid her face in Jack's chest. "Immensely. Do you mind, little sister? I'm kissing my wife." He wrapped his arms around Erin's neck, blocking her face from Kate and turned her away before kissing her again. Kate was grinning from ear to ear and a new levity lifted her heart. She didn't know *her brother* could be so much fun and playful and teasing. She hadn't foreseen that side of him.

Rounding the next corner was the beach. Shane and Allison were standing along the edge of the water, each holding the hands of their toddler as she splashed her little feet in the water and then laughed hysterically. Joey was floating on an inner tube. He raised a hand in greeting when he saw her, and she waved back. In that moment, Ben suddenly launched off the beach, taking advantage of Kate's distraction as he flipped Joey into the water.

Joey came up sputtering and coughing, the water dripping off his hair as he dove after Ben, who was already fleeing through the waist-deep water. That quick, they were wrestling in an all-out battle of youthful muscle and laughter. They were underwater, splashing and frolicking as Kate shook her head, laughing. On the beach, Ben's fiancée, Marcy, clapped too, raising one hand over her eyes to block out the sun so she could watch them.

Across the beach was Jocelyn. Kate glanced at her, surprised to see her there. She realized that all the people Jack employed were allowed free rein of the ranch as well as being treated like family. Jocelyn was watching the wrestling match as closely as Marcy. Kate followed her gaze, wondering whom Jocelyn was looking at, Joey or Ben? They were five years apart in age and great friends. Jocelyn's age allowed either possibility. Interesting. The seemingly quiet, rural, placid ranch had all kinds of drama and quirky interactions going on.

Cami sat on a big gray rock, pulling her legs up towards her chin and wrapping her arms around her calves. She rested her chin on her knees. Dressed in black skinny jeans and big, black boots, no matter how coolly Cami tried to play it, beads of sweat appeared on her hairline.

AJ sat on a log, amused by the frolicking boys too. Charlie was sedately sitting quite a way off from Cami, kind of staring at his feet.

Interesting... Anytime Kate saw Charlie, he was always doing something. He was eternally active and fun. She was surprised to find him sitting there all glum and old-looking.

Finally, he got up and entered the water, drawn in by his brother and uncle. Kate was nearly trampled, however, when Jack suddenly ran past her. Startled, she gasped, thinking something was wrong, only to see Jack grabbing Charlie before pushing him into the water along with his brother.

Jack stood there laughing and eagerly joining in all the horseplay. It wasn't long before Shane jumped in after his nephews begged him. Kate understood why: he was the only one who could take Jack on. Wearing cut-off jeans, Shane was instantly after Jack and everyone got all soaked in the fun and frolicking.

Erin walked up beside Kate. "Big boys, huh?" She nodded towards the water.

"They are. I didn't gather that. I thought they were always as serious as you all first appeared."

"Work hard, play hard." Erin fanned herself. "It's hot. No matter how many summers I spend here, I can't ever get used to the heat."

Kate nudged her shoulder. "Sure, that's what's got you so hot and bothered."

Erin ducked her head, smiling as she passed by Kate and entered the water without hesitating. She was soon swimming off by herself toward the high side, avoiding where the uncles and brothers were creating their own tidal waves with cannonball splashes. AJ turned and noticed her before waving her over to him.

She shook her head and tilted it toward the lost-looking waif, still sweating to death on the rock. AJ nodded, shrugging. He didn't know how to engage Cami either.

Kate set her towel down. She was wearing her bikini and she sat next to Cami, who barely even nodded at Kate. "Looks like they're having fun, huh?"

Cami didn't lift her head off her knees and her shoulders barely moved. "Whatevs."

Her favorite response to any question they asked. "You can't swim, can you?"

Cami's head shifted just a tad Kate's way, and she looked surprised. Kate smiled. "It's okay, you could still wade, or just float on one of the inner tubes. I'm sure AJ would be happy to tie it to the shore. And we'll all be here too, so if anything were to happen..."

Nothing. No answer. Kate sighed. "Cami, you have the skin of a ghost. You're burning up and now all that makeup is running down your face. It's too damn hot to keep trying to be so cool. Do you have a swimsuit?"

"No," she finally mumbled.

"Erin's as small as you are, I'm sure you could borrow a

pair of shorts and a shirt to swim in. We could get you a swimsuit, you know? It's no big deal."

"What—"

"Evs? I know. Seriously, at least, put some of this lotion on." Kate held the tube of sunscreen out to her. Cami finally took it, ducking her head down, and finally applying the lotion.

"Okay."

Kate's heart leapt with joy. *Okay?* That was better than a glowing review. "Let's go find you some summer clothes and we'll ask AJ to set you up to just float close to shore, okay?"

She shrugged. Kate took that *whatevs* as a yes.

"AJ!" she called out. He turned, leaping to his feet at her exclamation and racing over to her. He was so attentive, something she found flattering to the nth degree. Anytime she wanted something, needed something, or asked for something, he was all over it.

His shorts ended at his knees, a sedate dark color, no shirt and... and yes, the hat. It made her smile when she saw him. Then she almost wished the crowded beach would disappear as she stared at his chest. She wanted to rub herself against the hard planks of his muscles, and his hat with the shorts combination only further endeared her. It made her want to freaking cuddle up to him. Sure, he looked like such a dork, but the hottest dork cowboy that ever existed.

The boys' laughter and men's smack-talk, combined with the murmur of women's voices, was pretty awesome too, much to Kate's surprise. Raised an only child in a formal, mediocre family, there was never an afternoon like this in Seattle.

"I'm going to find Cami some beachwear. Could you dig up a rope and tie off that inner tube? Maybe get a life jacket too?"

AJ nodded eagerly. "Sure. 'Course." He turned and was

instantly off up the trails. Kate watched his quick steps. And his broad back. He was so obedient. Kate glanced at Cami. Did she realize that? Could she comprehend the power factor she held over AJ? He could cherish this girl and father her as no one else could. Kate just hoped Cami didn't abuse that.

She asked Erin for swimsuit help. Floating on the river, her hair slicked back, Erin waved at Kate, replying, "Go right ahead. You'll see my dresser. Pick out whatever fits."

"Thank you."

Cami got onto her feet, staring down, but she followed Kate without a word. They walked up the trail in silence until they entered the house Jack and Erin built.

"Will that work?" Kate asked as she handed her a bundle.

Cami took the garments with her into the bathroom. Kate waited, calmly staring out the window. The views were different from the main house. Pine trees crowded the landscapes and the river flashed silver through the red-barked tree trunks and green pine boughs. Far to the right, she glimpsed a pasture and some horses grazing.

Cami came out after clicking the bathroom door shut softly. Kate's heart was weary, but hopeful. It floored her that Cami would even come with her, or show any interest in trying to accept them. Maybe… no, she dared not get hopeful yet.

The black cotton shorts and dark tank top were garments that Erin probably wore under her clothes. The top hung a bit too loosely, but she was a tiny girl. She had to be if Erin's clothes looked big on her. But without all the layers and sloppy attire, Cami looked fragile, needy, sad, and lost. Kate's heart swelled, and she wanted desperately to help her. But… no. So no. Not her place. Still, the girl needed to cool off in the river before she melted like hot wax.

"Looks like that'll work. Maybe you should dab your

makeup off? The water will only make it run."

Cami accepted the hand towel that Kate took from the stove handle and handed to her. She briefly disappeared. Okay, still no words, but she was kind of interacting.

When she came back out clean-scrubbed, Kate wanted to croon how pretty she was, but that was not what Cami wanted to hear. So Kate just nodded and handed her the SPF 50 tube of sunscreen. The poor girl already had faint pink lines on her arms and around her eyes. She rubbed it on while Kate grabbed another towel from Jack and Erin's laundry room.

Back at the beach, AJ had just finished tying off the inner tube. It bobbed gently in the current with the long span of rope tied securely onto three branches of a tree, anchoring it near the shore. AJ held out a lifejacket. "This okay?"

Cami snagged the lifejacket and snapped it over her chest. "Yeah."

Kate and AJ exchanged a glance. Between the two of them, it was like climbing to the top of Mt. Everest. They managed to get Cami to join in, and even respond to them! They were both still wary and neither dared to trust her yet. Kate was waiting for Cami to flip off the lifejacket, or take a knife to the inner tube. She shook her head. Cami really wasn't that extreme, but Kate was still worried how far Cami might take her anger in her vendetta against them.

Cami entered the water. For the first time, a small smile lit up her face. She carefully, awkwardly backed onto the inner tube as she nodded to AJ. "I'm fine."

He released his grip and she drifted out. Staring hard at the surface for several minutes, Cami finally put her hands under the water and began to paddle around a bit. Then, relaxing in her newfound confidence, she tentatively laid her head back and seemed to be sunbathing.

"Wow, we actually got her to act normal," Kate muttered

to AJ.

He chuckled, watching her floating peacefully. "I can't imagine if we left her to do her own shopping, what she'd buy to swim in."

"She's so tiny. How could she be your daughter? There's *nothing* tiny about you." Teasing, Kate elbowed AJ's chest. AJ rolled his eyes and caught her hand in his but held it longer than he needed to. Her heart did an odd little tumble around her ribcage that it seemed to be doing quite frequently of late. Kate loved these little interactions of flirting and innuendoes. She even loved it when AJ sweetly held her hand. Together, they watched Cami enjoying herself.

Then, Ben noticed her. Kate immediately realized his intent. Ben didn't realize Cami couldn't swim, and Kate yelled out, "No!" But it was too late.

He dove underwater and easily flipped Cami over when he came up. Cami screamed as she got dumped. It wasn't a happy scream of fun and playing like Charlie's and Joey's were when Ben did that to them. Kate jumped into the water, but AJ was faster.

In three strong strokes, he reached Cami, lifting her out of the water in his arms, even though she was wearing a lifejacket. Everyone quit playing around and the shrill screams and laughter stopped all at once. AJ was holding the still shrieking girl in his arms. She was out of her mind with fear as the water dripped off her trembling body.

Kate was close enough to hear AJ trying to soothe her. "It's okay, Cami, it's okay. I got you. You're safe now."

Cami started to quiet down and AJ walked her across the swimming area to the beach, where he set her down. She was panting in sharp, shallow gasps. There was no doubt she was truly afraid and having a panic attack. Kate got closer to her and undid the snaps of the lifejacket. "Grab a towel," she said in a calm, matter-of-fact tone. Allison tossed her one. Kate wrapped it around the hysterical girl. She rubbed her arms and dried her off gently with the soft towel.

Ben was dripping water with his face drawn in sorrow. He stood at the edge of the beach.

"Cami, it's okay, honey. Shh," Kate said as she kept rubbing her arms. Cami was crying and her face was staring down towards the sand. AJ stood near her, looking miserable at her sorry state. "You were just dunked underwater. Ben didn't know you couldn't swim. No one was trying to hurt you," Kate explained as she tried to soothe the fearful girl.

Hearing his name, Ben came forward. "I'm sorry. I had no idea. I was trying to include you. You know? Because you're new here. I thought maybe you were feeling shy. I thought I could break the ice, you know, and just wanted you to have fun…"

Cami's sniffling slowed. Her face stayed down, but her trembling ceased. Then she lifted her face a fraction of an inch and replied, "Really?"

Ben put his hands up and squatted down until he was eye level with her. "I swear. I didn't know. I was kidding around. You were wearing a lifejacket, so I thought you were just super nervous. I had no idea you were really scared or couldn't swim."

"You wanted to include me?" Her eyebrows furrowed in disbelief.

Kate nodded. "He was just horsing around. And no one meant you any harm. They were just trying to include you as part of the fun."

Cami nodded. Burying her hands in the towel, she dried her forehead as streams of water dripped over her. "It's okay."

Kate had no idea if Cami were talking to Ben, Kate or AJ. That she was even talking was pretty huge, and apparently, not being mad at them was even bigger.

Ben put his hand out as if to shake hers. "Truce?"

Cami stared at his hand, then up at his face. There was a spark of interest in Cami's eyes and Kate's breath hung on her reaction. *Please*, she wanted to beg her. *Try.* Try to accept the friendship, and the inclusion by this family, this place, this father who wanted to provide for her if only she'd allow it.

Cami put her hand in Ben's to shake it. "Truce." It wasn't a declaration, but it also wasn't "whatevs."

Ben smiled and stood up. The rest of the onlookers took it as sign to continue with what they were doing and they all quit staring at her. Cami finally glanced up at AJ and said, "Thanks."

AJ nodded, squatting near her. "We wouldn't let anything happen to you."

She glanced at Kate, and Kate smiled, asking, "Why are you looking at me? Do you doubt I wouldn't?" Kate put her hand out as Ben had. "Truce?"

Kate expected the insolent, intolerant, rude girl to do or say something inappropriate or just go back to *whatevs*, but she put her hand in Kate's, saying, "Truce."

Kate smiled. "Good." Kate continued, "But where you fell in isn't any deeper than your chest. I think you should get back in now, or you might never want to again. And you just don't strike me as a girl who refuses a challenge or wusses out. You got guts. I think you should use them."

AJ's gaze whipped up to her. Kate was pushing again, and he opened his mouth to argue, but Kate shook her head just slightly, her eyes wide with warning.

"It's that shallow?"

"Yes. No one will bother you now. We all realize you can't swim and there's the lifejacket, along with AJ, who already proved he can lift you. Look at him. He could probably lift a bull out of deep mud. I mean, look at those muscles. He certainly won't have any trouble with a little tiny thing like you. Besides, I think all of them would like to swim with you," she said, waving her hands towards Joey, Ben, Marcy, Jocelyn, and Charlie. All of them were in the water as if obeying an unspoken fiat to continue having fun. They formed a chain of inner tubes by holding the handles of their neighboring tubes, in a circle, their asses in the water, and their legs and arms sprawled atop the round inner tubes.

Cami's eyes stared with undisguised interest at them. She eyed the pile of different inflatables still on shore. Addressing AJ, she asked, "Would you maybe, you know, hold my inner tube?"

AJ's chest slowly exhaled. He nodded with an unreadable facial expression, but Kate could see his surprise by his widened eyes and the careful way he held on to Cami's gaze. "Sure," he tersely replied. He also knew how to keep it easy and light. The request was huge coming from her, especially towards him.

Kate stood up and fell back onto a beach chair as AJ helped Cami into the water. He was holding the inner tube while she attempted to fall into it like everyone else. She peered down into the shallow water with some terror, but at least she didn't shriek or start running to shore.

Kate glanced up at Jack, who sat down next to her.

She smiled, and he reciprocated as their gazes looked out over the teens floating away… and AJ.

"She might come around after all."

"Well, at least, she stopped accusing us of being perverts. So… maybe."

Jack leaned down, sifting the sand through his fingers. "Any idea what she's been through?"

"No. Not really."

"Must be tough." His gaze traveled to Charlie. "I imagine Charlie being out all alone in the world without me…I can't stomach it. So much could happen. They are so innocent, and so much could go wrong."

"I think that's what happened to AJ."

Jack nodded. "He told you? About his past?"

"Parts of it. Can I ask? What made you hire him when you didn't know him except for his criminal history?"

"His sincerity and honesty. He told me right up front about it. First time I met him. Not many ex-cons are that honest. I doubt I would have checked into his background to find out. I respected his honesty and concluded if he'd tell me that, he'd be truthful about everything. And from day one, he's been faultless."

"I think part of why I like you is because you gave him a chance."

Jack smiled. "After you concluded I didn't beat up my wife?"

"A little before that."

"You're not here for me though, are you?"

She sighed. "No. Not fully, I mean."

"Yeah, I figured that out. He's a good guy. He just doesn't seem to realize it."

"Yes, there is that."

"Is she a deal breaker?" Jack nodded to the floating pair.

"Cami? I don't know. I mean… it's a lot to think of, taking on both of them."

"But aren't you already?" Jack pointed out, his tone level and dry.

"I—" Kate couldn't argue. She had already been handling the two of them. "I have no idea. This summer has turned everything upside-down. I was living in Seattle, running my company, and pretty content, or so I thought. And then my mom died, and I find out I have a sibling, and I come to this place, and now, a man is involved and his estranged daughter, who might hate me, and yet, here I am. I don't know why I'm still here. I just didn't think you knew that."

Jack shrugged. "I got eyes. I saw why you were here. It doesn't bother me. Strangely enough, after our initial mutual dislike, we seemed to mesh together pretty easily."

Kate glanced at Jack, a smile lingering on her lips. "We do. Are we that alike? Or just different enough?"

"Erin says we're alike."

"Well, shit, I'm sorry for you, Jack. Do you get accused of being hot-tempered, over-reacting, slow to change, often a jerk, and occasionally wonderful?"

He chuckled. "It's like you were quoting Erin about me."

"Yeah, me too," she mumbled with a sigh.

"The house is unoccupied, except for Joey who was traumatized by whatever happened that night involving Cami. I have an idea what went on, but Joey won't say. He called it 'inappropriate behavior.'"

"Cami was acting out. She has a lot of anger. Poor Joey is all I'll say."

"Have you considered staying permanently?"

"Here?" The shock and surprise competed in her tone. "No, no way. I can't live here. It's stupid to talk about. I don't belong here. I—"

"Not the way I see you. I think you make wherever you are belong to you. Anyway, it's just a thought."

"I think part of why I'm staying here is to avoid being in Seattle without my mom."

Jack nodded. "I can see that. Were you two close?"

"Yup. Like peas and carrots, butter and rice. So close, I had no idea she'd hide such a terrible secret from me."

Jack stared out at the river. "I can't pretend to know what she was thinking or doing, but I never missed her. I loved my mom, Donna, who raised me for as long as I can remember. I didn't know I wasn't biologically hers until I was ten years old. So, if it's any consolation, I don't wish my life were any different."

"I guess that makes it better. I mean, if she'd abandoned you to a life of misery, it would be impossible to forgive her. It's just so hard for me to reconcile."

Jack stretched his legs out. "I'm glad you showed up now. No matter what brought you here."

"Me too." She shrugged. "I just wish it didn't taint the memory of my mother so much."

Jack was silent for a moment, watching his sons. "I guess you should just look at it as your mother did the best she could. Sounds like she tried to make up for what she couldn't give me after she had you. Be grateful for that. I was okay, and you and I found each other. So maybe, in death, you can let her rest, Kate. Just love her as you remember her, and we'll let her rest in peace. You know what I mean? The older I get, the more I understand how imperfect each of us are. We are capable of things that don't always fit in with what we should do or be. I'm sincerely glad I got to know you, and maybe that's enough."

Tears filled Kate's eyes. "You're just saying that for me. You actually resent my mother for abandoning you, but you're stopping me from feeling that way."

He touched her knee and a soft half-smile appeared on his face. "I'm your big brother, right? Isn't it my job to try to make your life easier?"

A lump filled her throat. She nodded. "No, not all brothers…"

"Well, the kind I think I'd like to be."

"Thank you, Jack," she whispered over the lump and tears as she nodded. "I would like to just love my mother again. Because I did love her so much. And I miss her so much…"

"I get that. I still feel love for my first wife and my parents. I'd hate to have those memories tainted. I don't think your memory of your mother should be either. Okay? Let's just concentrate and revere what we have now. Regardless of how it happened."

She smiled away her tears and swallowed the lump in her throat. "I'm very glad it happened. I'm glad I came here, and so glad I found you."

"And AJ," Jack said as an observation, not a question.

Kate nodded in agreement, saying, "Yes, perhaps most of all, I'm glad I met AJ."

They stared out at the circle of floating loved ones. Finally, after several long moments, Ben leaned over to kiss Marcy and Kate asked, "Are you ready for Ben to get married?"

"Not in the least," Jack replied in a strained tone. He nodded at the couple, holding hands on the water. "What can I do though? I was the same damn age, and so was Lily. We were so sure, and so ready, or so we thought. But now? At thirty-nine, I can't think of a more stupid thing to do. It's so wrong. But what can I say? Who am I to tell him not to? Talk about a hypocrite. Anything I say in the way of advice will only push them into it sooner."

She sighed. "I think you're right. They're just so young."

"Tell me about it. You can't imagine the worry I have. It keeps me up at night. All the what-ifs. I just want him to have an easier life than mine was. You know? Even though I understand I can't live his life for him."

Kate stared at Cami, and similar thoughts and anxiety churned her gut, as they often did now. The teen was not her daughter, her blood or even her friend. Yet, Kate worried about her constantly. Softly, she said,. "Strangely, Jack, I think I'm starting to understand that. The helplessness, the worry, and the desire to make their lives better than our own."

Jack followed her line of vision towards Cami and

squeezed her shoulder with his hand. "Yes, I think maybe you do."

They fell silent as the family laughed and splashed all around them. They were the only ones still dry on the beach. And it was really nice. The nicest day Kate ever remembered having with a group in a very long time.

THINGS CHANGED A DEGREE AFTER THAT. Cami was allowed her own room because she got up in the morning. Sure it was late; but at least, she came out. Kate was specific about the chores she was expected to do and monitored daily that they got done. Ben and Charlie had a huge stable of friends, ranging in age from twelve to twenty. They were often hanging around in the afternoons and evenings when the heat of the day peaked. Cami went down to the river to hang out with Charlie and Ben, and they became much more hospitable to her since the day at the river. The young trio was often spotted floating down the river. Cami was all strapped up in her lifejacket, and Kate admired two things about her: the guts to face her fear of water, and her willing-ness to wear the lifejacket in front of others, given her quirky fashion trends. Cami even smiled sometimes when she was talking about it. Seemed she liked wearing it.

AJ and Kate often ended up down there too. It was too refreshing to resist a soak in the cool river. Jack, Erin, Shane and Allison, Rosie, and Joey were always in and out. Lots of screaming, yelling, laughter, and splashing all the time filled the air as people came and went.

One evening, AJ climbed up the big rock by the beach and jumped off it with an impressive cannonball splash. That set off Joey and Shane, who were trying to show him up. Even-tually, AJ convinced Cami to come up and try it. He carefully stood next to her, promising to hold her hand if she wanted to jump. She stood there for ten minutes, just staring down, pacing backwards, then forwards, only to stare again. Then all at once, she nodded, grabbing AJ's hand, and Kate, who was watching them, saw Cami count to three before they jumped in together, their hands linked as they flew through the air in the shimmering sunlight.

Kate managed to click a picture of them in mid-air. It was an awesome shot. They came up, and Cami was actually *smiling*. It was a huge accomplishment to see Cami looking so happy.

Kate cooked dinner because AJ and his baloney were too much for her to stomach. Cami always sat with them now. The first night, there was almost complete silence. Kate talked a little, but her lame, quiet days of staying in the house and working on her computer didn't offer too many exciting recaps.

When Cami left to go pee, Kate nudged AJ, "Talk to her. Ask her how her day went. How she's doing. You're her father. You're the one who has to ask. She isn't going to tell you unless you ask."

The stunned expression on his face was almost comical if it weren't so tragic to Kate. "I didn't know."

"Because no one ever asked you, did they?" she said gently. He shrugged. "You need to ask her. You're the one who needs to care. You're the adult."

AJ nodded vigorously and as usual, took her advice to heart. She could so easily convince him of whatever she chose to. His limited experience with relationships made him overly dependent on her. She wasn't trying to deceive him and hoped she handled his trust with the respect it was due. In true AJ style, when Cami came back out, he asked her how she liked Ben and Charlie. He also asked if she needed anything in the way of clothes.

"A swimsuit might be nice."

"Sure." He glanced at Kate, suddenly unsure. Kate internally sighed. She couldn't stop getting involved. "I can take you tomorrow."

"Thanks." AJ tried to give her money so she had to accept it. The shopping experience was a trip to hell. Cami must have taken three hours to decide on... a black swimsuit. But Kate patiently waited outside the dressing room, bringing in what felt like every single bathing suit they had in stock.

She did, however, have to kick AJ under the table when the very next night, silence prevailed. She tilted her head towards the girl, mouthing to AJ, *Speak to her.* He seemed startled by her tacit suggestion. Sometimes, AJ didn't realize that communicating with others wasn't a one-time event, but a daily thing to practice.

Kate made Cami come to church with them, which had become a regular habit now. Kate still hadn't decided how she felt about it, but it was so important to AJ that she made it her mission to urge him to speak to the community he now belonged to. He needed to make the teen feel like she belonged too. Cami's black makeup and the depressing clothes she still wore, no matter how freaking *hot* the days got, kept some people from approaching her. But the Rydell boys often came with Jack and Erin, and they all talked to her, and included her. Eventually, most of the others followed suit after the Rydells embraced the new, quiet girl.

Cami's style started to grow on Kate. Somehow it fit her. Jocelyn even complimented Cami on her unique look and the young girl blushed, growing flustered but appearing pleased by the comment.

Mostly because Cami needed any and all reassurance she could get.

She finally mentioned it to Cami one evening as they sat on the porch. They were watching Jack and Erin as they frolicked with some horses in the arena along with doing seriously cool things with them.

"You really have a knack for style."

"My mom hated how I dressed. She said my style made me look like a whore."

Um... Kate's open mouth would have revealed her shock if Cami had happened to glance her way. She had no idea how to reply to that comment made by the girl's dead mother. "Well, um, that's one opinion, I suppose."

Cami shrugged. "She wasn't trying to be mean. She was just like that. She was honest with her opinions. That was cool. You always knew where you stood with her."

There was honest and then there was mean and awful and inappropriate, but Kate kept that observation to herself at this point. "You miss her?"

Cami shrugged again. But neither did she reply with her typical, careless "whatevs."

"My mom died in April."

Cami's faced whipped around to Kate's, searching her gaze. It was a first, Cami actually showing shock and interest in something Kate said. "April?"

"Yes. She had a heart attack. Died. Then I found out I had a brother, but she had abandoned him. That brother was Jack. That's why I'm here."

"You didn't know all of them before either?"

"Not a one."

"My mom died in February."

From February to July before she showed up there? What happened to her? What was she exposed to? Was she safe? Cared for? Abused? Hurt? Desperate curiosity overtook Kate. She had to ask so they could know and understand what they were dealing with in this girl.

"I'm sorry. You're too young for that." Kate's shame was real. She was thirty-five and still couldn't handle her grief over her mom or her disillusionment. Kate couldn't imagine having a mother like Cami's and losing her at age thirteen.

"She lost custody of me a few times. She was a drug addict. It was better when she was clean, but it never lasted long; then..."

"Your dad's life was a lot like that."

"Not yours though?"

"No. Not at all. My parents were always with me and loved me." *They fed me, cared for me, kept me safe*, but Kate didn't say that to the lost little girl she saw before her. Funny too; no matter what a parent might do to a kid, the kid still loved the parent.

"What's that like?" Cami asked after a long moment, her gaze riveted on the view. Kate stared at the girl before her heart swelled in tenderness, sadness, and longing. Cami blinked her too-black lashes and kept her little girl face as neutral and tough as she could. Meanwhile, her voice wavered and she faltered at the question.

"It was very nice. It's a lot like what you've experienced this month here with AJ."

Cami's gaze shifted quickly at her, then she turned away. "And you."

Kate's breath stopped. She didn't expect that. She nodded and gazed out towards the view too. "Yes, with me too."

Whatever. At least, the girl didn't call her *crazy* or *bitch* anymore. She ceased all her insults. There was a wealth of untapped girl potential inside Cami. There was so much they didn't know about her, from her emotions, to her opinions about what happened to her. They didn't know how often she grieved or how much she loved. They knew so little. But the shift in her attitude, now that she just started to engage them, offered renewed hope, and someday, perhaps knowing nothing could change to knowing *something*.

CHAPTER 16

"*I* NEED TO GO HOME for a little while," Kate announced with a soft thump as she sat down on the couch.

AJ glanced at her, his attention fully engaged immediately. "Is something wrong?"

"Estate problems with my mom. I need to do something about her condo. It's a serious investment potential. I just... it's time. I have a former life there I need to get back to. A business to run, a condo I live in and I haven't... Well, this is not my house."

AJ kept his face carefully blank. "No, it's not." He sat back, setting his shoulders rigid. She nodded, riveting her gaze on the coffee table before them.

"We should probably talk about that."

She felt his gaze as he shifted forward, leaning his elbows on his knees. "Yeah."

"I can't stay here."

"I can't leave here."

She nodded. "I know. Seattle isn't for you. At all."

"River's End isn't for you."

"And now there's Cami. She needs you." *More than I do,* Kate thought, but she kept that to herself. Inhaling a deep breath, Kate turned to the side, her leg drawn up under her so she faced him. She touched his arm. "I started this with no thought of anything. But I'm glad I did. I have no idea what it means, however. You told me in the beginning you wanted sex to mean something. All I can tell you is *all* of what we shared turned out to mean *everything* to me."

AJ sucked in a breath, just barely glancing at her through the corners of his eyes before he leaned closer. "I didn't plan on it becoming anything either. But when you didn't leave, it became everything."

She rested her head against his big arm. His muscles tensed and he reached over and rubbed her head. She smiled at the gesture. "I'll come back."

"To visit," he stated, not questioning her intent.

"Yes. To visit."

He nodded. "I need to figure something out for me and Cami. She can't stay here alone, and I can't live in Jack's house. But the trailer..."

"What about that property you talked about before?"

He barely lifted his shoulders in a half-hearted shrug. "I can't afford that. Not right now, at least."

"I could." Kate kept her head on AJ, and her voice soft. She felt him tense at her words. He shifted and she had to lift her head up, sighing, as he started to overreact. "I can afford it. Is there any reason I couldn't buy it? Put something on it to live on, and you could rent it from me."

"You can't do that, Kate."

"Well, actually I can. You know what sucks? I know Erin stayed here after she and Jack got together."

"In the trailer I live in now."

"Yes, all of which Jack provided. But that's okay in your head. She's not a gold-digger or underserving of the life she now has, but if I'm the one offering you anything…well, it's just totally different, isn't it?"

AJ threw his hands up. "I have no idea. It just can't happen."

"I need a place to stay when I come here. Jack and I seem to get along well. There isn't much chance he, his boys, and his extended family around here are going to troop into my condo in Seattle, is there? So any visiting will be due to my effort. I can come for extended times; but I would need a place to stay. Why can't it be with you?"

He shook his head. "It can't be like that."

"Because of your pride? Cami deserves a stable place to live, AJ. Maybe some kids could move endlessly, but she deserves a permanent place to stay. So do you, to be honest. But face it, you've never once had that, not even for a year. I can provide that for you. You intend to stay here and Jack intends to keep you here as long as you want, I'd say, judging by the way he talks about you."

"What conversation are we having here? You leaving? We're done? We're together? Whatever it is, you're not paying my way."

"But again, Jack can pay for Erin? Fuck that, AJ. I had a lot of opportunities in my life, and I took them and never squandered them. I have worked for the past decade to accumulate the means for a healthy living and retirement. My parents also left me all kinds of money and investments. Lucky girl, right? Too manly to take my help no matter how practical, huh?" Mid-way through her rising temper, Kate stood up. AJ's eyes followed her.

"Maybe I want to do it. Maybe I want a place of my own when I come here. Maybe I'll do it anyway and fuck you if you don't take advantage of it. And we're so not done. But I am leaving. So figure out what the hell *you* intend to do with that."

She turned on her heel, stomped into her room, and slammed the door, nearly foaming at the mouth. Grabbing her suitcase, she started throwing her clothes into it. It soon became quite a pile of belongings. Not all of it would fit. She sat on the suitcase, trying to jam it shut when a soft knock rapped on her door. She gritted her teeth, not yet calm enough to apologize for losing her temper or swearing around him and being her usual, childish self. Later. Later she'd apologize and be calm and adjust her behavior to be more acceptable. Not yet. Not now. Now she was hitting, jamming, nearly screaming at her suitcase and the large bump of clothing that kept it from closing. "What?"

The door opened with a soft click. She sighed. It wasn't AJ. He would have just busted in. It had to be Cami. She jumped on the suitcase one last time before answering, "Hey, come in."

Cami walked in and glanced around. She glared at Kate with angry eyes, and her makeup was smudged. "I heard you."

Kate sighed heavily. She often suspected the clueless, careless girl knew everything that went on. Kate sat down on the edge of the bed. "I have a job. A life. As I told you, I came here to meet my brother. I never expected to find a boyfriend." *Or his daughter.* His wayward, sad, scared, scary, twisted, shy, sweet, crazy, secretive, angry, rebellious daughter.

"I thought he was your fiancé?"

She sighed. "I was mad that day. I only said that to get your attention. And then, he was living here, mostly to be near you, by the way, and it seemed okay to let you think that. But no, we aren't engaged. We just met when I arrived here. But I care very much about him." *And you too, little girl,* but Cami wouldn't let her say that. She wasn't trusted or welcome... yet. Kate believed more time and tolerance might help. But who knew what the future held?

"Did you mean it about the land stuff?"

"Yes. Sorry, you heard me yelling."

She snorted. "You could never be intimidating. You're like a puppy, all riled up and snarling at us."

Kate made a face. "I thought I was bat-shit crazy and scary acting. I try to be."

Cami shook her head. "No, I've heard scary anger before. And yours definitely isn't."

"No, it isn't." Kate sighed, staring down and feeling deflated.

"I think he should let you help him. And, you know, you deserve a place to stay here too, right?"

Kate's head lifted in surprise. "Uh, yeah. But he has this huge ego. Most men do."

"But like you said, Jack took in Erin, what's so different?" She wished Cami would ask AJ that question.

"I'll work on him and see if I can't make something happen."

Cami stood there, unmoving. Kate wasn't sure how far to take it. She had no rights with the girl and no idea how far their connection should go, considering she was nothing official to her. She felt nervous, and didn't want to push her luck. No telling where real life would take them as the summer ended, fall came, winter set in, and the sands of time smoothed it all over.

Still, she found herself promising, "I will be back."

Cami didn't move, but finally scoffed. "Whatevs, Kate."

Yeah. Whatevs. Kate wanted to wilt onto the bed or grab the girl in a reassuring hug and convince her she would be back. But Kate suspected this girl's entire life was filled with people leaving and few coming back, or even promising to. It seemed better not to build her hopes up. She didn't want to be another disappointment in Cami's life.

"I was just checking. See ya." Cami was biting her lip as she sped out of the room, the hallway, kitchen, and front door before Kate could even get to her feet. Sighing deeply, Kate watched the little pixie in black streaking across the yard. Off to where? To feel what? She wouldn't know. She couldn't help.

AJ entered when Cami slammed the door. "She heard us. I think she might actually care that I'm leaving."

AJ stared at her, and his shoulders relaxed as his eyes shut. "She's not the only one."

Kate's shoulders sagged and she nearly wilted. She stepped closer to him and curled up into his arms, placing her head on his chest, and listening to his heart. "Then don't be such a jerk about it. And she asked me why you couldn't let me buy the place. You tell me, AJ? You don't think that someday your daughter could have more money than whatever boyfriend she chooses? Think of that message you're giving her."

Kate thought he'd stiffen and push her away and they'd start again, but instead, his chest rumbled. "Kate. Give it up for now."

"I don't give up."

A deep silence followed her outburst and their gazes stared into the other's soul, or so it seemed. AJ finally whispered, "Well, maybe something won't end now."

"Do you mean that? You'll do this with me?" She nearly held her breath and crossed her fingers and toes in hopeful apprehension.

"Do this?"

"Long distance. Us together, even if we're not together all the time. So what if it's imperfect?"

He nodded and kept nodding. "Yeah, I think it's kind of a given. Unless you're done, with me, that is."

Kate suddenly threw herself at him. Why was he always so sure he wasn't the prize? Why did he always believe he wasn't enough? For Kate, he was more than enough, but he never embraced that. "I'm not done. I don't know how to ever be done with you, AJ, even if I desired that."

"You don't desire it? Not even a little?"

Again, his voice cracked with insecurity. Kate leaned back and touched her finger to his lips. "Not even a little."

"All right, then I'll see you when you next come back here."

She smiled through her anxiety; she hated leaving. "And I know I don't have to worry about other women, now do I, my celibate cowboy? That's one excellent thing about you, huh?"

He smiled too, although it was strained. "I'm with you, there's no one else I'd even consider desirable."

She leaned her head against his chest and swore she could feel him holding his breath, waiting for her response. He suspected she could not stay celibate. "You are wrong."

"About what?"

"It isn't hard for me to abstain from sex. The only time that's hard is when you're around. It's only you, AJ. I want only you. And if I'm not interested in someone, I can go for years without sex too."

His arms grasped her shoulders and he kissed her forehead. "I think I underestimated you."

"No, you underestimated yourself and how a woman can feel about you. So quit doing it and we just might make this all work out."

He took in a slow breath. "Work out to what?"

She didn't answer. Then she said, "Not sure yet, but I'm willing to see where it goes. Are you?"

"I am. Yes, I'm willing."

"Then, I'll be back."

"I'll be waiting. Actually, we'll be waiting. I don't think Cami wants you to leave either."

"No, but maybe it will be good for you two; give you more time to figure each other out. Your relationship with each other is more important than mine and hers or even ours."

AJ sighed. "When you say things like that, I think I can be with you for a long time."

She took his words to heart as they quietly held each other and let the silence fill the space between them. So much was still unknown and unanswered, but there was no denying the passion that existed between them. Kate shut her eyes, believing something had to come of this.

What that was, she couldn't name or understand. But she knew it was there.

THE DRIVE back to her condo had her heart aching in her chest the entire way. She kept biting her lip to stop her tears from falling. She didn't listen to any music lest it stir up emotions and make her chest ache even more. They did the whole goodbye scene, she hugged Erin, and even Jack embraced her, adding a *brotherly* pat on her shoulders. Hell, she now had a brother.

Cami just stood in the house, digging her hands into the deep pockets of her skinny jeans with little or no response to Kate when she tried to say goodbye. Finally, Kate sighed and hugged AJ after everyone else left and they had some privacy. They kissed, and hugged each other tightly. There were no promises, no I love yous or anything inappropriate. There was a distinct sense of loss and overbearing heaviness in

Kate, but she wasn't sure how to deal with it. It was just too much, too soon. Too soon for anything more, and she had a real life to return to. As well as a paycheck to earn in the city she loved.

All alone in the city.

That reality fell heavily on her mind.

Before last May, she didn't feel alone in Seattle. Of course, she had her mother then, and friends and co-workers. She thought her life was full and satisfying. Now? What? It wasn't just because she hooked up over the summer with a hot guy? AJ not only satisfied her physically, but even harder to imagine, he stirred up her emotions. No other man could do that.

Kate arrived at the condo and unpacked her suitcase, cleaned the house, paid the bills and ran errands. She emptied her kitchen since most of the perishables had expired. When she returned to work, she tried to keep the sad, heavy feelings at bay. But every evening found her alone. No one else was around. No mother to call for a chat. Complain to. Or gossip with. Grief over the harsh reality of her loss flooded her emotions. Yeah, the summer provided a brilliant escape, mostly from her true feelings. Her grief. Her sadness. Her anger.

How could someone she'd known her entire life keep such a terrible secret from her? No amount of hypothetical circumstances helped. After searching through her mom's personal things, there were still no answers. She found no secret diary or love letters. There was no answers. She left Kate absolute nothing but money. Except Jack's birth certificate.

Now Kate had the rest of her life to wonder why? How could she reconcile her former image of her mother into someone who was not so perfect, and actually made mistakes? How could a mother ditch her own child? But she didn't ditch Kate, and Kate had to live with that dichotomy.

Things settled back down as Kate gradually settled in. There was a certain relief and familiarity, however, as time passed and she resumed her former life. It was all exactly as she left it. She went to work, and spoke to a few friends, although she still didn't feel like responding to their invitations to dinner or even just drinks. She basically went to work and came home. Life was quiet. Flat. Boring. Forgotten. And lonely. She was so lonely sometimes, she ached at night.

Then one day, she got a call.

"Kate?"

She gripped the phone, AJ's voice sounded rough and rattled as he said her name. They talked often enough that she recognized the panic-stricken undertone. "What happened?

"Cami's gone. We've looked everywhere for her. She left school and didn't come home. I have no idea... Fuck!" He shouted into the phone. Bug-eyed, Kate swallowed her own terror. AJ sounded so lost...

Kate quickly gathered her scattered senses. "She ran away, AJ. So she's not hurt or kidnapped, she voluntarily went to wherever she's gone. That I know. Down in my heart. So we have to stop, think, and be smart. Where would she go? Do you hear me? She's okay." Kate drew in a sharp breath. She insisted that it be true. There was no other option her racing heart and sweaty palms could accept. "We have to remain calm and figure this out. Get ahead of her."

AJ's breath whooshed into the receiver as he replied, "Do you think so?"

"Yes." Kate calmed her tone. "Yes, I know her. She's punishing us. You. Me. Her mother. Her father. Foster care. A broken system. All the awful things that she had to endure. Just like when she got on top of Joey."

"We have to find her. Imagine the trouble she could get into. If she doesn't find it first. She's so small..."

"We'll find her, AJ. Pull out her file, the one that Nicola gave you. Sit down and read the fucker out loud to me. Let's start there."

She heard his breath slow down and her own heartbeat started to even out. They'd find her. Of course, they would. No other outcome was acceptable. AJ disappeared for a moment, and she heard some shuffling and muffled movement before he returned and started reading. She listened to Cami's long history with the state, but there was nothing that linked Cami to any particular place or person.

"Did she talk to you about anything recently?" Kate asked AJ.

"I found a new place for us. She didn't like it. She wants to stay here. I tried to explain that we can't live in Jack's family house. It isn't ours. She didn't understand why it was fine as long as you were here."

Kate closed her eyes. The poor girl's entire duration of stability was not even weeks old, and again, she was about to be moved. She sat up straight in her office chair. She has to be coming here. Kate suddenly knew the result. Cami leaving. Kate returning to Seattle. Cami was coming to her.

"Don't worry, AJ. She's coming here. Get in your truck and start driving now. Come to my place. I'll find her, I'm sure I will."

"How can you know that?"

"She's looking for stability. That was us. Together. We represented her first glimpse of stability, and then I left. She's punishing you now for letting me leave, and me for leaving. Just trust me. Come to Seattle."

"Where will she go? She has no idea where you live. She can't navigate a city of tens of thousands of people. How will she even get there?"

"The girl's been on her own all her life. I doubt a bus schedule would exactly stump her. I'm sure in all her thirteen-year-old brilliance, she hasn't considered that. She just associates Seattle with me, and thinks she'll be fine. I'll find her when the bus gets in. I promise, AJ. I'll find her. In the meantime, keep trying to get a hold of her."

"I'm on my way. God, Kate if you're wrong…"

"I'm not wrong."

"Or if you somehow miss her."

"I always do what I say I'm going to do."

Kate hung up, turning her chair to stare out over the city-scape of tall towers and square street blocks. She twisted her chair in half circles. Her jangled nerves began winding up her spine. What if she were wrong? But no. Nothing bad could have happened to Cami. She was simply taking a bus ride… here. Kate worked out a timeline, after some quick research online for the bus schedules. If Cami caught the first bus leaving River's End, she should be showing up at the bus terminal in another half hour. Kate would be there, waiting with bells on, if necessary. She got up quickly, grabbed her purse, and yelled to her secretary that she was gone for the day and to cancel everything. Nothing could stop her from her mission.

The bus station was huge. Buses kept entering and leaving the terminal constantly. It was gray concrete, dense with people at times, and at others only a trickle. Kate found the proper terminal and waited. She didn't pull out her phone or dare let her gaze wander. She simply stared at the spot where the bus was due to show up. Soon. So soon…

Finally, Bus #23 swung wide as it pulled into the lane and stopped almost ten feet from Kate. The passengers began to step right onto the curb of the sidewalk, and Kate was on her feet, moving within inches of the door. No one could get past her. Kate saw Cami standing at the top of the stairs inside the Greyhound. Her makeup was as black as ever, as was her hair. Her eyes gleamed when she saw Kate, but nothing on her face twitched in recognition. She took a step. And stopped. Then another. And stopped, her eyes never leaving Kate's. The man behind Cami grumbled and pushed her.

Kate aimed a scowl at him and snarled, "Hey." Kate stepped towards the man. "Get your hands off her. Back the fuck off! She's just a little girl. Let her have a moment here, asshole."

The guy, huge and tatted up, glared harder at her. He was maybe in his mid-twenties. Kate glared back. Cami looked over her shoulder, then back at Kate before she suddenly launched herself at Kate and started to cry.

Kate had to step back. She was wearing high heels and wobbled off balance as Cami pressed against her chest, wrapping her arms around her back. Cami's backpack held all of her worldly goods and it looked so heavy and bulky on her small, frail back. Kate found her footing and held the girl, eventually tipping her back far enough to look into her tear-streaked, black, running, made-up face. She held Cami's biceps in her hands and shook her gently. "What's the matter with you, you little fool? AJ's out of his mind with worry. If I hadn't guessed where you'd go, you could have gotten lost. Where the hell were you going?"

Cami didn't answer, her eyes glistening with tears. Sighing, Kate pulled her closer for a tight hug. Cami rubbed her face on Kate's white blouse, ruining it with the ridiculous mask of black makeup that was painted on Cami's face. Kate pulled back. "How can we keep you safe if you won't let us?"

"Us? There is no *us*. You don't want there to be."

"There is an *us*." Kate's tone was final. "And just because I went back to my job, and my condo and former address, doesn't mean I don't want you to stay *safe*. You have to know that."

"He's trying to move me."

"He has to," Kate replied wearily. "He doesn't own anything at the ranch."

"Then come back. You do."

"No, I don't, honey."

"You're Jack's sister."

Simple, teenage, selfish logic. Kate let out a breath of air and shook her head. "Let's go to my house. AJ will be there in a few hours."

Cami didn't respond as the people around them drifted off. Kate hiked Cami's backpack a little higher up before leaning over and gently running her hand through Cami's hair. "What made you run away today?"

"Shit at school."

"What shit, Cami?"

"Some bitch-ass girls talking smack about me. Whatevs."

Right. Whatevs as the girl took off across half a state she wasn't familiar with to a city she didn't know. Kate was sure there was talk. Nobody else looked like Cami at the small public school that Cami now attended. It included middle through high school and the total population of kids numbered less than five hundred. Everyone knew each other. Kate had dropped Cami off there one time and she scoured the crowds for anyone dressed similarly to the way Cami dressed, but found none.

Cami stared down at her combat boots. "If I went to school here, I bet I would fit in somewhere," she added softly.

But Cami, I'm not your damn parent, Kate thought. Of course, she didn't want to say it. Not at all. Even if it were obvious. Even if it were the right thing to say.

"Let's stop and get some food; come on, kid."

Cami obediently followed Kate without complaint or rebellion.

When Kate unlocked her front door, Cami put her backpack down. She spun all around, taking in Kate's condo.

"Wow," she whispered as she stared in visible awe, running her hands over the sofa.

It was rather small with a big master bedroom and a small second room that Kate used as a home office and extra closet for all her clothes. Cami walked around, only stopping before Kate's closet to run her hand over her shoes and boots, as well as the silk blouses, jackets, dress slacks, skirts, and dresses. Much of Kate's budget was spent on her wardrobe.

Kate wanted to reassure Cami, but she kept quiet, letting Cami decompress. Wandering around aimlessly, Cami finally sat down at the small, glass table and dug into the bag of fast food Kate bought her on the way home. Kate slipped her heels off and went into the kitchen in her stockings. She poured some wine to take the edge off, untucking her blouse from her skirt, and happened to glance up and catch Cami glaring at her. Her dark, smoky eyes made her glare all the fiercer. *What did I do now?* Kate wondered as she straightened up from closing the fridge.

"Why the scowl?" Kate asked as she took the chair opposite Cami and sat down, slipping her feet up onto another chair and cradling her glass of wine.

"What's the point of drinking that stuff?" Cami asked as she waved toward the wine. Kate sighed and set the glass on the table with a soft ping. Apparently, alcohol was also an issue. Along with everything else affecting this kid.

"Well, for me it is, I'm an adult who doesn't abuse it. Not you. Not some people, either."

"So just drink water, if you don't need it."

"Well, it's good to have an opinion on things. Maybe it will keep you from indulging in it before you should. But I can do it responsibly. I enjoy it. I take it you know someone who abused it?"

She shrugged, dropping her eyes again. The snippets were

all she gave away, like little crumbs she sprinkled around her, before clamming up, and keeping her real thoughts or opinions to herself.

"Cami?"

Her mouth was full of hamburger, but finally, she mumbled, "Anyone I ever saw using it."

Wonderful. Were there any positive influences in her young life? What the fuck was wrong with people? Kate studied the down-turned expression of Cami Reed. She was so young and small, like a naïve, elementary school girl sitting there. Except she wasn't. There were parts of her behavior, her vocabulary, her soul, and her experiences that far exceeded even Kate's.

Kate let the matter drop as she finished the wine, and didn't pour more. Seemed a fair compromise. Perhaps if she respected Cami's fears, she could show her a different way of handling intoxicants like alcohol.

Kate stretched out on the couch with her feet up on the coffee table as Cami sat on the recliner and watched reality TV about different music bands. Kate didn't know any of the bands or singers, and Cami started to explain why some artists were *soo* great and others weren't. Kate was pleased to see Cami so eager to talk about the subject. So the girl liked music. To the extreme. She never went without her headphones, listening to an ancient phone she acquired from a family who no longer wanted it. It was the only luxury the girl had.

"How come you never watched this at the ranch?" Kate inquired.

Cami shrugged. "I don't know."

That was part of the problem; the girl didn't know, nor was she comfortable anywhere.

A hard, impatient knock at her door brought Kate to her feet. *AJ.* Kate slid the deadbolt and swung the door open. He rushed right past her, harried with worry as he entered the room before stopping dead when he found Cami calmly sprawled in a chair, her legs swinging to the rhythm over the armrest. She had even smiled a few times over the last hour while educating Kate about *her* music. Her outright laughter at Kate would have been insulting if Cami weren't so shocked at Kate's apparent interest.

However, there was nothing fun about how AJ looked. His expression went from haggard to furious. Cami's easy sprawl in Kate's apartment made AJ lace his hands behind his neck as he shook his head. His temple throbbed and his neck muscles strained. "What the hell were you thinking? Do you have any idea what we went through? We had the police looking for you. Every person who lives or works at the ranch, along with about a dozen neighbors, are scouring the area. They were preparing an Amber Alert for you. A half dozen people saw you get on the school bus, only to get off in Patterson, where you don't usually, before you got into a car with a stranger. They had the entire city nearly shut down, stopping drivers, until I called with the news that you'd run off to my girlfriend's house. But even then, you had no fucking idea where Kate lived. And no way to find her. What did you think you were going to do when you got here? Huh? Just get off the bus and start walking? It's not River's End. Do you know what could have happened to you?"

AJ was shouting and pacing, his hands fisting the more worked up he got. Kate had never seen AJ react to anything, let alone with any kind of passion like this. She'd never seen fear on AJ's face either. So much, it practically emanated off him. He moved towards her and said, "Do you have any idea the things I was thinking might've happened to you?"

Cami's gaze widened, and dropped. She stared down at her black fingernails, which she picked at. The cuticles were shredded and she picked at white shards of dead skin. Ruthlessly, she pulled bits off. "It was only a few hours," she replied, but her feeble response merely incensed AJ all the more.

"Only a few hours? That's all it would take to lose you forever. For you to get kidnapped or taken or lost or taken advantage of... Dear God, you're just a little girl, do you know the things that could happen to you in *just a few hours*?"

AJ's eyes would have sparked flames if they could have. His hands rested on his hips, and his legs stood in a wide stance, making him look more powerful. Almost like the Incredible Hulk about to split his shirt. His muscles were straining and he seemed so intimidating, unlike he ever appeared before. Cami pushed into the cushion of the chair, biting her lip.

Kate stepped behind AJ and touched his back. "You're scaring her."

"Good! Maybe she'll listen for once. Maybe she'll understand that her actions affect others around her. And at thirteen years old, she doesn't get to go across a strange state, to a strange city, where she is all alone and vulnerable." He wiped a hand over his face. "Dear God, the things I've worried about happening to you."

They were the same fears that ate away at Kate the moment AJ told her Cami was gone. Being unsupervised and lost since no one knew she was actually okay were the same concerns Kate believed her parents would have had about her. Good parents worry about their kids.

Cami wasn't Kate's kid; at this point, she was barely AJ's. Only AJ's biologically speaking, since they didn't really know each other.

But their feelings were very real, Kate realized; and in the same way, Kate was beginning to think that was also happening between AJ and her. The feelings were there, but there was no time or opportunity to fully get to know each other. Time, of course, could render a solution to that.

Cami's small chest rose and fell quickly. She gripped the edges of the armrest, her fingers turning white. Taking a deep breath, she muttered, "You don't care what happens to me! You don't even know what to do with me without *her* around." The *her* was spoken with disdain as she narrowly glanced at Kate. Yet Kate didn't for a second believe Cami said it out of anger towards her, but rather, longing. Kate sighed heavily as her stomach clenched.

These two lost souls needed her. And strangely enough, she was starting to need them. But it was happening too soon. All so soon. There was so many miles between them, and so many other road blocks.

Except there was a little girl in the middle of it all.

AJ's massive shoulders that were so brazen and aflame with indignation, anger, and worry a few seconds before simply wilted. His head dropped in complete defeat. He turned and staggered to Kate's couch, slumping down. "I care what happens to you. Why do you think I had the police scouring the entire valley for you? Did you really think you could run away without me searching for you?"

She shrugged. "Dunno. Did it before and no one looked for me."

He closed his eyes, a deep, weary sigh escaping his lips. "I'm not anyone, Cami. I'm your father."

"No, you're not! You didn't want me."

"No, you're wrong. I didn't know about you. Those are two entirely different things."

"You don't like the daughter you got. You want me to be all cute and bubbly like that—that Marcy girl or something."

"Well, Cami, you're wrong again. I never wanted a daughter or began to think about children before the day I learned about you, so you're in luck, since I had no expectations of what I wanted. Not a one. My mind was a blank slate just waiting for you to step into it and be yourself."

Kate stood back and touched AJ's shoulder from the side. "Cami, could you give us a minute?"

Cami scurried into her room.

"She didn't run away to hurt you. She ran away to prove something. She wanted to see if you'd come after her. If you'd care. If there were any reason she should try to live with you. Did you stop talking to her after I left?"

"I tried, but she doesn't answer me. She doesn't talk to me. What am I supposed to do? So I… guess, maybe, I did."

"You keep at her until she responds. Question after question. She's not getting along well at school."

"What did she say?"

"Something about the 'bitches talking smack' about her. But I take that to mean she's not blending in well. She isn't the typical student at River's End, judging by what I've witnessed. She hoped she'd fit in here, or at least, find a segment of the school's population that accepted her. But mostly, AJ, she needs you. She needs to trust you're going to stick with her no matter what she does. If you feel that strongly."

"I do."

"Then find a way to tell her. I can't tell her for you. Maybe don't scold her so much now. Maybe just talk to her. I think she was looking for an opening and this could be it. This is her letting you in. So listen."

He nodded, staring at his feet. "So I should talk to her?"

"Yes." Kate went to her room and sent Cami out. Then she leaned against the bedroom door, her heart hammering. She hoped she was advising him correctly. She should give them privacy… but it was *her* apartment. And she could not bear waiting to know what happened. She kept the door cracked and leaned in to listen and peek at them.

Cami sat back down, slouching her posture and not caring. But Kate knew how she felt. And it was just the opposite.

AJ straightened up and squirmed while sitting on the edge of the couch. Then, clapping his hands together between his legs, he stared at them and said, "So, I won't yell. I'm sorry. When I got here… I was terrified. I couldn't calm down right away."

"You only cared that a person might be hurt. Not me, specifically. I know the difference, AJ."

He nodded his head slowly. "You're a smart girl."

"There's nothing you can do that I can't handle."

"I think there's a lot I could do that you actually can't handle anymore." He paused. His back rose and fell with a big breath. "Look, Cami, I didn't ask for you, and I was honestly stunned by your existence. I don't know you and you don't know me. But… that could change. We could work it out. All I can tell you is that you are mine. That is a fact. And nothing can take you away from me again. Consider me your armor against the world."

Her head started to slowly rise, and her eyes were solemn and untrusting. She tilted her head at an odd angle, but didn't believe him, although she was dying to.

"I can't offer you Seattle, and I know this city would fit you better. I realize that. I'm sorry, but as you can see…" He waved a hand at himself. He was sitting on her couch in ripped, dirty jeans, having raced to find her from the fields, and a stained t-shirt with his usual, dirty, white hat. "Seattle doesn't fit me. I don't have a lot of money. I only have a dumpy old trailer that I rent. But I have a job, and I always will. I also have strong back and I know how to use it. You'll never be hungry, or go without whatever you need. I swear to you I will do everything I can to earn a good living so that you can have whatever you want. It might take me some time, but I will find a way. I will never let anything or anyone hurt you, never again. I'll sleep on the couch of that place I looked at, and you can fix up the bedroom any way you want. All I can offer you is me, but you'll have me in every way you need until the day I die. I will do anything I can within my power. I know I'm not enough. I'm not smart or successful or interesting or cool or whatever, but I'll be there, every single day, every single night, and no one and nothing will ever harm you under my care. I don't drink, or do drugs, and women will not be coming and going. Kate was the only anomaly. *You* are now my priority. You will be the sole focus of my life. I'm rotten at knowing the right words to say to you. I don't know much about little girls, I mean teenagers… but I'll learn. I swear to you, I'm not stupid or an imbecile, I can learn it all. Everything you don't like about me, I can change and learn to be exactly what you need. You just… you just have to give me a chance."

Kate closed her eyes, but the tears ran down her cheeks. She wiped them, keeping the sudden knot that lodged in her throat quietly suppressed. She silently pleaded with Cami, mixed-up, screwed-up, distrusting, alone, sad little Cami to give AJ a chance.

Hearing AJ formulate that plea as a vow, and a commitment, and a promise made Kate's heart twist in agony for him. She wanted to scream, *all he had to offer?* He was so much more than any other man. What he had to offer was *everything*. It wasn't his location, his house, his portfolio, or his career. No, it was his heart, his soul, his integrity, and most of all, his love. It was all there inside him, just below the surface of that quiet nobility.

He kept thinking he had nothing significant to share with anyone, or if he tried, they wouldn't care. That was AJ putting himself on the line. There had never been anyone to even play the game with him. Kate closed her eyes, tears still brimming as she flattened her back against the wall and nearly slid to the floor.

Yes, AJ, I will give you a chance... Kate wanted to burst out of the bedroom and scream that before jumping into his arms. She didn't want AJ to spend another day alone and thinking, what? That he wasn't quite good enough. Not quite. Because he'd never been enough for anyone else. But he was for Kate.

She knew he didn't want her for her location, condo, portfolio, or career either, but only her heart, soul, integrity, and love. She realized that now. This man, who crossed the state in a panic of fear; the strong, bull-like man whose personality was so unthreatening, had so much fear building up over the loss of a daughter he didn't know. Kate fisted her hands and gasped.

Love. Kate offered love to AJ, and she believed he had as much to offer her. But. Cami. She was part of him, and therefore, part of *them*. It was so much to deal with at once. But Kate's heart was twisting as it swelled with passion. The desire to intervene was strong enough to place her hand on the door's edge, ready to pull it open. But it wasn't about her anymore. It was about a little girl, and that would always be.

Kate realized she could handle it in a sharp twist in her chest. She could handle Cami. She could handle River's End. She could... and they could.

She nodded with pride as if someone were there to see and agree with her. They could do this. Together. Her sense of relief was deep and strong, but first, Cami had to give AJ a chance.

Cami's voice was small when she said, "I was scared of you."

AJ jerked upright, obviously surprised by her response. "Why?"

"You're so huge. I was scared of what you could do to me, if you got mad."

"I won't hurt you. I'm here to protect you. My huge size will protect you from most everything. But I'll never use my size against you, or to hurt you."

"You really got upset that I was gone today?"

"I was terrified."

Silence. Kate peeked through the slat in the door. Cami was staring at her fingers in her lap. Several long minutes of silence elapsed while AJ was perched as if waiting to leap off a cliff, when Cami finally said, "I could give you a chance."

In that moment, if the angels in heaven started singing, Kate would not have been surprised. Or if AJ and Cami both jumped up and hugged each other in a tight, fierce embrace and celebrated their long awaited breakthrough and bond. Instead, AJ nodded just slightly at Cami, who stared at her fingers in her lap. So what if they didn't jump up and hug each other, and nothing else was said? In that moment, everything was said, and everything changed.

Kate took in a long breath, wiping her eyes as she glanced in the mirror to make sure her makeup wasn't crusting under her eyes. She smoothed her hair back and walked out towards the living room. AJ and Cami looked up at her gratefully since her entrance allowed both father and daughter a convenient distraction. Neither one seemed to know what to do next.

"So why don't I make you some dinner, AJ? You must be hungry. Cami already ate hers. Cami, do you want to relax in my room? There's a TV in there."

Cami nodded eagerly as she jumped to her feet and quickly disappeared. AJ stared up at Kate. He slowly rose and glanced down with a grimace. "Crap. I rushed in here with my boots on. I'm sorry, I was just so anxious to see her." Shaking his head with disgust, he leaned over and gently eased the dirt-encrusted cowboy boots off. They were old, worn, brown, and creased. Dust filled all the creases and dried crumbs of grass and soil were still stuck on the soles. He politely passed by Kate as he took the filthy boots towards her door and muttered, "I'll clean it up."

Bits of River's End were scattered on her pristine beige carpet. Kate stared at it, then at the man who so gently carried his dirty, soiled boots outside in his "white" socks. They were stained black in some areas from grinding the dirt in, and he had a hole in his pinkie toe.

AJ's disgust at himself was palpable. He cared so much, and worried so much. He didn't fit there. Or here. He didn't fit anywhere.

Kate rushed towards him, placing her hand softly on his arm so he turned in surprise to see her. She stared into his eyes, wordlessly locking his gaze with hers, and unsmiling. She reached forward and took his boots from him while his eyes darted down to her hands and back up to her face. She threw the boots at their feet and they landed and toppled over with a plop. More soil and dirt clods dropped off them in the fall.

"They're fine right there."

AJ stared into her eyes, then at her forehead, her mouth and her outfit, taking in every detail. Her blouse was untucked from her skirt, but the topaz and silver necklace with matching earrings and bracelet were visible. He closed his eyes, shaking his head again, just slightly. "That's probably not the best spot for them."

Her eyes grew more intense, holding his, as she softly replied, "They are. That is the best spot. It's where I want them."

"Why is that?"

"Because," she whispered, "it would make me very happy if your boots stayed right there on my floor."

He swallowed and dropped his gaze down, slumping his shoulders. "We—"

She stepped forward, her bare feet poised on the tops of AJ's sock-clad feet. "Should have dinner."

His expression pierced her heart. His love for her was so tangible in his eyes and his voice, hoping for her, aching to have her. She tilted towards him, and he suddenly scooped her up in his arms and held her against him. His lips touched the top of her head as her arms wrapped around his back. "I don't need any dinner."

Tears again filled her eyes as she sniffled and replied, "You do."

Releasing him, she leaned back. He touched his thumbnail under her eyelids and winced. "I haven't washed my hands yet either."

Kate grabbed his hand and kissed the back of it. "You're here. *That's* what matters."

He let her go as he glanced around the condo, his breath coming fast. Following her into the kitchen, he washed his hands and sat down at her table. "This place is really something. I didn't have a chance to say…"

She interrupted, "It would be like living in a tin can for you, huh?"

He glanced at the view that overlooked the city streets. "Yes. A little bit. But you are one hell of an impressive woman."

"Why thank you, AJ." She held his gaze until he smiled finally and so did she.

Dinner was leftovers she threw together. AJ gobbled it up; his hunger, as always, was more than substantial. When he finished, he glanced at her almost sheepishly. "It was so good."

She smiled as she took his empty plate to the sink. "You'd think anything that isn't baloney is good. You're so easy to feed. And easy to look at. And easy to be around." She kept staring outside and didn't turn towards AJ. Then she added, "Most of all, you're very easy to love."

She could see him sitting perfectly still. She leaned down and started the water to rinse his plate as her breath came in shallow bursts. Did she really just say that? So casually? So offhand? And while she was doing the dishes?

His chair scraped back and his tall form rose before he approached her. She stared harder at the plate before placing it into the dishwasher beside her. "Kate? Did you just…"

She was crouching over the dishwasher. "Yes, I just told you I love you." She straightened up while grabbing the dish-towel hanging on a hook nearby and started drying her hands. Then she carefully folded it and set it on the counter. Turning to face him, she rested her lower back on the lip of the Corian counter and admitted, "I'm in love with you."

AJ seemed to be looking around for the hidden camera. Kate shrugged with a gentle lift of her shoulders and clutched the counter for balance.

"Did you mean that?"

"Have I ever said or done anything to you that I didn't mean?" His smile was small as he shook his head in the negative.

Kate moved closer to him. He stepped towards her, and their gazes locked. A deafening silence in the moment seemed rare now in their interactions. Usually, Kate felt heat and passion, she was so physically and emotionally charged. This, however, was… real. Far more real than anything Kate had ever felt before.

"No, you don't do anything that you don't mean."

"Or say what I don't mean."

He shut his eyes. "I can't see how…"

"I don't know how it's going to work either. I'm just telling you how I feel. I listened to you with Cami, and heard what you said, and I don't think anything could break my heart more, or fill me with such hope and longing and love for another person. I don't give a shit anymore. Not about your job or mine, or your town or my city, or your trailer or my condo. I just don't give a shit about any of that. But you? I've never dreamed I could love a man like I've fallen in love with you."

"Opposites attracting and all?"

"No, AJ. I don't think we're opposites. I think we're actually quite a bit alike. We only say what we mean. We only do what we mean. We remain true to who and what we are. We both value loyalty, kindness, and integrity and readily offer them to those we love. So, some things about us are different. I'm loud, you're quiet. I'm outgoing, you're solitary. So what? That's not the bond at our core."

"What do you foresee?"

"Don't know. But we can figure it out."

"What about Cami?"

"Cami? I think she needs both of us."

"You're willing…"

"Yes. I'm willing. If you are."

AJ closed the distance between them and swept her up in his arms. Turning his face towards her, he gently kissed her cheek as her arms swung around his shoulders and grasped his neck. "I'm willing."

Tears filled Kate's eyes and streamed down her cheeks. AJ leaned back and touched them with his hand. "It usually takes more to make you cry."

"You do. You make me cry. Cami makes me cry. You two together make me cry. I'd like to be part of you though. What you said to her… about her being okay in the end? With you, and your commitment, she'll be okay. Whatever happened to her is significant; and we have a lot to learn about her, but when we do, we can both help her, we'll both be there for her and I strongly believe because of you, she'll be okay."

They shared a quiet hug in her kitchen with their voices muffled so Cami didn't hear them. There were no rash sex acts on her kitchen counter; only the contented smiles they both shared. Kate believed in her heart that they'd just committed their lives to each other forever. She could only wonder how that would look.

Then Cami ventured out and rolled her eyes at them. She flopped down on Kate's couch, and began flipping through the TV channels.

She didn't explain *why* she came back out. Was it to be with them? AJ and Kate exchanged a long look, a tremulous smile and separated, letting their hands linger for only a moment before AJ turned and flopped down just as dramatically as Cami did.

He wanted to be near her, and rested his feet on the coffee table before dissecting the music video she was watching, expounding on why it wasn't worth their time. Kate took the recliner, letting her mind wander while her heart thumped with passion. So much happened today, tonight, and now... There they sat, casually ribbing Cami on her choice of music while she defended her favorite bands. Musical artists brought out a Cami they didn't often see. Kate wondered how much more Cami had to offer. She slipped a glance at AJ, her heart twisting, and hoped, prayed, and longed now for the three of *them*.

"What next?" Cami asked finally.

They looked at her, then at each other. "What do you mean?"

"I heard you. In the kitchen. So what happens now? Kate comes to live with us? Or we stay here?" Tucking her legs under her butt, she rose with undisguised excitement.

"Uh..." AJ shot up straight. "I don't know... I mean, we

haven't decided anything yet. How did you know what we said?"

"I listened with the door cracked. Duh. How else would I know what's going on? Old trick. Although you two aren't usually all that interesting to listen to. Not like some of my other foster parents. But anyway… why can't Kate come with us? She's more fun to live with than you. You don't talk much."

"Neither do you," AJ grumbled and Cami smiled. She so rarely smiled. It softened her face and made her look so much younger. So fresh. So happy.

"I might if Kate were around more often."

Kate spun her chair towards Cami. "I might be around more often. But we have adult stuff to work out first. So no more listening to our conversations. We'll tell you what you need to know, when we know it ourselves."

Cami flashed a grin. "See? She's always balls-out and it's easy to know where I stand."

"And you like that?" Kate asked, her eyebrows furrowed in puzzlement.

"I like that. I like… you."

Like glass, Kate's heart simply shattered. She instantly replied, "I really like you too, Cami."

Cami shrugged. "You also seem to like *him*," she said, waving her hand towards AJ in a careless manner. "Well enough, so why can't you just come live with us? He seems hell-bent on not living in Seattle, even though that would be the better solution, so you need to come back to River's End."

"I have a job here. This place is my home. I have things to figure out first."

"Will you figure them out?"

Kate lifted her gaze to AJ, who watched her his expression seriously, his mouth a tight line. Kate held Cami's gaze. The girl's arms were crossed over her chest when Kate replied, "Yes." She eyed AJ, waiting for his silent permission. He gave the nod and she nodded back. "Yes, Cami, I will figure it out."

"Do you promise?"

"I promise." Without pause or regret, Kate knew in her heart that she was not making a mistake. A soft peace filled her mind. Yes, they'd all three figure out how to live together, where to live and still remain true to themselves. Together, they'd figure it all out.

"I've been promised a lot by a lot of people. No one usually comes through, though. Why should I believe you?"

She smiled. "Because I've never lied to you yet, have I?"

"No. That's almost why I believe you. I want to."

"Believe me."

KATE SENT AJ and Cami home the next day after sleeping with Cami while AJ slept on the couch. Cami hugged Kate tightly for the first time before silently waiting by the stair-well. AJ hugged her next, and held her longer. He brushed his hand through her hair. "This weekend then?" AJ asked.

Kate smiled at him. "Yes, I'll come back Friday night, right after work. I talked to Jack, and he said we can stay at the main house for a little while longer. It's absolutely neces-sary right now. When I get there, I want to look at that prop-erty across from the gate. I mean it, AJ. Cami needs a real home. A permanent one. And I can provide that for her... and for us. And believe it or not, you need a permanent home too."

He nodded, rubbing his neck. He didn't like talking about money with Kate. He'd have to get used to it. "Should we discuss the option of me moving here?"

"No. I appreciate the gesture and the offer. But I can work

from River's End. You can't work from Seattle. We'll make it fly somehow."

He stepped up, leaning forward to kiss her lips quickly, well aware that Cami was just down the hall, watching them. "I love you too." Then he left.

Kate let him go. Sighing, she closed her front door.

No, it wasn't a perfect situation. There was no throwing herself into his arms and saying *fuck it all*. There was her business to deal with, bills to pay and employees who relied on her. They needed a reliable place to stay, since her brother's hospitality would eventually come to an end. But for now, keeping Cami stable and happy were their only goals and focus.

Kate knew it would not be easy. Cami had an uphill battle. But Kate would not relent; and now that Cami came to them, she'd stay with them forever. There were just some details to iron out. And details? Those were Kate's specialty.

SIX WEEKS LATER, Kate showed up at the ranch on a random Wednesday evening. Cami and AJ were having dinner... together, as Kate insisted. Having spent the last seven weekends in River's End, she demanded they maintain the established routine. And talking. Kate stipulated they must interact whether she were there or not.

Kate walked in the door and dropped her bag down. Both heads jerked up with surprise. She hadn't called to inform them.

"Kate. What are you doing back so soon?"

"I've had enough. We need to be together and I need to be here. I hired a general manager for the daily business. I introduced the idea to everyone there last week, and spent all this time breaking her in. It's done now. I listed the condo with a rental agency. Did the same for my mom's apartment." She glanced at AJ, who was slowly rising to his feet, and pushing away from the table. "I'm now a landlord in Seattle," she said with a small smile. AJ smiled too. "And I'm now a proud landowner in River's End. My... *our* offer was accepted on the land across from the gate. Except I don't know what the fuck to do with it. So... get your working shoes on, 'cause you have a lot of work to do in order to develop that from raw land to a buildable home site."

AJ walked over to her and swept her up into his arms as Cami shrieked behind them. He planted a long, wet kiss on Kate's lips. "I'm pretty good at working out that kind of stuff, ma'am," he said with a teasing glint in his eyes. Tears brimmed over Kate's eyelids. She straightened up in his embrace.

"I still have to return once every week. I'll work that day, spend the night in a motel and work the next day before I come home. But I think we can manage that. Can't we... as a family?"

Cami's smile was huge as she nodded. "Are you guys going to get married?"

They glanced at each other with a broad, goofy smiles. "Let's not discuss that yet. Why don't we save something for me to decide? Kate's not the only one who can get stuff done," AJ said with a wink at Cami. Kate's heart grew so big, it seemed to fill up her throat.

First, there was Cami, and dinner, and Kate was starving. She couldn't wait to hear how Cami's science test went. All the snotty, catty girls who were teasing and bothering Cami were the next topic Kate wanted to discuss. Kate had a few choice words for them too, although she wouldn't allow Cami to say them. But they were making some progress in getting the girls to stop. Dropping into a chair at the table, Kate leaned over to steal a piece of chicken from AJ's plate.

Then she began listening to Cami's recap while eating the savory chicken and feeling a bubble of contentment, even excitement rise up inside her.

She silently marveled, that of all places in the world to buy a chunk of land with plans to put a home on it, she had purposely *chosen* River Road as the location. The road that AJ was so enamored to call his address, was now also, going to be hers.

And instead of resentment, annoyance, disgust or disinterest over that fact, all she could think about was the deep down gut-level feeling that she was finally home.

ABOUT THE AUTHOR

Leanne Davis has earned a business degree from Western Washington University. She worked for several years in the construction management field before turning full time to writing. She lives in the Seattle area with her husband and two children. When she isn't writing, she and her family enjoy camping trips to destinations all across Washington State, many of which become the settings for her novels.

Made in the USA
Las Vegas, NV
19 March 2024

87444160R00164